Portia's
REVELATION

Rich Tenaglia

Portia is insane. She is dead too, but not all the time. So begins the
revelation of a young Roman girl who has wonderful and terrible
visions of the future. Will her disturbing message ensure a future for
humanity, or is Portia's revelation the greatest hoax of all time?

Published by Richard D. Tenaglia
Copyright © 2015 by Richard D. Tenaglia

Title ID: 5384948
ISBN-13: 978-0692412640
ISBN-10: 0692412646

Address requests to mpluvius@sbcglobal.net

Printed in the United States of America
First edition: March 2015
Cover Photo Credit
"Sappho"- Fresco from Pompeii
Maintained by the National Archaeological Museum of Naples

Dedications

For my beloved Nammie, who saw clearly when I was blind.
How I need her eyes now!

Max Garrett

For my beloved husband, Marcus Pluvius, who Spiritae sent to
me.

Portia

For my remarkable wife and awesome daughter. They both fill
my life with rainbows.

The Author

Contents

Prologue

I REMEMBER THE MOMENT when I translated the first page of what has come to be known as the Capitoline Papyri or, more popularly, "Portia's Revelation." I was baffled. You just don't expect an ancient document to begin, "I am insane. My brother Cato has declared so publicly and now my life is ruined. I am dead too, well at least sometimes, but not always."

Little did I imagine the storm of controversy and ridicule I would face after I was foolish enough to publish my translation of the papyri two years ago. I should have known better. The Capitoline Papyri are a complete hoax, fakery of enormous proportions. They must be, as you will certainly agree when you read the transcript in this book. Purportedly, the papyri were written by a young Roman girl, Portia, during the reign of Emperor Commodus, circa 183 CE. Her "visions" are completely fantastic and too detailed in the descriptions of our times to be anything other than the work of an imaginative prankster.

My original translation was intended for fellow professional archaeologists. That version was a literal translation of the encoded Latin text, with extensive footnotes and references that made the document too pedantic for public consumption. Unfortunately, a yellow- press journalist heard of my work and published a poorly researched summary, which took a number of passages out of context and was simply erroneous in other respects. I had no idea that public reaction would be so strong—intense religious fervor on one front and moral outrage on the other. The most damning charge against me was that I represented the papyri as "authentic documents." Critics point to my work as a thinly veiled attempt at proselytizing. Such is not my intent. I make no claims for the papyri, other than my translation being an accurate representation of the writing on documents that remain available to others to study.

My colleagues charge me with faking the papyri in some pathetic quest for notoriety, and accuse me of being well situated to pull off such a stunt. I understand their suspicion. I am an assistant professor in the Department of Anthropology at a well-known university. My area of specialization involves forensic analysis of classical Roman and Greek manuscripts. Until this debacle, I had earned an excellent reputation for contributions in my field. The university leaders will probably dismiss me soon (as quietly as possible) for they abhor being embroiled in controversy.

Why in the world, then, would I publish this updated translation of the papyri? After all, I need more ridicule like I need another hole in my head. This will likely end my career, not enhance it. I don't stand to make any money from this publication. Because of all the misinformation floating about, I decided to publish a complete version that is accessible to general readers. Let me be perfectly clear: I have intentionally modernized the language in this version with the goal of preserving its integrity and charm. Others may fault my translation style, but nothing has been added and nothing subtracted in a manner that would change the underlying message. Hopefully, you will read it and decide what to think without having to listen to babbling heads on talk-shows who have never seen the originals.

Let me start by telling you how the papyri were discovered and deciphered, for this is an interesting tale in itself. After you read "Portia's Revelation," I will tell you how I have tried to uncover, sadly unsuccessfully, the hoax.

—Prof. Max Garrett

Discovery

I HAD THE GOOD FORTUNE, as a graduate student, to join a team of classical archaeologists doing excavations near the Capitoline Hill in Rome. Our team leaders got the plum sites, unearthing ruins beneath the medieval Sant'Omobono church, revealing what may be the oldest known Roman temple. We grad students were still polishing our field techniques and were assigned the grunt work, excavating nearby apartment ruins not really likely to contain anything much of interest. Tedious work, to be sure, as this region is at or below the water table, covered with silt and the muck of centuries from the Tiber River. But we were enthusiastic, eager to impress our professors. After each day's hard work, evenings were simply delicious, filled with wine, song, and the most delightful Italian beauties—rough life, huh? But I digress (sigh).

It took weeks of backbreaking work, using my pick, shovel, and brushes to sift down through my grid, seeking the tiniest pottery shard or artifact I could feel all puffed up about. No luck. Nothing fun unearthed except a small room with a floor of muddy stone tiles. Man, it was hot that summer—the kind of hot where your eyebrows drip with sweat, salt blinds you when you bend over, even in the shade. Gulping water, I poked around in boredom, tapping the floor with the end of my trowel, hoping that Professor Matson wouldn't force me to dig out all the floor tiles too. He had a well-deserved reputation for giving us busywork out of sheer malevolence.

As I tapped, the northeast corner of the room sounded faintly hollow. Curious, I pried at the cornerstone and—with a shock—exposed a crumbling wooden frame topping a hollow niche. Loath to thrust my arm down into God-knows-what, I chased down a flashlight and peered inside, dreading some snake or other nasty beastie might spring out at me.

Inside rested a small wooden crate, smeared all over with beeswax. Not a single seam could be picked out.

My excited cries brought the other students running and—hearing the ruckus—our professors too. We hoisted the crate gingerly, lest it crumble. It didn't look like much, just a big dirty black lump of wax. We took turns taking photographs documenting its removal, making sure we stuck in our faces to impress friends back home.

I was eager to tear into it, but Professor Matson had us relocate the crate to his field office for closer examination. To my chagrin, it was now "his" discovery, and he set about showing all of us how a "professional" examines an artifact.

Observing, I thought I would burst while he clawed away the wax with a small scraper, poking and prodding, until he finally exposed the seam of the lid. Silly, yes, but I imagined myself about to have—shall we say—a Howard Carter moment, glimpse "marvelous things" or at least something golden. But, when the lid was finally forced open, inside were large stacks of irregularly shaped sheets of scrap paper, which proved to be papyrus.

At first, Professor Matson was excited, explaining that few ancient documents survive into modern times, and the few that do are usually fragments rather than any significant body of work. Unfortunately, the papyri were in really bad shape, extremely fragile with broken edges, and so oxidized any markings were barely discernible.

With a magnifying loupe, he painstakingly examined five or six of the top papyri. I hovered over his shoulder snapping photographs whenever he moved aside. After what seemed hours, he backed dejectedly away. Shaking his head, Matson declared that these contained no message: they were merely practice sheets for lettering—the sort of thing a novice scribe might use to perfect his skills before writing on expensive vellum. The papyri *were* a unique find, but would not shed any new light on ancient Rome.

I felt deflated. The other students drifted away, each secretly happy I had not scored a big coup. Professor Matson ordered me to package the crate and its contents for shipment to his contacts at the Archaeological Field School in Vacone, for safekeeping and further analysis, as the Italian government doesn't look kindly upon removal of artifacts from the country by foreigners. The remainder of my summer was dedicated to poking around in more muck, and chasing *la dolce vita* at night.

I finished my dissertation the following year, and began contemplating postdoctoral studies in the hope of building my curriculum vitae to win a position as an assistant professor somewhere. Something was nagging me about the Capitoline Papyri, and on a whim, I inquired about a position in Padua, which, much to my surprise, was offered to me. I must tell you, Padua is a lovely city, maybe not a cultural center like Rome or Venice, but nonetheless alive with the youthful exuberance of its university students. Wine, song, and Italian beauties? Oh yeah, they hold their own with their more famous neighbors.

When I arrived in Padua, my new mentor, Professore Giberti, led me to the department basement. There on a pallet sat my little crate, relayed from Vacone, still shrink-wrapped and untouched from the day it appeared on the scene. Giberti curtly stated he had more important things to do than document some other professor's findings, and upon learning I had been on the discovery site jumped at the chance of getting this annoying chore off his plate.

Professore Giberti must have taken lessons from Professor Matson in coming up with busywork. Giberti decided that my first task would be to photograph each and every piece of the papyri. Even worse, any distinguishing characteristic had to be photographed more closely under magnification. This was onerous enough, but I had to develop special handling techniques for the fragile pieces. Some of the papyri were stuck together, and had to be painstakingly separated and transferred to the photo table without damage. I finally hit on a method, where I could float a sheet of papyrus onto a Teflon transfer plate with gentle puffs from canned air commonly used to remove dust from photographs.

Giberti was a traditionalist, and insisted that all photographs be done using glass-plate negatives for archival purposes. No digital photography for this guy. It took me more than a year, working many long days, to complete a catalogue of the papyri. Together, we published a short paper with selected photographs. I included several that matched the ones I snapped over Professor Matson's shoulder when they were discovered. Our paper failed to draw much attention, and a couple peers noted the contrast of the photographs was so poor that the writing on the papyri was barely discernible.

Though apoplectic over this criticism, Giberti privately agreed. I suggested enhancing the text with digital photo-editing software, but he simply couldn't stomach my approach. Instead, he came up with a more devious plan.

The Physics Department had recently acquired a new thermal-imaging camera, and needed someone to explore its capabilities.

Guess who?

Giberti gave me the assignment of figuring how to use this instrument to enhance the papyri text. Surprisingly, this proved to be fairly easy. Each sheet of papyrus was set back on the photo table under its hot lights, not too long because we didn't want more fading. The lights were turned off, and for a few brief seconds, the ancient ink and papyrus cooled at different rates. Snap the shutter at just the right moment, and the infrared/thermal camera revealed the lettering, glowing as if it had been recently written, but fading within seconds.

Once again, another year of my life evaporated, buried away in my photo lab, enhancing and recording each and every one of more than nine thousand papyri. I still see the damn things in my dreams. Just as Professor Matson had declared, each page contained random letters, beautifully written and carefully aligned, mind-numbing repetition assigned by some ancient taskmaster to a student who must have committed some terrible offense. All I could discern was that the writings all seemed to originate from the same hand and writing instrument, as evidenced by the similar patterns of wear marks along the side of each inked letter. Giberti and I published our enhanced version of selected photographs. Once again, few of our colleagues took notice. Gibberish from a student is not particularly exciting. I wrapped up my project, concluding it to be of little value.

Giberti seemed anxious to be rid of me, now that he had the papyri issue put to rest, and mentioned casually one day that he had contacted his "old friend" Professor Matson back in the States and recommended me for a recently posted teaching position. This suited me fine, as I was anxious to return home to be close to friends and my grandmother. I used my last month at Padua to make digital scans of the glass plates for both the original and thermally enhanced images, burning them to DVDs as a memento of the wasted years of my life.

I hurried home to America, eager to begin my career in academia. My DVDs migrated eventually to a cardboard box gathering dust-bunnies under my bed, where they languished for a couple of years in solitary confinement.

Insight

M Y GRANDMOTHER WAS A REMARKABLE WOMAN. A mother to me, more so than my real mother. My real mother had been a troubled teen, rebellious, who found herself a single mom and not very certain who my father was. She saw me as an "oops," and her maternal instinct never kicked in. The fast life was just too alluring for her to be saddled with a baby. Fortunately for me, my grandmother was everything my mother was not. I became, in her words, her "salvation child"—a second chance to get it right.

My birth mother burned too brightly and died of unnamed excesses in her early twenties. That same year, my grandfather died of throat cancer, and I think the twin tragedies nearly broke my grandmother's heart. She said she could never decide which of us rescued the other. We weren't well off, but my grandfather's life insurance made it possible for grandma Nammie to be my stay-at-home mom.

Nammie made the most of her second chance. I remember many loving moments with her, cuddled on her lap, learning to read. She played games with me endlessly, sprawled on the floor, mesmerized by anything that she could put before me to stimulate learning. She was my mother, father, mentor, confidante, and emotional coach all wrapped into one. Can you tell me of any other grandmother who would trot out ten yards on her swollen knees in a buttonhook pattern just to receive my wobbly football-pass and then crow with pride over my accomplishment?

I lived with Nammie until I went away to Padua. I like to think I helped take care of her as she aged, but she was fiercely independent, and more than held up her end of the bargain. When I could finally afford to help her with bills, she insisted, "Don't pay me back. Pay forward to those who need it." It had been a painful separation when I left for Padua, but she needed to move to an assisted-living facility where she could get more care coping with her arthritis than I could give. I was happy to return home so I could be near her again.

Nammie remained sharp as a tack, even as her body failed, right up to the week before she passed away peacefully in her sleep at eighty-three. How I miss her! Nammie read books like she was chain smoking, devouring them by the shopping bag from the library. She was amazingly humble, given her intellect, and held back in group conversations lest anyone would think she was "showing off." Alone with me, her conversations were scintillating, infused with dry country humor and sardonic wit. Nammie was obsessed with crossword puzzles, cryptograms, acrostics, Sudoku, and just about any other game that would keep her mentally agile. Hardly a week passed that I didn't stop in to visit and drop off new puzzle collections. After a while, it was tough to find puzzles she hadn't already bludgeoned into submission. She could do these things in her sleep, and probably did.

One day when I couldn't find anything new, I decided to pull a prank, which I knew would make her laugh when she caught on. I happened to think how some of the lettering in my papyri photos looked like cryptograms. I dug out some paper and copied a few lines of letters from a couple of them. I knew this was mean-spirited, but it would keep her occupied for many hours, and I could crow that finally she had been bested! Her eyes glowed with the challenge, as I handed them over with no explanation about their source.

When I saw her the following week, she greeted me at the door with a wry smile and a twinkle in her eye. "You ornery boy," she snorted. "I know full well you made this one up from random letters"—thrusting it back at me. "What a mean thing you are," she said chuckling. I grinned and shrugged. "And this one sure was a nice curve ball."

I blinked. "What are you talking about?"

"Oh sure, big man on campus, Mr. Ph.D. thinks poor addle-brained ol' Nammie can't remember any of the Latin she learned so long ago in high school."

"No, Nammie. What do you mean?"

She thrust the second sheet defiantly into my hands, and there in Latin her solution read: *Ego Portia filia Lucinio scribvm domino a Roma in anno avtem tertio regni Commodvs imperator.*

I burst out laughing. "Nammie, you are such a card! Leave it to you to turn the tables on my little prank."

She looked insulted and challenged. "No, that's what it really says! REALLY!" I could tell by her fierce glare she meant business.

"Why, it took me no time at all," she went on, "to see by the repetition that this message was in code, a simple Caesar's cipher with letters shifted a set number of positions, and just a little longer to realize that it wasn't in English. Since you made it up, and you know only one other language, *duh*, it had to be in Latin! It was a little tricky, since you didn't put in any marks to separate the words, but with a little trial-and-error, *Voila! 'Veni, vidi, vici'!*"

She beamed delightedly. "Ye of little faith! You silly boy, you even put the key to the cipher in those small letters off by themselves, as though I would need a clue. I should have seen immediately that the key said to shift the letters three positions to the left. Nice of you to use the classical Latin alphabet with 23 letters, leaving out J's and W's, and writing U's as V's." Nammie was absolutely triumphant.

I, on the other hand, could not speak.

How had I missed the code? I had considered the possibility, but after fooling around with the first seven or eight papyri, no message had appeared, even when I had run the letters through our department's code-breaking algorithms, most of them far more sophisticated than a simple substitution cipher. I left Nammie holding her sides, doubled over in laughter, telling me it would be a cold day in you-know-where before I would get her goat. I could only croak out, "Goodnight, Avia," as I waved goodbye, which only made her laugh harder, accepting my Latin word for grandmother as acknowledgment of my prank—and her victory.

I headed back to my apartment, and dug out my DVD collection from under the bed. I fully expected to find that Nammie had faked her message. She was pretty gifted at copying my handwriting, and I was sure that she had simply inked a new set of letters onto a piece of paper that devilishly matched her transcription. She would enjoy this episode all over again, once I discovered her deception.

I had copied lettering from the photo of the topmost piece of papyrus. For some reason, I had decided to give her the second puzzle, but had selected letters from a photo taken where the scattered sheets of papyri ended and neatly stacked bundles began. Not too surprisingly, the letters from the first piece had letters matching the paper she had returned to me. Nice feint, Nammie! What I discovered from the photo of the second piece left me stunned. The letters and the key to the cipher were exactly as Nammie had claimed!

I didn't sleep that night, and not much during the next several months. Pouring through the photos, and excepting the ten initial ones, it was obvious each had a message encrypted by the cipher key on the page. This demonstrated how the key also gave a numerical order to the papyri.

Abruptly, I suspected someone had monkeyed with my DVD. If so, they had gone to enormous trouble. I purchased some new photo-enhancing software, and decided to see if the original poor-contrast images were the same as my thermally-imaged photos.

They matched perfectly—all of them!

Any manipulation of the photo files was far beyond Nammie's capabilities and interests. She hated computers and would never own or use one. I had offered to buy her one to email her friends, and was refused. Nammie viewed computers as corrupting the fabric of society, something evil created to allow others to spy on you.

I was anxious to learn what messages my photos might reveal, but the task of manually decoding each papyrus was daunting. Happily for me, optical character recognition software has improved dramatically. I was able to automate the process, writing a code to recognize the lettering in each image, applying its deciphering code, and assembling the results into a word-processed document. I was even able to overlay a word separator routine developed specifically for Latin text, spending several weeks pouring through the output, manually editing phrases the software did not handle. My mind reeled....

Decrypting messages from a handful of the photos was all I required to confirm any forgeries. But why would anyone alter thousands of images with little potential gain?

Besides, photo-editing leaves easily detectable traces unless extremely sophisticated techniques are used, and these bore no signs of tampering. Had the glass plate negatives conceivably been altered, or replaced by forgeries before burning onto computer disks?

No, I told myself. Too much time and expense. Next, I checked my DVD images against the photos published upon discovery of the papyri, including one I'd snapped over Professor Matson's shoulder when the crate was first opened in his field office.

Drat! These matched as well....

When next I visited Nammie, she poked my ribs, asked whether I had any new pranks up my sleeve. I told her, seriously, that she had helped me discover something terribly important in my work. The more I tried to explain, the more convinced she became I was trying again to pull her leg. I think she never believed a single word of mine regarding the papyri. But she never tired of telling her friends at the home about the time she had out-maneuvered her smarty-pants professor grandson!

There simply was no getting around it.

I needed to return to Padua...reexamine the papyri directly. Since the days of my postdoctoral studies, Professore Giberti had passed away, truly a loss to our field of study. The new department chairman, Professore Bucelli, greeted me warmly and led me into the bowels of the basement storage area for old project artifacts. There, in one dark corner, sat my little waxy crate, fuzzed gray with dust. An old lab book scrawled with my investigatory notes still lay on top also grimed and cobwebbed. Everything appeared untouched since the day of my departure back to the United States.

Bucelli generously granted me unlimited access to their new labs and test equipment, a nice nod to a visiting researcher and former student.

I was dazzled by the modernization of the facilities, Bucelli justifiably proud of having spearheaded the grant requests to secure world-class forensic equipment. He hovered nearby while I opened the crate and started reexamining its contents, but appeared nonplussed by the nearly illegible condition of the papyri. He fabricated an excuse of afternoon meetings to depart.

I relaxed.

Working with someone looking over your shoulder is a royal pain at best. Using the lab's new thermal-imaging equipment, it didn't take long to determine that the lettering on the papyri matched exactly my photographs and DVD files.

This left only one possibility.

The papyri had been faked, planted in the Capitoline ruins prior to our excavations.

Nice hypothesis, but all my field experience pointed elsewhere. The apartment ruins had been buried under tons of river silt, clearly deposited in layer after layer, typical of hundreds, if not thousands, of years of annual flooding. The soil around the entire site showed no evidence of having been disturbed. I thought the only person who had a prayer of pulling off this stunt might have been Professor Matson himself.

But this notion didn't make sense either. His reputation didn't need any further enhancement. He was widely recognized as the best in his field, and had already been lauded time and again for his important discoveries. If he had been seeking some career capstone discovery to mark him as the best of all time, I doubt he would have left the crate for a student to find. Simply, he wouldn't have dismissed the value of its contents so quickly. He would have had to be Houdini too, as we arrived at the excavation site only days before beginning work.

I decided to confront Professor Matson, hoping against hope that he would beam his remarkable grin at me and admit how much fun he'd had pulling the wool over my eyes.

I found him at home, reposed in a wheelchair.

Matson's wife explained that he had Alzheimer's disease, but presently was having a good, reasonably lucid day. He appeared pleased to see me, a glint of recognition in his pale eyes, but kept calling me Sam—his brother's name. We had a nice visit, though, and he offered some accurate recollections of our "good old days" together. But when I asked about the Capitoline Papyri, he had little to add, as if recalling only fragmented moments of their discovery. Concrete memory, had it ever existed, must have evaporated long ago. When I asked if he had played any tricks on me, his expression shifted into apprehension like that of a lost child. Perhaps the papyri were faked, and buried, by some crazy monk scribbling in a Middle Ages monastery.

Nope; that cannot be. The messages from the papyri would be astounding if written only 25 years ago, let alone before the Industrial Revolution. Various other hypotheses circulating on the Internet are wildly fanciful. Did aliens from the future transport the crate into the excavations as a warning to mankind? Maybe it's a CIA plot, in cahoots with another ultra-secret Government organization to control our minds. Or Muslim extremists manipulating historical artifacts to discredit Western civilization. Maybe fundamentalist Christians conceived this as a means to disparage Islam, or atheists bent on rupturing all religion...or it's a communist plot. Don't forget the Democrats or the Republicans, and so on and so forth.

To preserve my sanity, I hold onto a thin thread of hope there exists a plausible explanation out there...somewhere.

The Capitoline Papyri are at once my Achilles' heel, the world immense on my shoulders, Pandora's Box, and Sisyphean boulder....

Since Nammie's death, I have returned again to Padua. Solving the hoax is my passion, even if that takes the rest of my life. Without further ado, I'll let the papyri speak for themselves.

Portia

I AM INSANE. My brother Cato has declared so publicly and now
my life is ruined. I am dead too, well at least sometimes, but not
always. Spiritae explained this to me, but I didn't understand very
well.

I am Portia, daughter of Lucinius, master scribe of Rome in the
third year of the reign of Emperor Commodus. I am 15 years old.
My family lives in a simple apartment near the river, not too far
from where Papa walks to work at the Tabularium in the Forum. My
mother is Aeliana. My idiot brother Cato is 16 years old, and my
younger sister, Antonia, is 12.

Papa says my head is injured badly, and I know he fears that my
mind will never heal completely. Mother thinks I am possessed by
evil demons. Maybe they are both correct. Antonia doesn't judge
me. She is sweet and sits beside me quietly, my little guardian angel.

My troubles began last year, shortly after Papa betrothed me to
Cassius. His father, Justus, is a successful merchant, trading in olive
oil from Baetica. Justus was kindly enough toward me, but Decima,
Cassius's mother, didn't care for me at all. She thought Cassius
would have been marrying beneath his station, and she was correct.

I didn't know Cassius very well. Although we were betrothed, he
was away at sea most of the time, learning his father's business,
which he will own someday. Cassius is ten years older than I. He's
not particularly handsome and has waited too long to marry.
Mother says Papa worked a miracle to make this match. I was not

sure about that but had little say in the matter. We were to marry in two more years, and I would go to live with his family. The future held few joys for me.

Mother told Papa that I was very lucky because I am so homely. She states the truth, but it hurts nevertheless. Mother was very beautiful in her day, and my aunt says Antonia received the blessing of Mother's good features. I, on the other hand, look more like Papa. His prominent forehead, large nose, and weak chin do not serve a young woman well. Papa was very angry with Mother when she said this, and defended me saying my gift lay in my intellect, which he claims is sorely lacking in the rest of the family.

Papa is the light of my life. He works terribly hard to provide for us. He is up before sunrise and off to spend a long day, every day, meticulously working on public records. Most evenings he comes home weary and works for several more hours by the dim light of his oil lamp. Papa came from a poor family. His grandfather was a slave for part of his life, and Papa's rise to his position is remarkable. His success comes from his dedication to education and hard work.

Papa talks with me—really talks with me, not at me, as though I matter. He alone makes me feel worthy. I worry about Papa. He is not well, and his eyes are growing dim from the strain of his work. I see yellow clouds floating in his large sensitive eyes. He knows this and averts his gaze whenever I try to look directly at him.

Papa hoped Cato would follow in his footsteps, but Cato is a dolt. He thinks he is Venus's gift to women. Trust me, he's not. His brains are in his testicles, and he thinks of little else than wenching and fighting. Cato would fornicate with a tree if it had a knothole and would stand still long enough. Mother says I am too hard on my brother. She says all men get the lust fever. Cato just needs to scratch an itch, and his affliction will pass soon enough. I remember when I had my first bleed as a woman, and Mother had the talk with me. I was appalled when she explained what men do to women to make babies. In the midst of my shock, she smiled tight-lipped and said that it isn't so bad once you get used to it. I had the distinct impression she was trying not to laugh.

Even more than whoring, Cato dreams of fighting in the arena. He is muscular and practices night and day with his weapons. He has the blood lust too. He is obsessed with gladiator fights and watching innocent people who have fallen from favor be torn apart by wild beasts. Cato goes to the fights at least once a week, and his eyes glint evilly when he recounts them to his friends.

Papa used to take me sometimes to the arena with him. Papa did not really like to go, but said he had to keep up a good public image, especially when the emperor was in attendance. Mother always refused to go, using the excuse she was too ill to be out in public so long. I hate the arena with a passion. If men wish to hack themselves to pieces with a sword, more power to them. But I cannot abide cruelty whenever a soldier chases and slashes some poor unarmed man or creature, just to hear them run shrieking in terror. Our Emperor Commodus is the worst of the lot. He likes to display his prowess, although he is never at risk. I once watched when he rolled into the arena on a tall wheeled tower brandishing a long pike. A large female bear was released into the pit, rushing about frantically looking for a way to escape. Soldiers wheeled the tower ever closer until Commodus was able to dispatch the hapless bear with a spear thrust through her heart. The crowd roared its approval when Commodus cut off her head and held it aloft to the cheers of the crowd.

I vomited. Cato laughed and said, "Wait 'til she gets a look at what the Christians will face today." Papa's face was gray, and we departed hastily, although not fast enough for me. He said I never had to go back, and he never did either. When Mother asked whether his absence would cause a problem, he said, "They can go to the Furies in Tartarus!" Mother blanched at his blasphemy.

Later, I asked Papa about Christians and why Rome seems to hate them so. He told me a story how, over a hundred years ago, a man named Jesus Christ had lived and died at the hands of Romans in a faraway place called Jerusalem. He had preached a doctrine of love and kindness. Some said he performed many healing miracles, and even brought people back from the dead. Some claimed he was the Son of God. He was whipped cruelly and nailed to a cross until he died. He asked God to forgive those who hated him and took away their sins.

I had ever so many questions. I asked Papa, "Was Jesus really the son of a god? Why would anyone hate him just for loving people? Wouldn't that god punish people for killing his son? Did he really perform miracles? Why does Rome punish people just for admiring and following a good man?" Papa looked at me sadly, more sadly than I had ever seen him. He said, "There is much evil in this world, Portia. Do not be blind to the goodness or the evil that can lie in men's hearts. Those who hated Jesus saw him as a threat to their authority, wrong as their rule may have been. There is a higher authority. I shall not tell you what to believe or not believe. Belief begins in your own heart and mind. Faith comes from within, not from without. Open your heart and you will know the answers." I will never know exactly what Papa believed or didn't believe. We never talked about this again, but I think he admired Christians, even at the peril of disgrace or a death sentence, given his position.

Papa has tried very hard to give Cato a good education wherever we have lived. Cato has had tutors to learn reading and writing, accounting, record-keeping, how to bind papyrus into scrolls, how to make our own vellum, and how to make our own ink. And Cato? Mostly, bored out of his mind and a poor student even when he does listen. But I listen and learn like a sponge soaking up knowledge. I want to be everything to Papa that Cato is not, even though I am just a girl. Papa notices me in the shadows during lessons, but he does not chase me back to my chores. He smiles and winks.

Over time, I began to help Papa at night, first secretly making ink and scrolls when his supplies ran low. He noticed and smiled more. He gave me a great gift, my own brass-tipped stylus, although he said it was worn out. He lets me practice lettering on a wax tablet and sometimes on scraps of his writing materials that were not nice enough for his work. He is a patient teacher, and I would do anything to make him proud of me.

Mother is very strict with me. She says girls should not be educated, unless they are the daughters of patricians or senators and not going to have to do any real work. Mother resents that we do not own any slaves to help do her work, although she says we could well afford some. Papa refuses to have any slaves and says slavery is morally wrong. No person should be a master; none should be a slave. Actually, Mother agrees, but life is hard for her. I worry about her too, because her arm trembles constantly, and sometimes it is hard for her to walk without limping. Her strength is failing, and physicians do not know how to cure her. Mother believes girls should not think so much—just busy themselves with women's work. Their lot in life is to make a home, make clothing, cook, and raise children. That's a full-time job in our house. I do not mind helping her, really I don't, but it's an endless chore except when she's resting or sleeping, which these days she does more and more. I love my sister Antonia dearly, but she doesn't catch most of the work or the criticism. I think Mother feels Antonia is destined for a better life because she is so pretty.

Mother is very religious, and we pay homage to the gods at her insistence at our little altar near the hearth and at temples on special days. Papa complains that she is overzealous, but she counters it is wise to worship and honor all gods. Why run the risk of drawing wrath down upon us, as so many stories of the gods tell us? She says Papa's indifference will be the ruin of us all.

Sometimes late at night, I hear Papa and Mother debating important matters. For a woman who claims women should love their place in the home, she is surprisingly knowledgeable and intelligent about worldly affairs. I do not know how she came to be so well informed, but I love listening to her, admiring her, when I hear her at her best.

Both Mother and Papa have a great deal of concern about the future of Rome. They fear that Emperor Commodus, through his excesses, is leading Rome down a path of debauchery and decline. They talk about uprisings of slaves and barbarians from the north and the east, and worry that Rome has grown too soft to defend against those who might wish to ransack our civilization. This talk scares me to death, and sometimes I cannot sleep for hours. After one such evening, I sat by our altar the next morning, and lifting up my hands, I prayed to know what the future would hold for us, and if any god would find favor with me, I wished to be used as an instrument of peace and harmony through my humble means. You must be very careful what you pray for!

One afternoon, I overheard Cato and Cassius planning a jaunt to the seedier side of Rome, no doubt planning an evening of drunkenness and sordid behaviors with prostitutes. Mother had been planning an outing to the market, so I offered to run her errands, all the while planning to look in on Cassius, just hoping to learn what sort of man he might be. I managed to get my best friend Quintina to join me and her brother Priscus to escort us. Mother doesn't permit me or Antonia to go about alone. Soldiers hang around the market, and they prey upon young impressionable girls. Quintina and Priscus were in on my little scheme, and didn't mind my furtive espionage.

Things went wrong in a hurry. Cassius and Cato were crossing a small alley, and I sneaked a peak around the corner of a fruit vendor's stall. My world exploded. I had picked the worst possible moment to put my face smack in the path of a cart being drawn by a horse taking its big chance for an escape. I was thrown heavily to the ground, my head cracking hard like a melon against the stones that filled the chariot ruts.

I came awake, back in my bed with my family hovering around me. Mother said I had been unconscious for three days. Quintina was frantic with worry and guilt. Her mother said she had been crying nonstop. Antonia hugged me repeatedly. My head ached like it was broken into a million pieces. I was seeing double, and a deep gash ran from behind my right ear across my cheek to the corner of my mouth. My bumps and bruises faded over time, but the cut on my face left an ugly scar, drawing the corner of my mouth up into a queer off-center grimace whenever I tried to smile. That wasn't the worst of it by a long shot.

I began having visions—dreams or nightmares—I'm not sure what to call them. I feel a compulsion, something inside me forcing me to write about them. I think they must be important somehow, but I don't know why. I am nauseous when I think about stopping. Writing is not easy for me. Papyrus is very expensive, and Papa can't let me waste his precious supply. Fortunately, Antonia has a friend, Marcus, whose father is a merchant selling sheets and scrolls of papyrus among his other goods. Marcus is about my age, and gets all bug-eyed whenever he is around Antonia. I think Marcus would like to find favor with Papa, so he can be a suitor for her hand. He is kind and handsome. I think they will be a good match. Antonia wants me to like him too, so she convinced Marcus to give me scraps of papyrus that are too poor to use in his father's business. He must have a good supply, and I think he gives me good pieces too so that Papa might think about buying supplies from him.

Finding time to write is not easy either. Mother keeps me busy morning and night until she goes to sleep. Papa thinks I am practicing my lettering late into the evening while he works on documents in the other room. He encourages me to practice diligently because he knows how valuable it is to write documents neatly and precisely. Antonia likes to watch me write, but has no interest in learning, so she dozes off most evenings pretty quickly. Much of what I write about my visions is very dangerous. I cannot allow my writing to bring harm to us, but I cannot seem to stop. I write with different letters, mixed up so that I can understand, but no one else can read unless they know how to put them in order. I keep sheets of practice-lettering on top of my true writings in case Cato starts getting nosy.

Having a vision is not easy on my body. I can always tell when it is going to happen. In the evening, my head starts feeling very woozy, and I can barely see my hand in front of my face. I excuse myself to go to bed early, and my visions begin after I fall asleep. My first vision was especially painful, but each time gets easier. Antonia says I cried out in my sleep, and she found me having a seizure, trembling with my eyes rolled back in my head, and wringing wet with sweat. My writhing stopped quickly, but she sat up all night holding my hand and sponging me with water, waiting to call Mother for help if I began again. She helped clean me because I was incontinent.

The next morning, I was exhausted, but in a deeply relaxed way, I felt at peace inside. Then I made a terrible mistake. I decided to tell Papa and Mother about my vision. Mother was horrified and turning to Papa said, "See, I told you the gods would punish us! Now they have sent demons to plague us." She was especially upset when Antonia told her about my seizure. Mother fears I have inherited her affliction, and doesn't want any blame. Papa looked stricken too, but he said sometimes this can happen when one's head is injured badly, that my visions will go away when my healing is complete. Antonia watched us with mournful eyes. Cato didn't say anything, but looked disgusted as though I was a piece of excrement. But later, he took his revenge. He blabbed to Cassius in front of his family how his crazy twit sister was having fits of madness, scaring the family with outrageous prophecies. Cato called me a name. [Author's note: no translation works well here, but the closest is "pissy-pants."] I was not shocked when Papa had a visit from Justus and Cassius the next day. Neither would look Papa in the eye. Cassius just kept staring at the scar on my face. Justus said he was sorry, but in view of the circumstances, our betrothal was off. Papa didn't argue. After all, what can a father say when his daughter looks deformed and acts so bizarrely? I heard Mother tell Papa later that she knew it would happen; now they would be stuck with me forever. I began to believe the bear in the arena had been lucky.

Afterwards, no one except Antonia wanted to be around me. Mother stopped giving me so many chores, I suppose, because she thought some demon inside me would jump out and bite her. Poor Antonia had to pick up the slack while I, on the other hand, had more free time to "practice" my lettering. I never breathed another word about my visions again to anyone. I may be crazy, but I'm not stupid.

Spiritae

MY VISIONS BEGIN IN A FOG, so thick that you feel disembodied, with not even the outline of shapes, only a brilliant white light. The fog dissipates slowly, and scenes began to appear until everything is completely clear. I truly am disembodied, only a wraith, a mental energy. I cannot choose where I become present. My destinations appear to be chosen for me—places I am supposed to see. Yet, I can move about with free will, flowing like the wind wherever I choose to go. When my vision ends, I grow drowsy and my awareness fades away into twilight until I find myself awakening the next morning in bed. My visions last days, even weeks, but I have never lost time when I return.

I can see and hear normally when traveling in a vision. Sometimes sense aromas and—concentrating very hard—even tastes. Temperature comes and goes, but I cannot touch or feel anything touching me. Hands and legs seem nonexistent...there are only thoughts. I cannot go through objects. When I try, I feel myself streaming energy around the constraint, like an invisible light bending around the outside. No one can see or hear me, no matter how hard I try. I am an observer, not a visitor.

On my first vision, I found myself staring at what must be a very large city. But *oh* what a city! I dared not move. Buildings of enormous height stretched out in every direction to the horizon. Rome is the largest city I know about, but this one would make Rome look like a tiny village. The buildings resembled stone, but they soared above the clouds. Each had marvelous mirrors all over the outside burning my vision with brilliant reflections of the sun, and clear mirrors in places where I could see people moving about inside.

There bloomed a fullness in my head. At first, I thought it was just another headache coming on, but there was the odd sensation of an outside presence, something conscious. I thought my mind must be splitting into pieces as though I were becoming two people. I knew great fear! Of myself, afraid of coming apart, and of inner demons like those I have heard about.

And so, I must tell you about Spiritae. My mind trembled. There followed surging calm...flowing through me. A sense of profound caring—something ancient and unfathomable, something sad.

I tried to speak but could not, so reached out with my mind, "Is someone there?"

Nothing.

After a while, I tried again, certain I was not alone. "Who's there?"

"I am with you."

If I stood upon legs, I would have fallen.

"Don't be afraid, nothing here will hurt you."

"Who are you? What is your name?"

Long pause. "I am. We are. We are one, I am many. There is no difference. I am who I am. I need no name."

So began the first of many frustrating convoluted answers to many queries. My mind—panicking—raced with question after question.

"What are you? Are you a demon, a god? Male or female? You must have a name! Are you real, or am I crazy? What do you want of me? Why are you in my mind? What am I doing here? What is this place? What! What?!"

Very long pause. "Calm down. I have been called many names, been many things to many people. Names have no importance. I am before the beginning of time, beyond the end of eternity. I am all things and nothing at all. What is real to one is not real to another. I am everywhere and nowhere, infinite and infinitesimal. Male? Female? I am less, I am more; this matters not."

"I don't understand! Must you confuse me with riddles? What do want with me?"

"You cannot understand my answers. The full measure of truth lies beyond you. You prayed. I am here. You prayed to bring peace, to have a purpose, and so you shall. I am here. Be not afraid."

"Umm, I remember now, but I didn't think this would come to pass. Not really. What would you have me do? I am frightened."

"Don't be afraid. I mean you no harm. See and hear, listen with your heart, your mind, your essence. Tell my message."

"What message?"

"Follow me. You will know my message when the time is ripe."

"But, but—I must call you *some*thing. Would 'Spiritae' offend you?

Weary pause. "'Spiritae' will suffice as well as any other, if you must."

I sensed "her" mild amusement, even if Spiritae won't own up to being a girl. She seems like a female to me.

I should explain. Spiritae doesn't "speak" to me. I hear no voice. Questions jump into my mind without trying, when I am confused. Sometimes there is no answer. Or, when there is, it makes no sense. Occasionally, after a while, a thought comes back to me that I take as an answer...not knowing whether this is my mind answering itself or answers coming from Spiritae. They *must* be from Spiritae, because some of these are too fantastic to come from *my* imagination.

Spiritae is not big on conversation.

She uses thoughts sparingly, and rarely elaborates when pressed for more details. When she says, "It doesn't matter!"—that's the end of *that*, time to move on.

I stared at the city below for a long time, uncertain what to do. I ventured a thought, "This must be the biggest city in the world!"

"Not even close. There are hundreds larger. People will not control their breeding."

Rebuked, I asked, "What is the city's name?"

Spiritae must have been in a really nasty mood: "I'll tell you one more time. Names are not important. I shall not tell you names of things, people, or places. Knowing their names would prevent you from seeing them for what they *are*, instead of what they are called. Make up your own names, if you must."

Whew! Bad attitude!

I wondered about the yellow-brown haze hanging over the buildings like a great dome. Spiritae thought at me, "The ambiance here is not so sweet. People foul the very air they breathe."

"Why, Spiritae, why?"

"Go and see. That's what you're here for. No time like the present. Get moving."

I didn't know how, or where, to go. "Spiritae, I don't know what to do. I have no body to move. Am I *dead?*"

Spiritae considered that for a moment with a brief mental snort. "Interesting. Life and death—given some thought, not so very different. It doesn't matter. Think about exploring and you *will*. Go wherever you wish. I will be there if you need me."

Chariots

So I WENT AND DESCENDED FURTHER into joy and madness. It would be far easier to tell you what little I did understand than try to describe all I didn't, but here goes. I must tell you of a place and a time when men have become gods, maybe demented and irresponsible ones, a place where life is paradise and the underworld wrapped into one, a time when life is easy and incredibly difficult, where the most common objects are terribly wonderful—or simply terrible.

The first things I noticed were the machinae.

I think they are alive.

Spiritae told me, "No, they were made by men. "She must be mistaken, for what manner of man could fashion such things? Besides, they acted as if alive. In spite of Spiritae's notions, I will give them a name—chariot machinae. They are marvelous creatures, with glowing eyes of brilliant white to show their path, even when they want to roam about at night. On their backsides, they have evil red eyes they flash whenever some other machina runs up behind too close. They run faster than a horse can gallop! I think they are slaves. Maybe there are no more people-slaves, only machina-slaves, for everyone seems to own several of all possible sorts.

Men, women, and children never walk anywhere here. They simply command the machinae to open their wings, and are swallowed into the machinae bellies to go wherever they command.

Machinae look like giant beetles, and come in many shapes, sizes, and colors.

I could tell they were alive from their fierce growls as they sped along, and from the frightening noises—bleating like goats or honking horrifically like geese—when they were mad. Machinae didn't like to roll on the dirt. Everywhere were long black ribbons of roads, smoother than earth, so they would not hurt their wheeled feet. Spiritae said the roadways were made of rotten plants, dead eons ago and mixed with rocks. She must think I'll believe anything.

They drink too—a lot.

I saw them stick a long black tube into a machina's mouth, while a filler machina spat a noxious liquid into the beast. Spiritae said they must drink about every week, and they gulp like camels. She tried to tell me their drink also comes from the same rotten plants that the roads are made from. Guess she thinks I'm an idiot like my brother does.

I don't think men make machinae. How could they? Besides, I see large groups of them clustered in markets. I think these are slave markets where you go to buy machinae after they are captured. Spiritae said I am hilarious, but I didn't know why.

I told her people should be careful or these machina might rise up in revolt.

Market

I WAFTED TOWARD WHAT I THOUGHT must be a marketplace, carefully slipping past the machinae who sat waiting patiently in row after row.

They looked temperamental, and I didn't want to get off to a bad start with them. Near the market, a blue-colored machina opened and spit out a woman and her daughter. Spiritae told me I was to see much of them in the days to come—that I would learn much from these two. This made me happy because they looked nice, and I followed them into the market, which was entirely indoors instead of being arranged in outdoor stalls.

An assault on my senses! I couldn't stop gawking.

The people were giants. I don't think I'm short, but everyone towered nearly a head above me. Interesting to behold, because they were all so unique. I'm not worldly, but in Rome, most of us look alike: olive skin, dark eyes and hair. We sometimes see black-skinned Africans or odd-looking slaves from far away provinces, but these are rare.

The urge to stare at everyone taunted me. There must have been plenty to eat, because many were, well, frankly obese like our fat senators who lie about on couches all day, spouting great thoughts and (according to Mother) doing little to earn a living.

I couldn't understand. The day was hot, but inside the market the air was cold. This didn't bother me, since I couldn't feel anything, but the mother and daughter shivered, pulled more clothing about them. Spiritae said people can control the air inside buildings for comfort, and even to prevent food from spoiling. She said this comes at great expense, though, as vapors they create through this process make it possible for the sun to hurt people. I do not understand what she meant. Her only explanation was mysterious: "Every luxury in life comes at a price."

I was in a scribe's paradise.

Everywhere, and I mean everywhere, was beautiful lettering—on banners, on boxes small and large, in every color of the rainbow. Perfect lettering, better than any I have seen. Spiritae said this was done by machinae. Oh, the poor slaves again! They must practice incessantly. People-scribes must no longer be employed here; the machinae do everything better. Spiritae insisted all machinae are only tools, made by people, to make every aspect of their lives easier. This made me wonder if people do *anything*. Maybe they won't need bodies much longer.

Spiritae said I'm starting to learn to see. I could not read any of the letters, although they were familiar. I couldn't understand the local language either. Sad, for I knew what this meant. Rome didn't exist anymore. The talk I heard sounded vaguely familiar, but guttural and rough, like the language of barbarians. Spiritae said not to worry. Rome was still here, but some things—for good or ill—had changed. The writing floated just beyond my ability to read, but gave me a feeling of vague meaning in each.

I begged Spiritae to help me learn, but she said I could understand well enough. Seeing is better than reading.

I was fascinated by materials everywhere that I didn't recognize. Most of the food in the market was not out on open display, but wrapped in the most marvelous casings. Spiritae said many of the materials were made by people, well, really by machinae made by people. Sure enough, she said those materials were composed of the same rotten plants that the machinae drink!

How many times is she going to pull *that* one on me?

Dryly, I thought: "If that were the case, society would run out of rotten plants quickly. "She said, "Exactly!"

Mother and Daughter commandeered a marvelously shiny basket on wheels. They must have been planning to buy enough food to last the entire year. I couldn't recognize most of it. There were no pens clucking with chickens, nor goats.

Daughter opened a box, and I was shocked to see twelve eggs neatly standing inside. The chickens must be kept out back. The two passed a large clear box filled with various meat and fishes, already cleaned and cut into pieces ready to cook. Preparing a meal must be a breeze. Mother read all the writing on everything she picked up. I figured this was because she couldn't see what was inside, but Spiritae said she was reading to learn if the food was healthy enough to eat. What? Why would anyone eat something if it wasn't safe? Spiritae said many people eat too much food, or food that *tastes* good but isn't nourishing.

When Mother and Daughter prepared to leave the market, they did not bargain with the owner to get a better deal. They were sure to be ripped off! I mean, who goes through life without learning to bargain? Instead, a boy grabbed each item, dragged it along a small moving road over a flashing red eye—another machina that quickly looked at each food and added up a total. I don't think I would trust a machina to do this, but it was as quick as could be.

Before you could blink, the food was packed in brown filmy bags and back in the basket ready to be hauled out to the chariot machina. Mother reached into her bag. I was expecting to see a huge bag of silver coins, as this bounty had to cost a small fortune. Instead, she produced a small hard rectangle of something with pretty letters (no doubt made from rotten plants) and showed it to another machina.

The machina trusted her to pay her account, for she scrawled something there and we were on our way.

Homeward Bound

D AUGHTER TICKLED THE MACHINA'S BACK, and it yawned, opening a large mouth into which she put all the food.

I hoped the chariot machina would not eat it all before they got to where they were headed. The wings flew open, and Mother and Daughter piled into the front. I had just enough time to flow in nervously beside Daughter to see what the machina would do. It coughed and growled awake. Daughter pressed something and it began to sing! Not just in one voice, but many, with thumping sounds and instruments I had never heard. I was stunned. I tried to see how a whole group of musicians could fit in such a small box.

Spiritae said people can capture sounds of anything they hear, and play them again and again whenever they want. What sort of sorcery is this? Mother sat in front of a circle rather like a wheel, which I think was the machina's bridle. She guided the machina left or right whenever she tugged on it. She also squeezed the machina with her foot to let it know when to gallop or to halt. I think it was raining, but we stayed dry. The machina kept blinking its eyelashes for us, swiping the rain off its see-through. Nice of it to be so helpful to Mother.

Despite being large and tough, machinae can be hurt or even killed.

Mother was guiding the machina along carefully when, ahead of us, we heard a terrible screech.

A sickening *crunch*—and machinae body parts were flying everywhere!

Two machinae had gotten into a fight over something and attacked each other. Both lay hurt at the side of the road. One billowed out great breaths of steam, and the other had some fire licking around its mouth.

Mother became annoyed when other machinae stopped to look. She kept glancing at something on her wrist. Spiritae said people are fascinated by time, and Mother's wrist machina would tell her how long she had been delayed. It seemed wrong to be so nonchalant when the machinae were so badly injured. Another machinae rushed onto the scene, red all over, flashing its eyes crazily, and howling like a demented demon.

Men poured out and dashed to the crumpled machinae. They pulled out two people, laying them on beds, and sped away with more yowling. The poor damaged machinae lay ignored.

I cried for them, but Spiritae said not to get all silly about a machina.

They don't matter. Spiritae can be pretty mean-spirited at times. Daughter was even worse. She held a little box in her hand during the whole trip, flicking her thumbs back and forth over its surface, making miniature letters appear. Spiritae explained that people can send messages to anyone no matter where they are. Talk to them, write messages, even *see* them if they want. She said these machinae were very smart, and could track down answers to any question merely by asking aloud. I thought this was wondrous, but Spiritae said, "All good things in moderation. People here can't tear themselves away from staring at the devices. They are becoming slaves to their own machinae."

I asked if the machinae were smarter than people.

She said, "Most of them."

I was exhausted by the time we reached Mother's house (or *palace*...for it looked much like the estates of our wealthiest patrons, maybe even larger). But theirs was not unique. There were dozens and dozens all along the road. As we approached, Mother reached over her head and abruptly a large door opened in the palace, admitting the chariot to a stall where it sleeps at night.

Mother stepped inside, while Daughter gathered all the food bags.

Although Spiritae admonished me about learning names, I listened intently to see if I could figure out those of my family. No wonder Spiritae said not to bother; names here are weird. Daughter's name is Christy. A man, who must be Father, came home, called for Becca, and gave Mother a kiss on the cheek when she responded. I heard her call him Allen. I mean, who would give people names like these? A large dog bounded into the room and scared the wits out of me.

Only very wealthy people in Rome keep dogs, big mean snarling ones to scare away thieves. This one, though, was friendly and beautiful, with long golden hair.

It smiled when it saw Christy.

She kneeled, and called the dog "Goldie."

The golden animal licked her right on the mouth. Yuck!

Most dogs eat garbage people throw away, and lick themselves in unsavory places. But this one must be part of the family. It crawled up onto a long piece of cushioned furniture next to Christy, as though it owned the place.

Becca loaded all the food into a large metal box. I could see its inside glowing, and ice too! How can ice not melt in the heat of the day?

Spiritae said most homes are like the market, having a machina just to keep their food from spoiling. I couldn't help but notice that Christy didn't help out much. *My* mother would be all over me if I wasn't doing most of the work.

I was so tired, and drifted away into darkness....

This was the vision I tried to explain to Papa and Mother. You can see why they thought I should be taken away to some asylum. Of course, I learned in a hurry that visions aren't the sort of thing you spread all over. People simply don't have a lot of tolerance for them.

At first, I had a vision almost every night. Later on, not so often. Sometimes, they would resume right where I had left off.

Second Vision

THE SECOND VISION TRANSPORTED ME into deep purple twilight. What I saw was beyond comprehension.

Lights came slowly on everywhere. One by one, the entire city came alive with a stunning display, lamps burning in every direction, in every color, in every size imaginable. Some flashed, others twinkled, others spelled out words—night became day.

Where could all the oil come from to burn so many lamps? Spiritae said people don't burn oil in lamps much anymore. What? She was giving up on the rotten plant thing? She had a new twist, claiming people have conquered lightning. They can make their own, force it into long strands of copper metal, send it anywhere! It is fed to machinae of every variety. I asked how they make their lightning. You guessed it, mostly from rotten plants! Spiritae has a one-track mind when it comes to humor.

I decided to explore more back at Becca's palace, and appeared there again just by wishing it so. Sure enough, Becca had many machinae, most with long brown or black metal-pronged tails she stuck into the wall to give life to the machinae.

Spiritae said I have to get over this—machinae are not alive. People have learned to create and use forces to animate lifeless things to do their bidding. I don't know why Spiritae thought this was any more believable. She said Becca lives in a home, not a palace, and many people live like this. The more time I spent there, the greater the wonders I saw. A hearth, but it did not burn logs.

Allen flicked a small lever on the wall—flames immediately licked logs without consuming them. I wondered what was burning, and Spiritae giggled, "A gas made from rotten plants."

Oh *please!*

Becca began to prepare dinner.

She took food from the box of ice, and put it into a door that opened in front of her face. She poked at the "fast-cook" machina a few times, and within scant minutes, the food was steaming hot.

I wasn't about to let Spiritae tell me this was the result of lightning and rotten plants again. I wish Mother could see how easy it is here to fix meals. Small wonder they eat so much.

Allen stepped to the box of ice and pulled out a blue metal cylinder. He handed a red one to Becca. They tugged at the top, both cylinders gave a loud wheeze, and they quickly put them up to their mouths so the contents would not spill. Allen drank several swallows of an amber-colored fluid, and gave a satisfied belch.

Becca's mouth scrunched with disgust. I concentrated, and wondered how the fluid might taste if I had a mouth. For a moment, I sensed a terrible tang—nasty!

Becca took a sip of the dark brown bubbly drink, and I tried hers too. Now I know! This could only be ambrosia, the legendary drink of the gods, sweeter than honey, tickling my imaginary tongue. Spiritae said the sweetness comes from plants, not rotten ones, but cooked ones that look like long poles. She is a terrific storyteller.

Christy insisted on drinking milk from the box of ice. I have no idea where they keep their cows and goats.

After dinner, Becca packed their dishes into yet another machina. This one washes them all by itself! Christy came back with a large armload of laundry. This seemed a big deal to me, as we must heat water over a fire for hours, and doing laundry is one of the worst chores. Christy opened the mouth of a machina, sprinkled in some powder, twisted a knob, and that's all there was to it. You'd think she'd have to go out later and hang the clothes out to dry.

Nope, she tossed them into a neighboring machina, and it blew them dry with its powerful hot breath. Christy even added a thin white cloth scented like flowers to make the clothes smell sweet. I'd wash our clothes more than every few months if it were that easy at home.

Becca walked across the kitchen and sat down at a large brown box.

She raised a lid, revealing many white levers topped with some black ones. She rippled her fingers over the levers, and the most beautiful sound I've ever heard came winging forth....

Peering at strange markings before her, Becca played one piece after another. Allen and Christy came over and joined in her singing. Christy showed off her pretty voice, soaring high above Becca's rich, expressive own, the sort you yearn to hear soothing you into sleep.

Allen joined with an enthusiastic male counterpart. Honestly, he was not as tuneful as he thought he must be, but Becca loved having him nearby. After a while, she stopped playing, slumping in exasperation, and I thought she had saddened because her performance wasn't all she had hoped.

This was crazy. People from all over Rome would have come to hear me if I could play like *that!* Sweep me into the presence of the emperor, and shower me with golden coins too. I'm not exaggerating. Apollo himself would beg me for lessons.

Becca reached below the row of white levers and pushed the front of a glowing box on the music machina.

I almost passed out....

The machina begin to play all by itself! I wouldn't have believed it, but it played even better than Becca. With her hands, she had pressed five or six levers at a time. The music machina went wild, dozens of levers going up and down at great speeds that left me breathless. I couldn't decide if Becca had taught the machina to play as her student, or whether the machina was teaching *her*.

Spiritae said, "Don't get too excited. All she did was give it some instructions on that little round thing she stuck in its mouth. It's not intelligent; it blindly follows the instructions."

Not *intelligent?* Geez, *I* should be so dumb!

I faded off to sleep, the music of the gods ringing in my ears, echoing through the chamber of my skull.

Utter bliss....

Christy's Academy

CHRISTY WOKE EARLY, before sunrise, and got ready to go somewhere.

Allen and Becca rose even earlier, and had already departed.

I think Allen went to his work, but I'm not sure about Becca.

I really like Christy, and wanted to follow her all around today. I wish I had an older sister like her.

Christy is absolutely beautiful, even prettier than Antonia. Tall and thin, with long golden hair woven into a single loose braid dangling down her back. This lovely hair is adorned with a strand of brilliant pink, and another of metallic blue. I had no idea hair could be grown hair in these colors. She has the largest pale blue eyes I have ever seen. I cannot imagine a more perfect face. High cheekbones, thin finely-chiseled nose, and fair skin without any blemish. Full lips, too, and I love her generous smile. I cannot help but stare at her perfect teeth, glowing brilliant as if from an inner light.

Christy finished her breakfast, a thin slice of bread cooked in a machina with lightning, and pieces of some type of fruit. She sipped a dark brown liquid in a cup made steaming hot in the fast-cook. This smelled great, but tasted pretty nasty to me.

She headed to a small room to perform her morning ablutions.

This house is amazing. They do not have to go to public toilets or even use pots at night. They not only have a toilet in their house, they have *three*.

I didn't mean to invade Christy's privacy, but was so curious, and she would never know.

The toilet was incredible; white and shiny, like a beautiful throne. She opened the top and I saw it had water inside. I don't think she had to haul it in here, either. She did her business, and cleaned herself with small pieces of scented papyri and moistened cloths scented like flowers.

Can you imagine? Being able to waste precious papyri that way? I kept waiting for her to use a wet sponge on a stick the way I do, but no, that's not the way it's done there. She pulled a silver lever on the side of the toilet, and it gave a great *whoosh*, swallowing everything in one tremendous gulp.

Questions formed in my mind, and Spiritae interjected, "No, the toilet did not have to eat the waste. Don't start feeling sorry for it. It sends everything to a place where the water and waste is cleaned, and put into the river."

What? It's not buried, or collected to fertilize crops? Sounds pretty nasty for the people living downstream!

Christy scrunched up her face at the mild smell she made. She should get a whiff of the public toilets sometime. I have to hold my breath when I go there. She grabbed a tube on top of the toilet, waving it back and forth, while it spit out a fog, filling the room with the heavy scent of a pine forest. What will they think of next?

She shed her night clothes, and prepared to bathe.

I think people here bathe a lot, maybe even every day. Don't they know how much water this takes? Besides, any more than once a week, and you're bound to catch a cold. They must have more water than they could ever drink.

Christy is very curvaceous. Venus can't have much on her. I am envious as I think of my pole-like shape. She stepped into a small clear room, touched more silver knobs, and was pelted with a rain storm.

I thought she would jump from the cold water, but no, the water was warm and steamy. Spiritae started to explain, but all I got was that there was a giant tube-shaped machina somewhere in the house that takes care of making all the hot water.

How? Yep, she started the talk about burning something from rotten plants again....

Christy's skin is flawless, and I saw a colorful image on her shoulder, pretty butterflies and a small bird in green leaves. In her navel was a small jewel crowning a fine gold pin piercing her flesh. I bet that hurt, but it looked very pretty. How can it be that a girl here can have so much?

Spiritae thought rather tersely that people are created with perfect bodies; nothing they do to themselves makes them any prettier. She was not impressed.

Christy looked like she was drowning, and covered herself with white bubbles emanating amazing fruity fragrances. People here must think they really stink. She ought to check out some of those walking around Rome.

Christy dried herself off, and put on a filmy blue undergarment that barely covered her butt. This had an image of a black-and-white bear sewn onto it. She pulled on an undergarment, very delicate and finely made, with cups that covered her breasts and thin straps gripping her shoulders. I didn't understand why this was needed, but it *was* quite pretty, and she admired her looks, staring into a large clear wall bearing a perfect reflection, much nicer than our polished hand-mirrors.

Clothing here fascinates me. Christy didn't dress in a tunic. First, she pulled on a black stretchy fabric that covered her legs up to the waist, leaving her feet exposed below the ankles. This conformed to her body like she was dipped into wax. I have no idea where they find sheep with wool so stretchy. Girls here have lost their modesty, and no one seems concerned when they show off every curve or private part, if even a token effort is made to cover it.

Next, she pulled a tunic-like shroud over her head, down around her waist, but barely covering her backside. Christy owns a whole room full of clothes, all the most amazing colors and styles. Not even the wealthiest women in Rome have clothing dyed so brilliantly with every color imaginable. Probably she could wear a different outfit each day of the year!

She produced yet another machina, and it blew hot air through her hair for a long time, while she raked with a comb. Her mane is thick, lush with many subtle shadings. I know women who would kill to have hair like hers.

It sure took a long time for Christy to get ready, but it was worth it. She pulled several pretty rings onto her fingers, dazzling jewels worthy of the princess she appeared to be. Finally, on went her sandals. Well, not really sandals. Her clothes room had more of those than you can shake a stick at. None bore any wear-marks. Apparently it was important for each to match her clothing, or have some shocking color to attract attention. Some had little platforms under the heels to make her taller. She already is a giant.

Christy pulled out a series of jars filled with powders and dyes. Artfully, she brushed her face with various shades, blending and highlighting, and carefully applied a dark fluid onto her eyebrows. The results were sensational. She didn't look like a painted whore from the streets of Rome. You would swear she hadn't put on anything, yet she looked exceptional. Spiritae opined that she looked fine simply the way she was made.

Eew!

Christy capped her fingertips with two pieces of glass, squirted water on them, and—unbelievable—shoved them into her eyes.

I couldn't imagine how much that must hurt! Why did she want to cut her eyes to pieces? She'll go blind!

Spiritae said, "Oh Portia, don't be simple. People here make glass lenses that correct any weakness in their eyes. Some put large pieces of glass on their noses held in place by fine metal wire around their ears. Christy doesn't think she is as pretty when she wears these, so places small pieces onto the surface of her eyes. They are very smooth, so she isn't hurt one bit."

I might be willing to try putting something around my ears. Of course, everyone in Rome would know I had gone crazy just by my looks. But I certainly wouldn't jam any glass into my eyes even if it meant I could see clear across Rome.

Finally, Christy was ready to go.

My stars, it turned out she had her own chariot machina sitting next to where Becca's chariot slept.

She likes to make it run faster than the way Becca does. I wasn't happy when she whipped out her far-talk, and sent some messages with her dancing thumbs. She should keep her mind on where the chariot is headed in case it decides to make a run for it.

I was excited when I learned her destination—an academy of learning.

I could scarcely believe my eyes. Boys *and* girls get to be educated here! The students move from classroom to classroom, and have different tutors for each subject.

Her first class began with an owlish man talking, writing symbols with a short yellow stick on a slate covering the room's front wall.

Few of the students paid much attention. They sat slouched...completely bored.

Two seated at the back of the class, one of them Christy, sneaked far-talks out of their bags and sent messages to each other, stifling giggles. I suspect this was not permitted.

I wafted into an empty seat, and watched the tutor intensely. I would have given anything to be able to understand.

Spiritae said I had seen as much as I needed to know (sigh)....

Christy's Race

Today "is"—"was"—well, "will be" a special day for Christy. I'm beginning to see what Spiritae means.

Time is relative. Her "It makes no difference" makes more sense when I realize that time depends on who is thinking about it, and it really *can* be the same.

In any case, I was excited to be headed to an arena today with Christy and her family. Not for fighting. Here, men *and* women, boys *and* girls play athletic games—and Christy is an athlete!

She can run like the wind, and ran an important race today. I am her biggest fan. Many people came to watch, colorful banners were flying everywhere, and tremendous excitement filled the air. All around were competitions...boys and girls running, jumping over fences, launching themselves into sand pits, and throwing heavy stones and spears. Everyone cheered the winners, and a woman handed out wonderful golden statues to the triumphant and smaller ones to athletes who almost won.

Soon it was Christy's turn to race on a large oval course surrounding a grassy field. The track had a reddish-orange, spongy-looking surface on which I would have liked to try bouncing. The raceway had stripes, and each runner had to stay in the proper place at the start, and no one was allowed to cheat, or make an early start, lest they end up losing.

Christy appeared in her running outfit, far too immodest, I'm afraid, the shortest garment conceivable.

Cato would have a lust-stroke were he to see her. But the other girls were dressed this way too, and no one seemed to pay any attention. Christy's best friend, Tanika, was running in this race too. They are friends, but also fierce competitors. Tanika is an attractive, dark-skinned girl with the friendliest smile you ever saw. It makes me happy just to look at her.

She has the craziest hair, which she tried unsuccessfully to tie so it wouldn't flop around when she ran. Tanika is powerfully built, with muscular thighs and broad shoulders, rather like a horse bred to run. Christy, on the other hand, is built like an antelope, long-legged, thin with graceful strides, and incredibly agile. All the girls wear special shoes soled with nails that bite into the earth.

The girls crouched on the raceway, feet braced against special pads for a fast start.

Christy and Tanika looked at each other, baring teeth in mock ferocity, growling and giggling.

A man raised his arm, holding some sort of machina. It erupted with a jarring bang and a cloud of smoke. The girls burst from the braces. Tanika and Christy held back, saving energy, letting the other girls surge ahead. As they rounded the great curve they moved to the front, passing their competition.

Abruptly both girls exploded into an amazing sprint—huffing and gulping air, feet thundering side by side toward the finish-line. I wanted to shout, "GO CHRISTY!" but of course couldn't. Christy stumbled—collapsed hard onto the track grating hands and knees as she rolled into a ball.

Tanika at once halted, turned, and rushed to Christy's aid. The other girls rushed by in a pack toward the finish.

Christy stood limping, blood leaking from her knee. She feigned bravery, but her eyes brimmed, and a tear spilled down her cheek.

Tanika's face tightened with concern, and she stooped, shouldered Christy's tottering form. Together they limped across the finish- line...dead last.

Becca came down from the seats, gave a cursory inspection of Christy's knee. *Only a minor scrape*, she told herself, *but it sure did bleed!* She crooned motherly words of sympathy. Christy hugged Tanika and kissed her cheek, eyes brimming with gratitude.

I thought, "How remarkable Tanika would give up a win to help her friend and rival, when she could have run a few more paces and gone back. She shouldn't have lost."

Spiritae whispered, "Neither girl lost. *Both* won more than you imagine."

Becca brought Tanika and Christy home to have lunch.

They sat at the table, thoughts of the race long gone, and chatted away as though they hadn't just spent the day together the day before.

Becca brought out some remarkable treats.

First, they had thin slices of snow-white bread, cut perfectly—doubtless!—by some machina. This heavenly stuff looked like it would melt in your mouth. The three smeared some light-brown goo across the slices (honestly, this resembled something a baby might leave behind). But it smelled nutty and delicious. Becca opened a jar emblazoned with an image of grapes, and containing wiggling purple stuff she smeared atop the nutty layer, followed by another bread slice.

I couldn't help but try to taste it.

Fantastic!

I actually tasted grapes, but this was sweeter than honey. Becca produced a plate of a special treats, chunky circles of sweetened grain flecked with soft white nuts and dark nuggets of something truly amazing. Whatever that stuff was, it was to die for!

The trio washed this down with tall containers of milk—probably served up by another machina far, far away.

Antonia

TONIGHT AS I WORKED ON MY WRITING, Antonia sat in the corner watching sorrowfully.

She often is quiet and reflective, but tonight especially silent. I had to admire her. At 12, she is already a beauty, long brunette hair thick and luxurious, with a gentle braided to twist gently around the right of her face and looped down her back. Sapphire eyes, soulful and expressive, adorn her visage. She's so lucky. A blemish wouldn't dare flaw Antonia.

Those high rosy cheekbones and lips plump for a ready smile are the envy of Venus.

Already, Antonia is developing womanly curves. In a few years, she will drive men to the brink of madness. When sad, she is beautiful. When happy, she is absolutely stunning. She might be nicer than she is pretty, if that's possible.

In her presence, I am a candle beside a roaring fire.

Antonia has been an awesome sister to me, and I love her so much. She has nursed me through tough early visions, comforted me during seizures, mopped my burning brow and gripped my hand when fear shook me. I cry out in my dreams, but Antonia never breathes a word to Mother or Papa.

So I had to know what troubled my dear sister.

"What's the matter, Ants? You look like you have the weight of the world on your shoulders."

"Oh, nothing, nothing important," she sighed dramatically.

"C'mon, c'mon, this is me, remember? Spill it Sis. Your face will burst if you hold it in." This earned a small laugh.

"I was admiring what you are doing. You know, helping Papa with writing and all. You're so smart! I wish I could be like you."

"I can help you learn, if you want."

"If only it were that easy. But Portie, I know I'm not gifted that way. I can't seem to make myself be interested in anything when I have to concentrate very long. It's not that I don't want to. I'm just not that bright."

"I think you're plenty smart. And I would give my right arm to look like you, you're so pretty."

"That's the problem. I'm just another pretty face, someone who will be auctioned off in marriage to some fat old man who lives in a nice villa, and I will be his brood mare to foal his stable of heirs. He will use me up until I can't walk anymore. He won't care whether I can think or even feel. I will be a fancy cat, kept in a golden cage. No man will ever see behind my mask because men are blind. Even Mother can't see beyond my exterior."

I burst into tears and ran to hug her. "I had no idea you felt this way!"

No wonder...what a lonely life she envisioned....

"Antonia, so long as I live and breathe, I will not forget who you are inside, for you are made of solid gold. Your beauty will never sink inside like Papa says, because it has no better place to go. I am your sister, and darned proud to say so. No matter where you go, no matter what your life holds, I will be your best champion. Woe to any man who takes you for granted, for I will take him to task!"

Sniffling softly, we held each other for long minutes....

The love of a sister is precious indeed.

Becca

BECCA MUST BE A SPECIAL MOM, a special woman. I've learned she goes to a job every day like Allen. I thought at first she needed to work too to afford all the marvelous things they own. But the truth is more wonderful. Becca makes her own contribution to the family, in fact the world, and is not second-class to anyone. Allen accepts and loves her for this. How hard she works!

I can see where Christy gets her good looks.

Like Antonia, she has copied her mom pretty closely. Becca is still beautiful, even with the lines showing in her face. These must be badges of accomplishment, which render her lovelier still.

I decided to follow Becca to work, before the sun comes up, and she guided her chariot into a resting place at a very large building complex. People greeted her with awe, which told me she is a person in command. A physician, a healer!

Becca didn't waste a second, washed her hands over and over with a foul-smelling reddish-brown liquid, and put on some artificial hands that snugly fit over her own.

After this, she headed to a room where others clothed her in a loose-fitting blue gown that entirely covered her. Hair tight-pinned, she donned a partial head-piece with another veiling her mouth and looped over her ears. Finally, some clear material snugged across her eyes, secured with a strap. This outfit was terribly hot and confining. My mind roiled with questions.

Spiritae whispered something to me, but I understood only that she couldn't allow dirt and bugs from herself onto those she favored with her healing. Becca had bugs? I don't think so. She had several helpers, each protected by blue gowns.

She entered a brightly lighted room, its space a scatter of silvery machinae.

A woman, seemingly asleep or unconscious like I had been, was rolled into the room on a metal bed.

What was wrong? I couldn't say. They covered her with a large blue fabric, only a small square hole opening over her abdomen, and washed her with the nasty liquid (Spiritae said this was bug-killer—oh please!).Becca plucked a small sharp knife from a silver tray, and cut a straight line into the woman's belly.

What a shock! Blood spurted everywhere, but no one even got excited!

They leaned closer and sopped it with sponges, and kept going.

Becca slipped a long black tube into the woman, and glanced at a glowing machina before her. A miracle indeed, for I realized she peered into the woman's body.

At once I was fascinated and queasy. Becca worked on the woman a long time, inserting tools and cutting, extracting blobs of flesh seemingly corrupted with disease.

Finally, she busied herself sewing shut the woman's insides like some mad seamstress.

The helpers finished the job, and cleaned away the bloody mess.

Becca had no time to catch her breath, before moving on to another patient in a different room.

Later that day, perspiring and exhausted, she pulled off her gown. She didn't go home yet, but checked on the people she had so busily tried to heal.

She found the first woman, sitting up in bed and still drowsy, but talking with family.

I could tell by their relieved expressions that Becca told them the woman would get better.

They gazed at Becca in awe like she was in fact a goddess.

In her own way, I think she is. I would love to be like her. I would study all day, all night, if I could even be her helper.

Young Love

C HRISTY HAS A BOYFRIEND! I wondered why, at her age, she was not betrothed, especially since she is gorgeous.

Things have really changed here! Spiritae said fathers and mothers here don't make marriage agreements for their children. Children are permitted to make their own choices about marriage, although the parents try to discourage them if the match is not to their liking. Sometimes the children marry even without the blessing of their parents!

Finding a good match on your own must be very difficult. I mean, how is a girl to know whether her new family is prepared to take care of her and their son's children? Children here "fall in love" first, and then think about marriage. Mother says making a good match for the family is one of the most important things a parent can accomplish, and "love," if it is meant to be, will come in time. I think she is right, and can see that Mother and Papa love each other.

In my time, women do what the man wants according to his wishes.

Of course, these wishes can be swayed most of the time, but must be done craftily so he never loses face by not being in control. After all, if the man sets us aside, we are fallen, and life becomes nearly impossible. Here, women have more opportunity, and some even live alone, raising children born out of wedlock, earning a living much like a man. This must be very difficult. Here, women express their opinions more openly, even forcefully. I'm sure this doesn't always bring peace and harmony. More like tying the tails of two cats, and may the better cat win!

Christy's boyfriend, Paul, is a very handsome young man, maybe one year older than she. He has shaggy black hair and dark brown eyes. Tall, with wide shoulders and a smile that glows white like Christy's. I can see in their eyes they are wildly in love, and never stop glancing at each other, grinning and blushing. Becca and Allen like Paul, and Becca likes to give the couple her delicious treats whenever they can be bothered to sit down at the table in the cooking area.

Today, Paul and Christy were off on an adventure. Apparently their parents trust them not to need chaperones. I tagged along, since they couldn't see me being a third wheel. They were headed to a large public building. Inside were large glowing walls designed to entertain large groups. Room after room of walls, so there were many choices.

Paul bought Christy a treat, a small box of dark brown beans. I stole a taste, and decided they must be shriveled grapes covered with that same brown stuff in Becca's treats. Highly addicting! They also bought a large tub filled with some puffy white stuff, gooey with yellow sauce and salt. Woo-hoo! No wonder she loves him so much!

The lightning lamps were turned off, and a booming sound filled the dark space. Paul and Christy snuggled into their cushy chairs and munched their treats.

I didn't understand much of what I saw, but liked the moving drawings. These resembled people, but not exactly, like some of the moving images I have seen on the far-sight machina. Spiritae claimed these come from the imagination, whatever that is.

Christy sat riveted by the wall, gazing at a young empress who lived in an icy world. She must be a goddess, because all she had to do was thrust out her arms and immense showers of ice flowed at her command, freezing into buildings and bridges and beautiful wintery scenery, accompanied by expansive singing. If only I could have understood the words! I sensed an inspirational declaration—freedom from what others expect you to be.

Paul paid little mind, and lovingly fixed his gaze on Christy's face, arm draped over her shoulders. His hand probed for places it probably shouldn't have gone.

I thought Christy might get angry, but no, she snuggled her nose into his neck. Time for me to head out of there. Some things I didn't need to see. I think Christy would be well-advised to keep her toga tightly about her, if you know what I mean.

Papa

Tonight I was feeling glum, musing over Christy and Paul and how they were free to pursue their feelings of love without being married off in a family quest to better their parents' status and fortune.

After dinner, I joined Papa in his work room, sitting in the corner to copy some documents he had turned over to my attention. Mother and Antonia had slipped out to visit with some neighbors and Cato, as usual, was out for the evening with "friends." I was proud that Papa had trusted me with some real work, although I knew it was far from anything important. Mother doesn't like me to call Father "Papa" as she thinks this shows disrespect, but when we are alone, he encourages me to call him by the name I first learned as a baby. Mother was never "Mama," always "Mother."

I tried to focus on doing my best lettering, but my mind wandered. Papa is usually immersed completely in his work, but tonight he kept glancing at me with concern. Finally, he set aside his stylus and said, "You are quiet tonight. Are you still hurting from Cassius and Justus calling off your marriage?"

"Not really, Papa. I have a lot on my mind."

"Come on, little one. This is Papa you're talking to. Tell me what is troubling you."

"Oh Papa! I don't care about losing Cassius. He didn't care about me. His father only wanted him to make some heirs for his business—some that he could acknowledge as his children instead of the ones he's so busy making all over Rome."

Papa winced. "Yes, I'm afraid he and Cato are up to no good. I admit, it wasn't the best match ever made, but your mother had high hopes that it would turn out for the best given some time. I shouldn't have given in to her wheedling. I'm sorry."

"I feel terrible that you and Mother are stuck with me now."

"Stuck? Stuck?! *I* don't feel that way. Portia, you are a treasure in my life, perhaps the best thing that has ever happened to me. I have never looked forward to the day when you would leave our house."

"But Mother does. I heard her say so to you."

Papa's eyes narrowed in anger at the memory. "Your mother has an unfortunate habit of letting some words slip out of her mouth before they pass through her brain."

He nodded, as if reaffirming the notion. "In spite of what you might think, your mother does love you and wishes you all the best. However, her vision of what is best is what *she* thinks is best. She means well, but is very rigid and opinionated."

"Papa, do you think the day will ever come when girls will get to choose who they will love and marry?"

"Hmm. Don't know. *Maybe.* I think that might make for some really good matches and some really terrible ones. But you have a point. There are good and bad matches made the way we do it now."

"Mother says you don't have to love to get married. Love comes in time. You love Mother, right? Did you love each other when you were first married?"

He shrugged, as if asked why the sky is blue. "I've never told you much about those days, have I? Your question is not easy to answer. There are many forms of love, and these change over the course of your life. There is the hot passion of youth, the allure of romance and physical attraction. You may find the love of a partner who is your best friend, your confidant, the person who completes and complements you. Another love is born of deep respect for each other and mutual compromises. Love can be shared memories, experiences, and the joys of raising your children together.

"Sometimes love means you do not always need to talk, as you already know what the other is thinking. Your happiest moments are those when you are together, and you even grow similar in appearance as though you were created just for that person. There is the bittersweet love of facing life's troubles together and surviving. You love growing old together, caring for the other when you are needed, holding hands as on the day you met. Love does not die, for there is love after death, when your dreams turn to the day you will be reunited.

"So yes, we have come to know many of these. But it was not always so. When I was about Cato's age, I was completely smitten by a young girl, Marina, who was the daughter of a baker in my village. We were wild about each other, and I thought of her night and day. To me, the sun rose in her eyes. My father and your mother's father, Seneca, were the best of friends. Together they decided we should wed. Your mother and I looked at their decision as a disaster. I ranted and raved how I wanted to run off with Marina. Your mother was a beauty then, and still is. She had imagined a life of luxury, and being married off to a lowly scribe was not her idea of good fortune. But our fathers were adamant. In the midst of all the turmoil, Marina's mother intervened. She stated publicly that Marina was too young to be betrothed, and in any case, she could not abide me as a suitor. I never saw Marina again. To this day, I wonder what happened to her. Guess I'll never know. "How different life might have been. But in the end, Aeliana and I were wed, much to our chagrin. You might think, as did I, our marriage could never work. Somehow it has. Not always easy, but no marriage is. Marriage takes work, commitment, and compromise. As I look back, I feel blessed. Your mother is a good woman, has given me three fine children, and made a good home for all of us. Without her, I would not have you, which would be a real tragedy. I only wish I had made her happier."

"Oh Papa!"

I embraced him, and buried my face in his shoulder. It made me sad to think how he had acquiesced to expectations instead of following his heart.

He held me at arm's length, and with a penetrating glance asked, "How have you been feeling. Still having visions?"

I was wary, but didn't want to lie. On the other hand, it would serve no good purpose to worry him with more examples of my insanity.

"Sometimes I still have vague dreams, Papa, but they aren't hard on me anymore. I really think I'm almost well now." He seemed relieved, and I changed the subject. "I don't mean to say mean things about people, but I don't think Cassius is a very nice man. You know about his carousing at night, don't you? I think he has a bad influence on Cato. Jaw set, he said, "I'm not sure who is the worse influence, but I've had harsh words several times with Cato about this matter. He has a strong will, and doesn't heed my advice much. I do not condone their behavior one bit. Cassius was not a good choice. I'm sorry I let myself be convinced otherwise."

"Papa, I wish I could have been your son. I would have made you proud and followed in your footsteps."

He seemed flabbergasted. You are the finest treasure in my life. I could not be more proud of you. I would not trade you for a son by any stretch of the imagination. I think a day will come when women will be accepted as scribes. Maybe you will be the first."

"Papa...what Cassius and Cato are doing frightens me."

He regarded me with a squint. "You mean you are frightened about relations?"

I nodded. He said, "Your mother talked with you about this a couple of years ago, right?"

"Yes, I know all about how babies are made, but...but, it sounds so, well, *nasty.*"

"I know it is not easy for daughters to talk with their fathers about such things. Not easy for me either. It is natural to feel timid.

Boys feel timid too, although they don't like to admit it. Maybe I can help, not about the 'how' of it, but what to seek.

"Sexuality can be one of the greatest gifts in life or one of the worst burdens. A lot of the outcome depends on your attitude and self-respect. It should not be feared, nor treated lightly either, for fulfillment of this aspect of life calls for responsibility and commitment to a special person in your life. This subtlety has eluded Cato so far, but I still have hopes for him."

He paused and blankly stared, as if searching shadowy halls of memory.

"Men who see women as conquests, who spread their seed like they are pollinating flowers do little to honor the gift the Creator has bestowed upon them. Women who thrive on the art of seduction for money or status also do themselves a disservice. Many people have pitfalls. Men are drawn like moths to a flame by feminine charms, with no regard for their inner grace and intelligence. Women fall for men with wealth or powerful physiques, without consideration of their character. Children are eager to become adults, and behave as such with no capacity for mature responsibility."

He paced, but no more than usual. I hoped this wouldn't change. I simply watched and listened.

"Men or women who become enamored with their own appearance, who leverage their outward appearance at the expense of their inner qualities are no better than Narcissus. They will find no better fate in the long run. Beauty fades with time. I like to think of beauty retreating inside as we age, leaving wrinkles to show where it once lay. Later in life, you have to look deeper for beauty, and you must work to make your insides beautiful."

I had to smile at that imagery.

"But the importance of sexuality in a relationship should not be ignored either. Sex is a human need, not merely an act for having children. It can be abused so that it fails to be a pleasure, or even a need. A man who treats his wife like property, someone to be used at his pleasure, will never know the joy of a good relationship. If he wears his wife out bearing children, he will leave her devoid of spirit. But, a wife who disdains sex or withholds her favors to gain what she wants does herself and her mate an injustice too.

"You will find extraordinary happiness when you find that special person who you care about more than yourself, whose happiness is everything to you, and he feels the same about you. When you come together as one, you should each give your love and receive the gift of pleasure in equal measure. There is no need to feel shy, even when you feel civilization stripped away from your senses and you are immersed into instinct. Be as comfortable with your mate as you are with yourself. Don't fault or judge. Affirm and fulfill. Sex is more than a physical pleasure. It is a melding of your minds, your hopes, your inner selves, as though you join two candles to burn as one. When that love creates a child from the glow in your eyes, there can be no greater pleasure in life."

"Papa, that sounds so beautiful. You give me great hope."

"My wish for you is that you will have a daughter exactly like yourself. Promise me something special—our secret. A day will come when you are together with the man who is the love of your life. I will help you to find that sort of man if it is the last thing I do. It may well be my most vital act. Do you remember our secret glade, the intimate garden meadow on the far side of the river we used to explore in your youth?"

"Of course. It is so pretty there."

Now it was Papa's turn to smile.

"When the time is right, take your husband there on a night when the moon is dark. Make love in the soft grass beneath all the flaring stars above. Your souls will dance together, and you will receive the Creator's gift for your daughter. At that moment, you will understand these words...."

I blushed to my very core, for he was telling me how I was conceived, in love, under a canopy of twinkling stars. "I love you Papa, so very much."

With that, I padded off to bed, and sank into the vast strange symphony of dreams...aware I would be seduced onto another path of visions....

Far-Sights

THE FAMILY SETTLED FOR THE EVENING in their gathering room. Becca arrived late from the healing place as usual, but Christy helped cook a meal. She doesn't practice often, but I think she will be a good homemaker unless she decides to work elsewhere like Becca.

In minutes, she had food containers opened from the box of ice, loaded into the fast-cook and—just like that—meat and several vegetables steaming on white plates.

After dinner, Becca rushed around putting clothing into the machina for washing, while Allen entered his special room where he does night work, like Papa does most evenings.

Christy vanished into her sleeping room, where I think she was supposed to study work from the academy, but she spent most of her time on the far-talk making kissy-talk with Paul.

Later, everyone changed into night garments and settled onto the couches around the far-sight.

I thought they might gather to talk, but no, family conversations are a lost art. I had seen the far-sight when I first came to the house, but had not realized what it does. Becca doesn't like to see it glowing all the time, and she dictates when this machina will be used. Now I understand why. It is very powerful, and should not be used unwisely or too often.

The far-sight has amazing capabilities. Sometimes there were people talking and showing sight-captures or moving captures. I think they were discussing important matters from far away, but I couldn't really understand. Then someone showed sight-captures with symbols about weather, as though they knew what the weather would do in a few days!

I think maybe they can control the weather and are telling people what they are planning to do. Goldie too curled at Christy's feet watching the far-sight. Tilted her head back and forth, ears perked up whenever some animal appeared.

It frustrated me to realize that Goldie understood far more than I. Christy paid no attention. She was too busy poking her far-talk. Women walked into view and talked about games at the arena. They got right up in the face of the gladiators and poked a black stick in front of their mouths, which made them sound much louder. I didn't understand any of this, or any of the rules, but the contests must be just as popular here as they are back in Rome. This was the only time Allen put down what he was reading and paid attention. Not sure which he liked best, the gladiators or the talking women.

Becca had a black stick too, but she used it to tell the far-sight where to look and how loud to talk. She wouldn't let Allen touch it. I think the far-sight can look anywhere in this world, and she changed its vision quite often. Spiritae said I must be extremely careful trying to learn from what I see on the far-sight. About half of what is shown is meant to entice people to buy things, and they behave in crazy, weird ways to get your attention.

The far-sight showed us the same images over and over, as though we were too stupid to get it right the first time, and wanted to pound it into our brains. Though I don't speak the language, I got the idea quickly enough, and watching this grew quickly tiresome.

Spiritae said people pay money to make you watch this stuff, so you don't get much choice. Otherwise, you're not allowed to watch anything more worthy. More importantly, Spiritae says it is impossible to know what is real, what people want you to think is real, or what is purely from the imagination.

I'm not confident what imaginary means, but I think it's like guessing or pretending. She said I must not jump to conclusions, and not everything I see is happening at present.

The far-sight can store images for as long as anyone wants and then spit them out whenever desired. Spiritae said some things I saw happened in the distant past or only yesterday. There was no way for me to know. I asked if the far-sight could see into the future. Long pause. Spiritae said, "Not exactly." If I get it, she means some pretend things might come true and others might not. Like having a vision, I guess. In my heart, I think maybe all the things I saw were real, but she didn't want me to know about bad things—and I saw some extremely shocking scenes.

Let me describe some of these.

I saw a giant fish with glaring eyes come up out of the sea, roaring, and attacking some people. It bit the leg off a boy when he swam nearby, and his leg sank to the bottom in a cloud of blood. The fish had teeth bigger than my hand and blood dripping down its chin. I am not going into the sea ever again. I'm not about to take any chances that there is even *one* of these monsters living in the ocean.

I watched a giant ape climb to the top of a sky building holding a tiny woman in his hand.

I feared he might eat her, but he kept looking at her with bug-eyes like he was in love or something. Some metal flies attacked him, and he swept them to the ground whenever they bit him. Later, he got into a fight with a giant lizard that bellowed and spat fire from its mouth! An entire city burned to death instantly with a piece of the sun that was thrown onto it, which grew into a terrific-size mushroom of fire.

There was a talking green frog in love with a girl pig. Palaces perched on beautiful white beaches, surrounded by skinny trees with leaves only at the top, waving gently to and fro above the loveliest blue-green water you ever saw. And men in flying machines that hovered like dragonflies. When they settled to the ground, others dressed in green with bubbles on their heads jumped out. They carried black sticks and sprayed people with instant death. I think one man could kill an entire Roman legion with one of these.

There was a horse talking to its owner. I'm sure it was smarter than he. I hope!

And a man in a blue suit and red cape lifted a huge puffing machina over his head. He jumped and flew into the sky. This guy would be a terrific gladiator in the arena. I saw men climb inside a machina that breathed fire, and step out onto the Moon! Also thousands of men saluting their emperor stiffly, arms extended as one. The emperor had a small mustache, and shouted all the time. I saw terrible sights of starving people, piled as they died into big openings in the ground, and men spit death at them with their sticks. Then a big machina pushed soil over them to hide their bodies. Some of them were still screaming. There was a man capturing lightning and making a monster he had stitched together come to life. Given the easy access to lightning around here, I think this scared me the worst.

I saw places where families were happy, and everyone laughed hysterically at almost everything the other said. And a storm on the ocean knocked a giant boat upside down, and the people were drowning. I saw a place where terrible people came staggering into the city at night, walking with stiff legs, and the flesh was rotting off their faces. Another image had athletes competing against giant machina. They had to run, jump, climb, and finally the machina would knock them into water far below and everyone cheered when they made a big splash.

I saw men kissing men, and women with women too. I think this happens sometimes in Rome, but we don't sit around watching it. Becca likes to watch shows where people are cooking food, and I liked these too. I thought maybe the far-sight would let me taste the food they were making, but I couldn't figure out how to do this. Sometimes there are contests, where the winner looks very happy. The other contestants walk away sulking.

I asked Spiritae about everything I was seeing, but she wasn't very cooperative.

"People watch the damnedest things. There's no accounting for the crazy stuff they come up with. You'd think with all the beautiful things in this world handed to them on a silver platter (weary sigh)...."

Obviously, Spiritae thinks I should not waste much time with far-sights.

Dance Party

CHRISTY IS VERY POPULAR at her academy and has many girlfriends. It must be wonderful to have so many friends. We are so busy at home that we can only make friends quickly at the market, or when we are washing clothes together.

Today was Christy's birthday, and I counted seventeen candles glowing atop the sweet treat Becca had baked for her in an oven. It was sweet, soft bread, dark with that wonderful brown stuff they put in treats, and covered with a swirled creamy topping. I couldn't decide which tasted best. No matter, everyone took pieces that had both! Everyone sang happily to honor Christy, and then she blew out all the candles with a big whoosh of air.

No one seemed to care that she spat onto the treat when she blew them out.

One candle kept lighting itself again and again even after Christy blew it out, and Becca laughed like this was some old family joke. Maybe it was.

Christy received a special gift—a celebration party with her friends. Becca and Allen have a cherished room at the bottom of their house for gatherings, and they invited seven of Christy's best friends to have fun and spend the night.

Becca made plates of various enticing treats for the girls to sample.

I know Christy's friend Tanika, but I couldn't keep the others straight. They looked alike, and their names sounded all the same.

Allen and Becca stayed upstairs and left the girls to their fun. Becca peeked once in a while, out of sight, to make sure the girls didn't sneak in any wine or boys.

Christy turned on a far-sight, and I wondered what sort of weird things they wanted to watch.

But this far-sight was different.

It taught them how to sing and dance. A woman dressed in garments painted onto her body started to explain and demonstrate movements. The woman must dance all the time, as she was very fit.

The girls watched intently, and soon were doing a great job of mimicking the instructor's techniques. The music was loud and rhythmic, and very intoxicating. I think it must have gotten into each girl's arms and legs, and hips, in the most outrageous way. I could imagine Allen upstairs rolling his eyes and covering his ears at the racket, but he put up with it as part of the fun. Goldie flitted back and forth among the girls grinning, gathering pats of affection, and occasionally barking her excitement.

The girls stood in a line, danced and bobbed and swayed in perfect synchrony.

I imagined, "pretended," that they had included me too, inviting me to jump in at the end of the line.

Even without limbs, I felt myself bouncing, swiveling, and rocking about like the crazy woman I am. No thinking, just letting the music guide my body wherever it desired. I don't think I've ever had so much fun! The girls sang at the top of their lungs. They knew every word, too. I wished to join the singing, and I managed, if only in spirit.

Finally, they were satiated, and collapsed onto the floor in gales of laughter.

One girl sneaked up behind her friend, raised a sleeping cushion, and whacked her in the head!

Soon, a terrific battle broke out—everyone wrestling and shrieking in the middle of flying cushions. After a while, Becca appeared and gave a stern look, although everyone knew she didn't mean it.

When she turned to leave, she heaved a cushion at the back of Christy's head and dashed upstairs.

For a few minutes, it was chaos again, but the girls were winding down. Each brought out her own cushion bed, which were unrolled across the floor. The wee hours of the morning found them sound asleep, exhausted by their reverie....Girl power at its best!

I know each of us will remember this night for the rest of our lives.

Allen's Work

Today was Allen's turn to be followed by a wraith. I had no idea what he does for his job, and I suspect that Becca and Christy don't either.

Like Becca, Allen leaves the house before sunrise and puts in a long day at work. He starts his day sitting at a table and sipping a cup of that nasty brown liquid that Christy likes too. This is usually accompanied by a visit to the front door, where Allen collects a scroll of papyri covered with exquisite writing by scribe machinae and some sight-captures.

I asked Spiritae to help me understand what he was reading, but she said that would cause more trouble than it was worth. She would only say the scroll reveals what has happened or is planned to happen. That sounded quite interesting, but she said no, there's precious little of value inside; it contains mostly bad things about people, and I would get a distorted view of the world. Better, in her opinion, to go look for myself.

I couldn't decide if Allen's job was hard or not. Mostly, he sits all day in front of a glowing machina, reading and pecking away at a board that makes symbols appear on the light-board before him. This must require considerable concentration, and I would be bored to tears in a few minutes, let alone if I had to do this for year after year.

For much of his day, Allen is seated in gathering rooms and listens to people making speeches and observing symbols cast onto glowing walls.

I saw a remarkable machina. Allen had a piece of papyri covered with beautiful writing. He slotted this into the mouth of the machina, and faster than you can blink your eye, it spit out an exact twin. I don't think I'll get too close. This place doesn't need *two* Portias.

While he was in the room with the twin-maker machinae, a woman came in, acting very friendly with Allen—too friendly, in my opinion.

She appeared exotic and was dressed in fabulous clothing. She got up close before him, blocking his way to the door, and repeatedly touched his arm and plucked at the front of his...not sure what you call a tunic here.

I wanted to fly at her and slap her silly.

How dare she act like a harlot? I'm not about to let anyone hurt Becca or Christy! But Allen shook his head *no*, and moved the woman aside, none too gently. She sashayed off, swinging her hips and looking back to see if she was making him sorry. Good for him. She wasn't working any magic.

I was about to drift away looking for other adventures when Allen finally left his chair, his work area, and headed to where hard work was being performed.

Maybe his job has something to do with it, maybe not. He walked a long way through many doors to a building so large that I couldn't see walls on the far side. This was only one of many such buildings. What I saw inside was truly frightening. There were great vats of liquid fire metal, white-hot, so bright that I could not look directly at it without leaving purple spots in my eyes. Maybe this is what comes out of volcanoes from deep within the Earth. Mother would call this Vulcan's workshop.

Everywhere I looked, ribbons of fire leaped, emitting showers of sparks and fumes. The noise was deafening, the pounding of hammers so hard it vibrated your bones. The stifling air burned, thick with smoke and ash you wouldn't want to inhale. I wanted to ask Spiritae what manner of underworld this was, but I doubt that she will ever come into such a place, and I couldn't have heard her above this din anyway. All this seemed to have one purpose—to produce great expanses of red-hot metal that machinae use to make other machinae.

I followed Allen all the way through this building to others far distant, yet connected. Here, my senses were assaulted once again. I saw machinae making chariots! Dozens of machinae with giant arms waving about in an evil synchronized dance. These raised pieces of chariot bodies, placing them where they belong, and fixed them in place with fiery showers of sparks. Quickly, as if never tiring and chased by demons.

I saw few people here, only machinae doing many chores: lifting, carrying, cutting, forming, and much, much more I could not understand.

I see what Spiritae was trying to tell me.

Machinae are not alive in the way people are alive. No. They are faster, stronger, harder-working, and getting smarter all the time.

I am glad I will not live long enough to actually dwell in this time. A period of people living in a golden age, cushioned in luxury, oblivious to the mysteries of an underworld where machinae toil away.

What horror! What melancholy!

I sense a time when people will no longer be relevant.

Quintina

QUINTINA FLOUNCED IN THIS MORNING, sprawling over the couch in our gathering room and flopping her arms and legs like a crazy woman.

I've known Quintina since we first moved to Rome. She's a hoot and my best friend. Quintina said, "Father and his new wife booted me out of the apartment for the day—well, you know why, and she rolled her eyes pretending a bewildered innocence. Father gave me some money and told me to make myself useful at the market. He means 'Don't show up around here before dark'," and she barked an ornery laugh.

Quintina—just looking at her—makes me giggle. She can imitate anyone and says the most outrageous things. If she were a man, she could make an easy living in the theater. Her every expression ignites laughter—with leering eyes, grimaces, nose scrunches, or any of a million other gestures.

"What do you say, Ports? How about if we head down to the market and blow some of Father's sex-bribe money? I heard your mother and Antonia are away for a couple of days visiting your aunt."

"Yeah, they're not coming back until late tomorrow, but Mother left me a boatload of chores to do."

"You're not still having those headaches and crazy visions, are you? It will do you good to get out for a walk." She gave me a penetrating look, as though really wanting to see if I would explode into some insane rant.

"Naw, no more visions or demons," I lied. "Guess my head is nearly healed."

"C'mon then. Let's not waste the day. Besides, I'll give you a hand. We'll be done with your chores in no time."

She wasn't kidding. When Quintina wants some free time, she can work like a whirlwind. Of course, she takes shortcuts that Mother would force me to redo if she caught me doing anything not in accordance with the way she thinks things ought to be done. But with Quintina's help, we were ready to frolic away the afternoon in less than an hour.

Quintina loves to shop. I'm not sure which she enjoys more, fingering all the merchandise or flirting with the young men who attend her in hopes of making some big sale. She dresses the part, so they all think her parents are wealthy nobles. For the most part, they ignore me when I tag along. She simply lights them up with her personality, and I have fun imagining that I'm her twin sister which, of course, I could never be unless we were named day and night. Quintina is attractive, not stunning like Antonia, but so vivacious that people cannot take their eyes off her. She really knows how to command attention."

Mother has taught me how to bargain at the market, but no one, and I mean no one, outdoes Quintina.

The first stall we visited displayed beautiful bursts of flowers: pink roses, narcissi, oleanders, violets, lilies, gladioli, irises, and poppies, all artfully arranged in colorful urns.

Quintina sauntered over acting disinterested, and said to a handsome young man, "Oh, it's you, Rufus, isn't it?" She knew darn well it was, we've seen him a dozen times, but he clearly warmed to her recognition.

"I see the season must be getting a bit too hot and dry, not good for business."

His eyes widened in shock, as the flowers were fresh, singing with fragrance and fully bloomed.

"Philo, across the market, has such nice fresh flowers, but it's probably easier for him to get water from the river. Still, I would rather buy from you than have to walk all the way back there. You are so nice. Do you have something lovely that doesn't cost too much?"

By now, Rufus was stammering, trying to think of a reply. Finally, he thrust a massive bouquet into Quintina's arms, and asked a pittance for them. Seeing her hesitation, he insisted on putting several of his best roses in our hair, no charge of course.

Quintina beamed her best smile, and the lad knew paradise. She left him guarding her flowers until we could retrieve them after finishing our shopping.

Quintina decided we were getting hungry, which seemed to coincide with passing a stall displaying honeyed wine, boiled eggs with pine nuts, and fish sauce.

Another young man with startling coal-black eyes was her next victim. We walked on with more than we could eat, and she had hardly broken into her father's stash of coins.

"Quintina, don't you ever feel guilty playing boys this way?"

"Oh sure!" she lied, assuming a perfectly contrite expression without trying. "I feel just awful when they throw everything they have at my feet. Of course, they feel obligated to do so since I am their goddess." She distorted her face into an amusing grimace that said, *You are such a novice, Portia!*

I laughed helplessly at her charm.

Quintina flirted our way up one side of the market and down the other, mesmerizing every male older than roughly ten years.

Dusk was dimming the scene when she remembered that she had been asked to bring home some fish for dinner. Quintina told me her father has a passion for eels, and began a hilarious comedy routine about this. She mimicked eels with gaping mouths talking to each other while waiting patiently for their heads to be cut off. "Look at this man's new wife, Eelo! She's almost as plump as you!"

"Yes, Fish Breath, she's a fat one all right, and her skin is scaly like mine too!"

She agitated her wrists and flailed her fingers like eels' mouths— which cracked me up.

Quintina doesn't care much for her stepmother, and apparently the feeling is mutual. Her birth mother died about eight years ago from a fever, and Quintina hasn't warmed up to her father's new choice.

She launched into a new routine, this one about how her stepmother eats octopi tentacles only to make her father happy, since he enjoys them so much. She mimicked her stepmother sampling one, the suckers sticking first to her tongue and then to her cheeks, making all sorts of spitting sounds and disgusted faces while she tried to pry it off. I was nearly howling over that, and Quintina appeared not to notice we were drawing stares. Of course, she full well knew this. Exactly her intention.

She stepped up to a fishmonger's stall, where stood a handsome young man beaming at her. "Hello Quintina."

"Oh, do I know you?" Of course she did; she's shopped here frequently.

He didn't stand a chance, because she wouldn't be caught dead hanging around someone with Remus's odor.

His face drooped with defeat. But Quintina reeled him in. "Oh, yes, *now* I remember. You've given me good bargains before." Casually, she stretched out a leg from beneath her long gown to reveal a delicate ankle and shapely calf. Yeah, right, as though she isn't careful about maintaining a modest appearance.

The poor guy almost swallowed his tongue.

Abruptly, Remus's mother appeared from behind—lanced him with fierce dark eyes. At once she dispatched him to some chores, and he dashed out of sight.

A smile hinted around her lips like it hurt. "Quintina, so *nice* of you to stop by. How can I help you today?"

She obviously intended to remind Quintina that her reputation preceded her, that she now was pitted against a foe more formidable. Quintina didn't miss a beat. Actually, she appeared energized by a greater challenge to her skills.

Quintina stepped forward, pressing her finger into the flesh of an eel. "Oh, these poor things! I guess they don't get much to eat at this time of year, and these seem to be sad for having sat out in the sun too long!"

The woman narrowed her eyes. Nonetheless, they shone with amusement over the ancient game. "You *know* these are excellent, Quintina, fresh and the very best of the season."

Quintina shifted strategies. "Well, maybe not so bad, but the ones farther up the market are nicer, and cheaper too. But I hate to walk back so far."

The woman smiled warmly. "But it might do you good, dear. It would keep that pretty leg of yours in fine shape. Besides, I keep good tabs on my competition, and my fish are the best value for the money. But you know that, you clever girl."

Quintina slowly wilted, as the woman made clear her game was all too recognizable. Quintina decided to move to the endgame. "Perhaps," not conceding defeat. "What is your price for four eels and two octopi?"

The woman named a fair amount. Quintina contemplated offering less, but appeared weary and agreed. As the woman wrapped up her purchase, she added an extra eel and cheerily said, "Give your father my regards, and thank him for sending his charming daughter to me." Walking home, I had to hide my amusement at seeing Quintina meet her match.

I didn't wish to hurt her feelings. We quickened our pace, and I saw a tear glint on her cheek, figuring she was embarrassed. I was wrong.

She turned to me with liquid eyes. "Portia, I want to have a mother like Remus's. I want to grow up to be exactly like her. You don't know how lucky you are to have a mother and father who so care about you—enough to teach you how to behave. My father has forgotten me, and I'm in his way. My stepmother wishes I would disappear. Your mother would tan your hide if you acted like I do, and well she should. My mother is dead, and I miss her so much. How can I ever learn the grace of living within boundaries? I can't seem to help myself sometimes. I wish I had someone to love me like you are loved. I envy you so much."

My eyes stung, and I swallowed hard.

"I love you, Quintina. You are and will always be my best girlfriend."

We walked along in silence, arm in arm, and I mused over my strict parents in a new light.

Iulius Holiday

Today must have been a holiday, because Allen and Becca didn't go to work, and Christy didn't go to her academy.

It felt like a birthday, but I couldn't figure out whose. Outside, Allen and Christy were decorating the house, this time with colorful red, white, and blue flags. Christy had a large bag full of small flags on sticks, and she was busy sticking them all over their grassy yard. Goldie romped and barked, tried to pull them up and undo Christy's work. She laughed and tackled Goldie headlong, rolling over and over, which the dog clearly loved.

Many people started to arrive.

I think they must have been family and friends, since they all knew each other and exchanged warm greetings. Allen was in charge of cooking a meal outdoors. I hadn't even guessed that he could, or would, cook. Our men wouldn't lower themselves to cook food, as that is women's work. But he had a machina to help, of course. He tickled a fire into it, and within minutes had a blaze glowing inside the black metal box.

Spiritae playfully asked, "Wanna guess where the fire comes from?"

No, I didn't.

Allen arranged pieces of meat onto the hot-cook. Spiritae explained that the disk-shaped cuts were made from ground-up cows. Also, there were tubes of meat she claimed were composed of ground-up pigs and cows, and stuffed inside intestines.

"Well, not really anymore," she said. "People use machinae to make artificial skins and stuff them with meat."

This sounded completely bizarre and disgusting. Most of the men congregated around the hot-cook and drank from brown bottles filled with that nasty-smelling amber liquid I had tasted before.

Christy was inside helping her mother make other dishes of food, bowls heaped with greens and some type of diced white tubers that looked like turnips mixed together with eggs, although the mix didn't look like anything I know.

Back at the hot-cook, Allen tried unsuccessfully to quench a fire that had erupted. Amidst swirling smoke, the meat smelled delicious. After this spectacle, the meat was served on soft white bread, making it easy to eat without dripping fat onto your clothing. Everyone ate until you'd think it would have come out their ears!

Later, everyone lounged around with their stomachs about to burst, when Allen announced it was time for his special treat.

I have heard rumors of exotic icy treats prepared on great occasions for emperors, but here, the secret of such delicacies is available to everyone. Becca prepared a mixture of milk, eggs, and sweet stuffs, and Allen transformed this inside a freeze machina...into cream-ice.

Christy eagerly accepted a bowl-full, and drizzled onto her treat the mysterious dark-brown liquid she so rightly adores.

Wow! This time I had sensation in my disembodied mouth. Cold! Very! If I had possessed a head, surely it would have ached. But what a sensation! Well worth any pain.

At twilight, full of their day of visiting, most of the guests began to head home.

Allen, Becca, Christy (and Paul, ugh!) seemed to be heading out for another celebration, as if the day hadn't been exciting enough. A huge crowd was gathering near the center of the city where the buildings grow so tall.

It was quite dark now, but we waited a long time for something to happen. Children scampered and giggled playing tag—fantastically adorned with luminous necklaces. I cannot come to grips with the notion that children here wear such finery. If our empress showed up in one of these, she would be the topic of conversation for years!

All at once thundering voices echoed through the night sky, and light speared up from the Earth, meeting first in the sky, and shining like daylight on a huge red, white, and blue flag spread down the side of one of the tallest buildings.

Everyone stood. Many lay a hand over their hearts, and began to sing. I think I understood now. This must be a birthday celebration for their city! I have to admit, while we have plenty of special days in Rome, these people really go over the top with their celebrations. A *whump* sounded, followed a few seconds later by a tremendous explosion that ripped open the starry sky, glittered it with fiery red streamers bursting like flowers centered by a rumbling boom.

I nearly pee'd my invisible garments!

There ensued open warfare in the sky among all the immortal beings....

I hunkered down, hoping to shrink my spirit.

This clearly annoyed Spiritae. "What's the matter with you? This won't hurt anyone here, let alone someone without form!"

Ouch! She can really lay you low.

The fire-fight was supported by music from the heavens too, timed for great effect. The crowd *ooh'd* and *ahh'd* each time a new piece started.

I asked Spiritae why the people felt so strongly about their city. She tried to explain, but I only understood some of what she said. People love all their land, not just this city. They love it because it belongs to them, not to their emperor. She said there is no emperor, and people here *choose* who will be leaders. She called it a land of the people, and claimed, "This is not a new idea; the ancient Greeks tried it too. Doesn't always work well for everyone though, but is a darn sight better than most of the alternatives."

I'm not sure what alternatives there are. But Spiritae said the people here fought long and hard for their *ideals* and the right to live their lives the way they want to. Wish I knew what ideals are, and what freedoms they want. I asked why they had to *fight.*

"Freedom is not free," she said. "The freedom to speak your mind, the freedom to worship as you will, freedom from deprivation, and freedom from being afraid—there are those who would take these liberties from others for their own benefit, and sometimes people must pay the ultimate price for such rights. These people are honoring their country, and those who have paid this price for them."

Her comments humbled me.

Gradually, I stopped trembling, and tried not to lose my wits each time the sky turned inside out.

It was beautiful in a terrifying sort of way. Magnificent golden showers, screeching bits of rainbow-colored light darting all over the sky, and even a face that smiled at me. That one had to be a demon!

At the end, the entire sky flashed and rumbled with the immortal warfare. The lights and thunder-bursts shook the Earth like a dog shaking a rat. Maybe Jupiter throws lightning rods, but if he comes up against this stuff, he's a goner.

Joyous, the crowd shouted and clapped, and to the best of my ability so did I.

Mother

MOTHER—as usual—cornered me this morning with her list of chores, asking: "Can you do me a favor? I need help with a couple of things."

You have to understand that she doesn't always say what she means, as this would sound too harsh. What she means is, "I have lots of chores you must do today. I'm not asking—I'm *telling*. You need to get started right away, and do everything the way I showed you. I'll probably think of more things throughout the day, so don't wander away when you think you are done. When I say you will be *helping*, I mean you will be helping by doing it all."

No sense being upset, as it has been this way forever.

Honestly, I don't mind. I like to stay busy, and doing the cleaning, the cooking, and the mending aren't all that challenging. But my mind wanders when I'm doing menial jobs, and soon I'm off on flights of fancy. Of course, that means I'm always messing up something simple, and I get bawled out for being stupid or forgetful. Mother is a perfectionist, especially when it comes to what she expects of *me*. There is only one way to do something—her way. She's great at giving orders. Not so much at accepting the suggestions of others. I suppose it's because I have messed-up so many times, but all her instructions are given with great detail. Be sure to do *this*, or be sure to do *that*, even when I've done the job a million times. She sees this as being helpful, not annoying, and if I get short-tempered and object, she gets mad at my impertinence.

I know Mother isn't well.

No one can figure out why her arm trembles so. I can't help but notice it does so more obviously when she wants me to do something. I'm not saying she uses the arm as an excuse, but suspect she sees her health as a greater limitation than it might be.

You might think I don't love or respect my mother, but that's not true at all. I suppose we have the usual mother-daughter head-banging. I love her very much, even when she drives me nuts, and I know she loves me too. It's hard for her to say so. You know when she pays you a compliment you've really earned it, for they are about as rare as dragon's teeth.

I must be fair and tell you Mother's good traits too, as she is a formidable woman. Fiercely loyal to her family; free with criticism, perceiving this quality as a shaping influence rather than merely being negative. Indeed! Let someone outside the immediate family say something negative about one of us, and Mother transforms into a she-wolf protecting her young. I know, too, she is proud of us, often boasting of our accomplishments. She attempts to keep us out of earshot during such moments, lest we get too full of ourselves.

Mother is a good teacher too, justifying things be done her way, as those methods rarely come up short. She is compulsive about attention-to-detail—not much escapes her scrutiny. Her inner eye for wrongness can spot any shortcut in an instant, but such steely influence has been good for me. At my age, I can run a household as well as most grown women, at least when I put my mind to it.

Mother is quite intelligent, although she likes to say that women should not be educated and ought to focus on *doing*, not thinking. She is surprisingly conversant with a number of topics, and during discussions with Papa, his respect for her opinions is touchingly visible. I learn a lot about our home, and the world, eavesdropping on them whenever they debate Rome's affairs late into the night.

Mother also is skilled at making friends, and strangers don't long retain that status. When first meeting someone, she is overtly engaging and friendly, intensely inquisitive, and they soon warm to her. Within minutes, these new friends are revealing life histories and intimate memories so you might presume they were childhood buddies.

If someone needs help, she's first to lend a hand. Of course, this usually means having one of *us* give a hand too, but that's okay because it draws me out of my shell and makes me a better person. If everyone (let's face it) had a mother like mine, the world would run much smoother. She has strong opinions about nearly everything, and is quick to express them. While possessing a strong sense of right-and-wrong and standing up for what you believe displays muscular moral character, Mother is not always easy to live with.

Then again, great people rarely are.

After giving me my daily assignment, Mother didn't saunter off as usual, but pressed in on me. "Portia, have you been having any more of those demon dreams?"

Leave it to Mother; she doesn't beat around the bush.

"Now, don't *lie* to me. I heard you calling out last night in your sleep. I asked Antonia about it, but she insisted she doesn't think so, because she is never disturbed by you anymore. I'm not stupid. She's covering for you—love for big sister and all that."

I used the same white lie I told Papa. "Mother, it's true that I still have some vague dreams once in a while, but I think any lingering demons must have left. I don't feel troubled anymore. If I cry out, it's probably nothing, like a sleeping dog yipping. Sorry if I disturbed you."

She eyed me with a skeptical squint. "Well, I want to spend some time praying with you this morning. We must burn our offerings to Vesta at the hearth, and ask her to use sacred fire to purify you of demons."

Ugh! So I spent an hour kneeling beside Mother before our private hearth altar, tossing bread crumbs into fire and listening to her droning supplications....

I sensed Spiritae nearby, and could hear her mental smirk: "Shaking out all the demons, huh?"

"Well, if it gets Mother off my case, it's worth it. What do you think of this approach?"

"Rather a waste of time. But the bread smells nice. Could be worse."

I agreed.

When Mother finally stood, she regarded me with a rare loving glow. "Portia, I know you don't spend all your time at night practicing lettering. You might fool your Father, but that doesn't convince me for an instant."

Uh-oh!

I'd been found out, and braced for the inevitable assault.

Instead, she floored me. "When you write about your dreams, do it well. Write the secrets from your heart, for I know they are important somehow, part of who you are. I love you...you are a worthy daughter."

I think that's the only time she's vocalized that. An amazing mother, yet an enigma to me.

"I love you too, Mother."

I meant it.

Arena

ALLEN TOOK CHRISTY TO THE ARENA TODAY to watch the games. Unlike my reaction to the arena, she seemed excited to go. I wondered what sort of killing some sadist would dream up today. Still, I decided I would go and find out how killing has advanced. Maybe men and machinae would fight it out to the death.

The arena was not what I expected. This seemed to be more of an athletic contest. Actually more like a pitched battle between two armies. There were two teams of gladiators, dressed in fantastically colored armored garments with a bubble on their head resembling a metal helmet, but different. Most of the gladiators had a shield or a guard over their eyes, probably to keep out sword thrusts.

But I was confused. None of the warriors had a weapon. They just rushed at one another at great speed, slamming into their opponent's legs or hauling them to the ground with their massive arms. Just like at home, the gladiators were very muscular. I don't think ours would stand a chance. These men were behemoths, so tall and wide and heavy I couldn't be sure whether they were actual men, or perhaps machinae built in male form.

I'm guessing many of these gladiators—judging by appearance—were slaves captured from Numidia or Africa. Most ran as if possessed, faster even than Christy! But Spiritae said I'm wrong, that these men are free, and born to this place. Highly revered, they are paid princely sums of money to play this game competing for fame, fortune, and sheer love of the sport.

I have no idea about the rules...if there are any. They tossed around and even kicked a funny-looking brown ball with striped ends.

This might have been a dead piglet. It sure looked like one.

Sometimes one man clutched the ball and ran while others tried to tear it away. Other times, a man heaved the ball to another, who tried to catch it while opposing gladiators made to smash him to smithereens.

After lots of falling down, one man carried the piglet mummy near the end of the grassy area, and there was great cheering from the crowd. He slammed the piglet into the ground, pointed his fingers skyward, and performed a wild celebration dance. His team rushed to him, jumped high into the air trying to knock each other down again.

I asked Spiritae what the man was doing. "Hard to know. Sometimes, he is thanking God for bestowing athletic abilities. Other times he might be praising God for helping with the victory, as if God cares a whit about who wins or loses. Like the *Creator* has nothing else to worry about than helping some infinitesimal speck run over another speck! Once in a while, though, the gladiator merely is indulging himself...showing off for the crowd. Remember what *that* did for Narcissus?

Later, one man was knocked to the ground, and everyone rushed out to help him.

He rolled on the ground in pain until, limping and moaning through a sweaty grimace, a few non-warriors guided him out of the grassy area. I couldn't help but think he was making too much of this. What would he do in Rome if he sustained a whack from a sword or pike-poke in the belly?

Bet he'd cry like a baby.

Other parts of the contest were more interesting. I liked how the people in the crowd wore the colors of their favorite gladiators.

Some were pretty crazy-looking. Some painted their faces with the same color as their outfits. Others ripped off their garments and displayed symbols painted on their chests. Thankfully, no women seemed inclined to do this, but I wouldn't have been surprised. No one was supposed to bring in wine, but I suspect—judging by their behavior—a whole lot of wine-drinking was going on. Either that or they'd been consorting with Bacchus well before the contest started. Not much difference from Rome in that regard!

At one end of the arena, a monster-sized far-sight cheered and urged the crowd into even greater frenzy. Its booming voice nearly split my ghostly eardrums. Sometimes, it even showed what had happened moments before. Maybe the crowd was too drunk to remember and had to be reminded.

Each team of gladiators had supporters dressed in their colors, cheering and tumbling in amazing feats of agility. I liked how the men would hoist a girl completely overhead and dangle her from a foot! Faking loss of his grip, he would catch her an instant before she crashed to the ground. Often such men would throw a girl high into the air, so high that if they missed catching her, surely she would be squashed!

In the middle of the contest, the gladiators took a rest to plan the remainder of their fight strategy.

A group of people dressed in identical costumes and carrying musical instruments marched onto the grass to entertain the crowd. As one, they danced and maneuvered in intricate patterns. Most of the crowd didn't bother watching, and headed to stalls where they could use the public toilets and buy food from grinning vendors.

When the game resumed, the crowd stood as one and formed an arena-encompassing ring cheering and undulating like ocean waves. Incredible! I think all this was intended to excite their favorites into a sort of crazed warrior lust. I felt mounting energy...a force that might turn the tide of the contest for the favorite.

Spiritae wryly noted: "The force of will is powerful indeed when all focus in the same direction. Imagine how powerful were this concentrated toward a more worthy cause."

Apparently, the favorites won the battle.

Most of the people were happy and chatty, including Allen and Christy. A mammoth bell tolled, proclaiming victory. Probably it could be heard for miles.

Imagination

"SPIRITAE, HOW DID I DIE? I can't remember."

"What?! Really, Portia, you ask the dumbest questions sometimes!"

Ouch! Spiritae clearly was in one of her moods. Timidly, I asked again.

"Well, I don't have a body."

"You keep returning home, for the most part alive, don't you?"

"But I don't know what is real and what is imaginary. Is this all a dream?"

"You are a traveler. Imagination is a first step. If something can be imagined, it can be realized. If it cannot be imagined, it cannot manifest. A dream is a wish your heart makes...Hmmm, I think there's a song in there somewhere. But people forget the second part. A nightmare is a fear your head makes. Today, your travels will take you to a place where everything comes from human imagination, so you will learn precisely what this means."

I appeared in a room with Christy and Tanika.

They were very excited, and busily packing clothes into a large bag with a leather handle. Becca was taking them on an adventure. Allen couldn't go because he had to work.

Becca drove them to a hulking cluster of buildings sized like a new city. Leaving the chariot machina in a pen with thousands of others, they jumped onto another machina that gathered other travelers. We entered a large hall chaotic with hundreds of people dragging bags of clothing and poking glowing machinae, before someone took away the clothing. The girls were sure to be upset when they found their clothes missing!

Next we queued in a very long line, designed to take us past grim officials who prompted the girls to remove their sandals and outer garments, and place their bags into a machinae that somehow peered into them probing for bad objects. I didn't know what "bad" things they might have carried, but these machinae sure were snoopy. Finally, they were through, and everyone looked rather frazzled. If this was an imagination adventure, I didn't see the point. We walked some distance, again found ourselves waiting. I wandered over to the window, and got quite a scare.

Outside lurked a monster-sized machina with giant wings!

In fact, lots of them.

Spiritae said the nearest one out there would take us far away, flying high above the clouds. I was sure we were going to die.

Didn't she know about Daedalus and Icarus? You get up too close to the sun, and the gods get all upset. You're going to take a big plunge down to the sea! "First of all," she said, "that was imagination, and second, people here fly in machinae all the time. Trust me. Riding in the chariot machina was more dangerous."

Well, maybe that is so, maybe not. But having your wax wings melt off and falling from the clouds into the sea, where one of those big nasty fish is hanging around waiting on a snack, is not my idea of adventure. Trust me? Oh, sure!

The girls chatted excitedly, appeared unafraid. So, I was not about to leave them now. After a while, we got into another long line and entered a square tunnel, at whose end waited the bird machina with gaping mouth and whining impatiently. Inside, we were greeted by friendly women who pointed us toward row after row of cushy-looking chairs.

I had a problem, as there were no extra chairs. But I considered how I didn't actually need one, and simply spread myself around where the girls sat. Sometimes it's nice not having a body.

Once all the people had crammed their bags above them and were seated, the giant bird machina decided to roll around. Not too bad after all. Somewhat noisy and bumpy, but I thought I could get used to it. Abruptly, the bird decided to make a run for it, slowly, then faster and faster...louder and louder.

Peering through small clear spots in the bird's skin, I could see buildings rushing past in blurs! The silver bird leaped into the sky roaring like a berserk lion. I don't have a clue how these tremendous birds fly. No wing-flapping could be seen, yet we climbed quickly until inside the clouds! I had never wondered what being in a cloud might be like. Now I knew. Like thick fog. You couldn't see a darn thing.

After a few minutes, our bird peeked from the clouds and soared into boundless blue sky.

Zooming above the clouds was incredible; they spread out below in the most fantastic patterns. No wonder the gods choose to live on Olympus, if this was their constant view. Spiritae seemed a little put out with me.

Now the adventure seemed truly fun. A man and a woman rolled along the aisle a metal box jittering with drinks and treats. Becca had a drink made from oranges, while Christy and Tanika went for the fizzy brown ambrosia from red cans.

Outside, I occasionally could see other bird machinae rushing along, exhaling long thin cloud tails behind. I wondered what the bird machinae ate, but immediately killed the thought. Spiritae would have started with the rotten plant thing again.

I suppose the bird machina grew tired, and had to land. Must take a pretty mean tree to support one of *these* birds.

Gradually, it slowed...glided down through the clouds. I could see it must have planned to land on a very long black road. Down, and down, and down....

The earth came up frightfully fast. Finally—with a jarring screech —our bird touched down, roaring louder than even before.

Did this mean it must be temperamental? Clearly something made it unhappy. Our bird rolled right up to a tunnel, and fell immediately asleep. The girls nonchalantly gathered their bags, and everybody lined up to step again through the bird's mouth.

Apparently, we were here. But I wasn't sure where "here" might be.

Inside the receiving building, Becca stepped toward an older woman who stood behind a dais crowned with a black whirring machina whose flat face glowed blue. The woman's fingers clicked lettered tiles arranged atop a tilted base.

Becca conversed with the other, who had a mean scrunched mouth. The woman waved papyri painted with images of chariot machinae. When Becca showed a small card of money, I told myself *she's buying another one!*

It's not like these things grow on trees. Probably I got it wrong, but after she lettered some stiff papyri, they did give her a chariot.

She drove us to a massive apartment building just like ours in Rome, except these units were gorgeous inside. I guess this was to be a home away from home during their adventure. The first home seemed good enough. I didn't understand the excitement over coming to this one. I supposed they were spoiled.

Each got her own living-space, indoor toilet, and rainmaker room. Christy squealed when she saw that hers also had a fat white tub, probably for swimming. Spiritae said it would make bubbles when the girl bathed. Does that sound like a good idea? Being boiled alive when you are just trying to get clean?

We headed to a clear room near the building's entrance. A long snaking machina slithered to the curb hissing, opened its portals, and released its chatty riders. Others who had stood waiting climbed on. Weird!

People here are obsessed with a myriad of riding machinae. Perhaps that's what imagination is all about. The snake machina didn't weave back and forth; it glided along smoothly with a quiet hum. Spiritae claimed everyone here would be much better off with fewer chariots and more snake machinae. Everyone buzzed and gestured with anticipation, and I wondered what new machina lay ahead. No, no more traveling.

After a few miles, we arrived at our destination, a city of magic and imagination. So hard to believe that an entire *city* exists devoted solely to the purpose of entertaining people.

Christy and Tanika clapped their hands and jumping up and down as we walked in. Everything was so clean and bright with lights, reminding me of a giant market, except here each vendor had a large indoor stall filled with wonderful goods. But this wasn't what had so excited the girls.

They spied a fabulous palace in the distance. Now I understand why Spiritae said it was funny when I thought their houses were palaces. *This* was a palace, painted blue and gray with great soaring spires...more beautiful than anything I had ever dreamed of. Unfortunately way too many people milled around—pushing and shoving for a spot alongside the roadway where they could sit.

Spiritae said we were about to see a great procession, and she wasn't fooling. I thought the Emperor's victory procession in Rome was spectacular. Nothing like this.

Even the music here was happy!

The procession blazed with actors wearing outrageously-colored outfits and masks. At least I *think* they were people wearing masks. I saw a boy mouse and a girl mouse with giant heads. A big duck and a dog with a tongue as long as my arm. Hundreds of people danced and sang and smiled throughout. The women were amazingly beautiful. One girl with brown curls danced with a terrible fanged monster. Another girl with flaming red hair and a fish's tail sat among dancing sea creatures. Yet another with short black hair was followed by a group of diamond miners who were no taller than children, and a terrifying old woman offering a piece of red fruit. Men on long legs stiffly walked high above the crowd.

My favorite, though, was a clear round chariot shaped like a gourd. Seated inside was a young woman, who must have been the most beautiful in the world. Her golden hair was bound up in a swirl, and she wore a garment shimmering as if studded with all the gems of the world. Her chariot was drawn by delicate white horses, prancing because they were so proud to carry their precious owner.

Finally, she daintily stepped out of the halted chariot, waved to all the children, and was guided down by a fabulously handsome young man who gazed adoringly. I too was gazing rather adoringly at him—along with Christy and Tanika, maybe even Becca, although she was too demure to stare.

This young empress wore clear sandals, and you could see her lovely feet. I guessed they knew only the fluffy kiss of clouds.

It is hard to recall all the wonders there.

I know you'll think I'm daft or making all this up. We rode flying baby elephants, holding feathers in their trunks. We listened to bears singing and playing instruments. We went on a boat ride among dolls dressed in fantastic outfits. The music during this trip stuck in my head, and I think I'll be humming it forever. We climbed up ropes to a house in a giant tree, and rode another boat on a river where we were attacked by huge river horses that bared their teeth at us until the oarsman scared them off with a bang machina. We went inside a mountain where we left the Earth and had a crazy spin through the stars. I think I would have puked, if I were able.

Christy and Tanika were indefatigable, but Becca was looking a little worn around the edges. I thought this was one amazing city, but no, *one* was not enough, so we jumped back on the snake machina and headed to another imagination city.

This one had a giant ball looming over it, covered with protruding triangles that made me dizzy. Spiritae said the first city was all about fun imagination, but this one was more about learning imagination. Not sure what she meant, since it was all new to me. Everything I saw blew me away.

We headed into a large hall where many chairs faced a glowing wall.

This had something to do with the Earth when it was young. The seats abruptly shifted—coming apart in long sections. Was this an earthquake? It sure felt like one, but I couldn't tell whether it was real or not. Slowly, the chairs lined up again section by section, and we began to travel toward a dark tunnel. I had been fooled. This was yet another fantastic machina taking us on a further adventure. This vivid world seethed with fire and heat. Volcanoes erupted everywhere we looked. I began to get a funny feeling like someone in my head waited for my reaction. I refused to give in, but knew this was all about how plants from ages long ago were taken into the Earth and, with immense pressure and heat, transformed into the substances these people use to power their machinae.

I played ignorant, even though I could tell Spiritae was silently amused.

In the distance wandered huge creatures. I mean HUGE, as some would make elephants look like small dogs. I'm glad they were far away, since they looked so scary. At that moment there came a terrible roar, and a giant reptile head thrust close by our faces, with glowing red eyes and gaping mouth.

Tanika shrieked with such force they might have heard it in Rome. The beast dripped its evil saliva onto us and puffed out foul-smelling breath that reeked of infernal underworld fires. I was going to have a heart attack from all this imagination stuff!

But it pulled back, and the girls collapsed in a fit of laughter. Apparently, I had been fooled again. Simply another machina with no other purpose than to scare girls like me into the next world.

After waiting in another long line, we found ourselves hanging in long flying benches before a massive glowing wall that transported us into the middle of its images.

With shocking suddenness we made soaring swoops, smoothly gliding as if transformed into birds. We birds flew over the most beautiful scenery I could ever have imagined. Yes, I know now what it is to envision flight over snowy mountains, along the seashore, over deserts and fragrant trees. Wind rushed over our faces. I see why Daedalus and Icarus wanted to fly! Birds are blessed. Some things make you cry aloud at the sheer beauty of their creation. I could tell Spiritae very much liked my thoughts....

Evening purpled the sky. We exited, and stood once more before the beautiful palace, now aglow with floods of serene colored light. The sky erupted with a spectacular series of bright explosions. This time I wasn't as nervous, and could relax and enjoy the spectacle with everyone else.

Near the end, a small woman in a winged green suit flew down from the palace, whooshing over the crowd and waving a sparkling stick as if blessing us with magic fire dust. Perhaps she was.

I returned with Becca and the girls back to their home away from home, our energy spent and deliriously happy. I faded out, while Christy boiled herself in the tub, immersed in scented flowers and clouds of bubbles.

Rotten Plants

T HE FOG HAD LIFTED, but today I was not with Becca or Christy. Instead, I stood at the edge of a vast field.

Ugliness was everywhere, and a noxious odor hung in the air. All around me, there were large black machinae with heads like giant birds. They were bobbing up and down, piercing the earth with their beaks, as though they were trying to pull worms from the ground. In the distance, I saw men running and shouting with excitement. A metal structure sat above the ground, and suddenly it vomited a thick black liquid high into the air, which rained down upon them, covering them with a black slime. They danced happily, but worked hard to make the machina stop being sick.

Not too far away, I gravitated toward a metal city. I saw large tubes sticking up into the sky, and tubes crisscrossed on the ground, above the ground, everywhere. Small tubes, large tubes, it looked like a big mess. In the air, there was a foul stench, like something long dead being cooked. I started to tremble when I thought how it smelled similar to the liquid fed into Becca's chariot machina.

Spiritae asked, "What do you think they are taking from the Earth?"

I hesitated, not really wanting to answer, for I had a sinking feeling. "Rotten, oily plants?"

There. I'd managed it. I swear I heard a faint, "Told you so."

Give Thanks

As I faded in, I saw that Becca, Allen, Christy, and Tanika were piling into the family chariot machina preparing to head off to an adventure.

I presumed the idea was to have me tag along instead of babysitting Goldie, so I flowed in around the girls barely before they slammed the machina's wings shut.

The day was shivery cold and blustery, and the machina slipped several times on the slushy snow building up on the road. We passed over a river, through some woods, and snow drifts were mounded up along the way. I had a funny feeling we were headed to see Becca's parents, but I couldn't be sure. I thought I heard Spiritae suppress a laugh at my thoughts.

But no, I was wrong. Turned out we were headed to a squatty building with a large room holding several huge cooking machinae. Six women and one man were already there cooking up a magnificent feast. At a glance, I realized something didn't make sense. The amount of food being prepared would feed an army, literally several hundred people, not the dozen or so here. Why, they would explode if they tried to eat one tenth of all this stuff.

The cooks greeted the family very warmly.

Spiritae flowed in and explained that the food was being prepared to give to homeless poor people. She said Allen had done something very kind. Usually, the food fed to the homeless is very plain because it costs lots of money to feed so many. But Allen had said this was a special day of celebration to give thanks to the Creator for all the blessings people have received, so he had insisted on a very fine dinner, no skimping on what the poor would eat today. Allen had personally visited the market, purchased all the food, and delivered it to this hearth room for preparation.

The pungent aromas wafting from the cooking machinae were out-of-this-world, and I watched carefully as the cooks opened the mouths of the oven machina to see whether the food was ready.

One machina held tray after tray of the largest roasted birds I've ever seen. I'm not sure what they were, but larger than any goose. Their legs were trussed with thin ropes, and the cooks repeatedly basted the birds with rendered fat. After a while, they turned deep golden brown, and I sneaked a small bite. Heavenly!

I didn't recognize most of the foods.

There were orange lumpy things covered with brown ambrosia and white puffy pieces, cooked until everything became soft and gooey. Oh my, even better than the giant birds!

One woman was using a machina with slender silver fingers that whirled at great speed to mix some white lumps. She added something that looked a bit like the butter barbarians use in their food up north. I thought the creamy-looking white mounds would taste rancid, but no, this was just as awesome as everything else. Another woman loaded a tray with bread chunks, celery, and spices. The man scooped a portion of this mixture and began stuffing it up the butt of one bird that had not yet been roasted.

One of the women pointed at a tray she'd reserved for this. Thank goodness! That would have tasted nasty!

They had better be careful. Celery is a powerful aphrodisiac, so the homeless party might get rather out of hand!

At least I recognized the baking bread, although it was *very* white and delicately soft. If I could learn to fix any of this stuff, I could land a job fixing food for the emperor!

Finally, the meal was cooked.

Oven machinae were switched off. Food loaded onto metal trays, and snugly covered with shiny sheets of thin metal crinkly and flexible. Sensing my fascination, Spiritae advised this was to retain heat, but I couldn't see how this method achieved that.

The considerable bounty was packed into several chariot machinae, ready for delivery to the people without homes.

We rode in the chariot machina quite a long while. We passed through areas in the city that didn't look nearly so nice as the area where Christy lives. In fact, many of the buildings stood faded and crumbling, the area casting a dark aura of menace, rather like the seedier parts of Rome.

The chariot hauled itself up to one particularly sad-looking building, and heaved a sigh of rest.

Four men sat outside chewing on fire sticks, and rubbing their hands to stay warm. These men, with their ragged clothing and worn faces, sadly resembled some of the people who haunt the fringes of the Forum. Our soldiers usually chase them away when too many gather in one place.

The men appeared eager to see us, and rushed forward to help carry the food. We followed them inside, and I could see we were here to do more than provide sustenance. We were part of a team serving those in need, the very ones seated hungrily at long tables, sprawled on worn couches, even on mats spread across the floor. Many stared at a large far-sight that glowed and jabbered from a corner. Confused, I consulted Spiritae, "I thought you said these people were homeless. This place *is* a large home. Maybe no privacy, or very attractive, but nonetheless a home, isn't it?"

"Not exactly. They're only allowed to come in here for dinner, and sleep on the floor until morning. It's a temporary shelter, not a home."

"I don't see any women. Is it only men who don't have homes?

"No, there is another place not far away for women and children."

"Are we going to feed them, too?"

"Not tonight. Another group is doing that, but I'm sad to say they won't be dispensing nice dinner that Allen picked out."

"Oh... But what about entire families without a home?"

'These people have it tough, Portia. They have to split up. Too many problems letting men and women sleep together."

"Maybe they could try doing without the celery." Spiritae didn't seem to catch what I meant, but passed it off without comment.

"All of these people are homeless?"

"Actually there are many more, but they are too embarrassed to come here for a handout. They would rather scrounge through trash cans than accept charity."

"Oh Spiritae, that's so sad. Where do they go? It's getting terribly cold outside. They might freeze to death."

"Once in a while, some do. They huddle together, sometimes in vacant buildings, sometimes on benches covered with anything they can find in the trash, or under bridges out of the wind. Many people think of them as human refuse."

"What happened that they can't have homes like others?"

"There are endless causes of human misery. Some have trouble finding or keeping jobs to earn money. Some have fallen into addictions they cannot shake, which robs them of dignity and money. A large number have emotional or mental problems and trouble fitting into a society that's failed to figure good ways to help them. This costs money, and there aren't enough people in better circumstances willing to share their extras with those they wish would go away. This is a problem in your time, and apparently one for the ages."

I was really depressed, thinking about what she told me.

One man seemed to be in charge of the building, and he announced on a loud voice that a prayer would be said before they could eat. The men edged forward respectfully and humbly, most of them pulling off their tattered hats and clasping their hands together. Some pressed closely to the front of the line where the food would be served.

I saw a nervous Christy being pushed forward by Becca. Spiritae said, "Christy gets to give the prayer blessing for the food. I'll help you understand what she says." Christy gulped, and began in a timid tone: "Dear Father, we ask your blessing on this food we are about to receive. On this special day of Thanksgiving, we join others throughout the world to think of the many blessings in our lives. Let us be Your hands to help those in need. Help us to remember those who cannot be together with their loved ones tonight. Amen."

A chorus of "Amen"s rippled quietly through the men.

I was proud of Christy, and asked Spiritae if she had done a good job.

"Yes, Christy did well. All these helpers have done well. The prayer was nice, but it's not the words that impress me the most. You see, the vast majority of people in this land are at home today, having nice dinners with their families. They say the same words. Then they laugh and gossip with their friends and family. Many eat like hogs and retire to couches where they fall asleep in a food coma while watching some athletic contest.

"They don't put their prayers into action. Christy asked, 'Let us be Your hands to help those in need.' That's exactly what I need and want. I am spiritual in nature. I can't fix all the wrongs and miseries that befall people—but I can inspire them, if they'll listen, to help others. It isn't terribly hard. A little help goes a long way. This is precisely what Christy's family has done: put the needs of others before their own pleasures."

The men pressed forward, eager and hungry.

The servers dished out generous portions, and remembered to greet each man with a smile and friendly comment. Some responded warmly and appeared happy that someone had bothered to treat them as human beings. Others merely grunted thanks, or looked away sadly, as though it was painful to receive kindness.

"No matter," Spiritae said. "The kindnesses shown here today touch deep inside."

Many of the men had eyes only for Christy and Tanika. Why wouldn't they? Both girls are stunning and outgoing. But these gazes were not lecherous. The men regarded them as if though beholding illuminated angels come to walk among them. Perhaps the men were right.

They wolfed down their food as if they had not eaten in weeks. Many expressed surprise at its high quality. Allen grinned every time someone blurted a compliment. He stood near the end of the food line and served drinks from jugs brimming with a cool, muddy-looking juice.

I took a quick swallow. Delicious, of course. I don't know where they get so much ambrosia, but they put it in just about everything.

When every man had been served, they were permitted to go through the line again. Most did.

Many also took food with them for later, when they returned to the cruel streets. The small loaves of bread were especially popular. One man even tore a leg from one of the remaining huge birds, stuffed it into a slot in his clothing, seemingly heedless of the meat's juices soaking him.

Spiritae said that he wanted to take it to his little girl at the other shelter, and he would walk there in the bitter cold just to make sure she got it tonight.

Becca figured this out, and made a special box with all the leftover roasted bird. The leader of the shelter promised to leave right away to take any extra food to the women and children.

Hearing this, the man began to weep. So did I.

As soon as the servers finished and cleaned up their supplies, they ventured out to sit at tables with some of the men.

Spiritae said this was one of the greatest kindnesses of the evening. People need to feel human contact and to know that even in the midst of their troubles, someone cares and is willing to listen to them.

Slowly, some men began to talk about their lives, their families, and interests. No one mentioned any troubles, only their joys. One man was an artist and showed some of his sketches, which displayed considerable talent.

During the ride home, everyone stayed quiet.

Finally, Christy said, "Mom, that was a lot more fun than I thought it would be. I mean...not fun...it was *moving*, and I feel good inside about doing it. Thanks for insisting that I go."

"Yes," Tanika added, "me too."

When they arrived home, Becca hugged both girls tightly. "You are awesome young women."

She beamed at Allen, and he grinned back with a look that told her he knew he was married to the greatest woman in the world.

And I think he probably is.

Cato

I AM FURIOUS!
Mother and Antonia went visiting this afternoon, and Papa went to work as usual. I slipped over to see Quintina, and Cato had the place to himself.

But Quintina wasn't feeling well, so I returned home unexpectedly. When I went to my room, I found Cato rummaging through the writing supplies on my bedside table. He scrambled guiltily to his feet. I was terrified he had discovered my secret writings—and became almost hysterically angry. Knowing any outburst would work against me, I cornered him. "Just *what* do you think you are doing?"

"Whatever I please. Thought I'd look through this junk and see if you were writing anything about that crazy vision that got you into so much trouble. Any more *demon* tales to tell us? You sure screwed up your life with that last one."

Clearly, he was trying to get under my skin. He had decided to put me on the defensive so I couldn't focus on his snooping in my things. I was up to the challenge!

"Yeah, thanks to you and your big mouth, you had to run right over to Cassius and tell him about a private talk I had with Mother and Papa. You had *no* right to eavesdrop on us, you have no right to touch my belongings, and you know it."

I was extremely relieved to see that he hadn't yet discovered my secret cache of writings hidden in the floor niche under my bed.

Antonia, of course, knows about it—but she'd never tell anyone, let alone Cato.

Fortunately, I had had the good sense to create a ruse: A scatter of practice sheets on my table, marked in gibberish produced by my best handwriting.

I was anxious to draw him away, lest he notice the small crack in the tiles where I open my hiding place. I decided to go on the attack myself.

"You know, Cato, if you had any sense you would learn Papa's work, and *I* wouldn't have to bother learning something you're too stupid to do."

He tensed, and I could see his blood rising to a boil. Exactly the reaction I wanted.

"Bah!" he said spat. "Scribe's work is no work for a *real* man. I have no intention of wasting my life scratching out public records. I'm a warrior! I'll be the one who earns fame and glory for this family. Reputations are made on the field of battle."

He knew how to attack me too, for I cannot abide his disrespect for Papa.

"Some reputation. The only one you will ever earn is the one for whoring all over Rome. You'll die in glory all right, not on the battlefield, but with a mind rotting from the whore's disease."

For an instant this threw him. I suppose he thought no one in the family realized how he spent his evenings.

"It's *nobody's* business how I spend my time. I don't care what anyone thinks, especially Father and Mother. They are idiots just like you. Besides, you'll never know what sex is like. No one will ever want to plow your frozen wasteland, especially with your face all twisted up like that."

"Perhaps you are right. But then, my goal in life isn't to go around poking every woman I meet with some small twig." A low blow, I knew, and of course had no interest in knowing whether Cato is a twig or a log. But I had worked a hunch and scored a direct hit. He came rushing at me in a terrible fury.

"I'll...I'll *kill* you, you crazy she-devil!" He raised his fist as if to deliver a punch. I knew he could probably kill me with his little finger, but I stared him down defiantly.

"Do your worst, Cato. I'll be happy to drag myself to the Centurion and show him your handiwork. I hear he isn't too impressed with men who like to beat on their family."

He stood there swallowing, blue veins bulging his neck, face purple with rage. Finally he picked up my practice sheets and ripped them into pieces. He turned to go, and there stood Mother in the doorway. She said nothing, but glared at him with naked rage.

I'll never forget. Cato couldn't meet her fierce gaze, so stomped off in defeat and left the house.

Mother came close, laid her arm across my shoulder, and said, "That was a dangerous game Portia."

"I'm sorry. Truly. I know he's my brother, but he made me so angry."

"You stood your ground well. He was *wrong*. But remember, there are some words said in anger to win a point that can never be retrieved, never forgiven nor forgotten. Choose your battles well when you must do this, for words are more powerful than the blow of a sword."

I have a lot yet to learn from my mother....

Hiems Celebration

GREAT ANTICIPATION WAS IN THE AIR.

I arrived to find Christy, Becca, and Allen busy with holiday preparations. Snow silently fell...fat flakes that filled your palms, and buffered all sound into a magical hush.

I guessed it might be Saturnalia, based on the snowfall and the mood, but instantly sensed Spiritae's jarring bristle.

Allen and Christy brought home a pine tree they had cut down in a nearby forest and lashed atop Allen's chariot like some beast after a successful hunt.

Becca bustled indoors, cleaning, straightening, and preparing a special place for the tree. Somehow, she found a moment to switch on the singer machina, filling the house with joyous sounds. My mood brightened.

At that moment, the world could not have been a better place.

Allen and Christy dragged the tree into the main room.

It barely fit through the door, and they had to wrestle with it quite a while. Finally, they raised it in its place of honor, tip mere inches from scratching the ceiling. The house filled with a lovely scent, like when you are deep in the forest and by inhaling its incense, realize you belong to the good Earth.

Now I understood. They were going to worship the tree.

I didn't know why. I didn't even know there *were* any tree gods. But Becca hauled out a large box filled with the most beautiful tree adornments you ever saw.

They hung golden balls, red berries, and shiny baubles all over it, thick as could be, every so often pausing to stand back and admire the jeweled beauty. Back to work, they laughed in shared memory of various ornaments thought long lost. Christy has very long arms, and Becca employed her to place a miniature white-dressed lady atop the tall tree.

Finally, it practically sagged as if one more decoration might send it toppling to the floor.

Allen stepped to the wall, stooped, and stuck the end of small green rope into the lightning box.

Had I one, my mouth would have gaped at the mesmerizing vision like stars come to Earth. Behind the decorations, thousands of points of light came alive, intense and hypnotic. A galaxy of lights glowed red, pink, yellow, and green, but I liked the deep blue ones best. They made me feel all serene inside. When I looked up, the face of the lady on top the tree was glowing, and she moved lighted candles in her hands back and forth. Her dress was lighted from within. When I looked closer, I could see she was an angel from paradise, greater than mere mortals. She had feathery wings folded behind her back. Now I really understood. The family was going to worship *her*, and the tree was just a home they had prepared for her. I wished I had known her name so I could have worshiped too.

Becca, Allen, and Christy disappeared for a few minutes, and returned carrying large piles of gifts. These were wrapped in stunning papyri, so colorful, with beautiful images all over. If only I could show a piece to Papa! He would think *he* was the one who had gone crazy! Their packages had glorious silky ribbons and golden flowers, and they arranged them around the tree's base. I wondered if the angel would come to life and venture down to accept her tributes. Or, maybe, they would show them to her, offering up sacrifices. But no, maybe it was not yet time.

Outside, night was unfurling, and Allen led Becca and Christy into icy air where he had been working all morning before going to get the tree.

They shouted in expectation, and he moved a small lever inside the door.

At once the house, trees, and bushes blazed with lights like those on the tree, but *millions* of them, I think.

You've never seen anything like this. I expected the house to float fly straight up into the sky and outshine the ancient constellations. A jeweled treasure that had come to life. On the lawn away from the house stood two deer covered with white lights, heads shifting.

I wondered if Becca and Christy too would burst into light.

The family stood outside a long time, growing colder and colder, but watching arm-in-arm as lights began twinkling on all the other houses. Everyone in the neighborhood had turned their dwelling places into a fantasy land of light.

Spiritae was as quiet as the snow....

After a short while, the family moved back indoors and prepared to go somewhere. This was odd. They had just made the most beautiful place in the world, and they were planning to leave? But Becca and Christy were dressing in their prettiest garments, putting on their most treasured jewels, and their loveliest sandals. This is what we would do if we were called into the emperor's presence.

Allen reappeared and was all dressed up too, in a strange but attractive black outfit, dangling from his neck a long cloth. He prompted Becca to help him tie this into place with a big knot. She admired the tiny pictures of wreathes and berries all over it, helped him like a little child, and warmly kissed his lips.

We piled into the chariot, and headed off to our destination.

I kept looking through the clear walls trying to guess where we were going. The roads were treacherous with ice and snow, and the chariot occasionally slipped as it rolled along, which fluttered my stomach when I imagined it falling down at such high speed.

Finally, we approached a large, brightly-lit building, where hundreds of people were congregating. We were visiting their temple! Now I was really excited.

I tried to decide whose temple they had chosen. Jupiter? Juno? Maybe Apollo, or Diana? I could almost hear Spiritae roll her eyes. She cast abrupt thought my way: "Nearly every place of worship in this city is a *Christian* church." Clearly, the Christians have risen to power, just as Rome had feared. They sure are into building temples, as there is one on nearly every street corner. Now even the Roman gods have been vanquished. Mother would be heartbroken. I decided I had better just watch for a while. The congregation gathered in a great hall rowed with long wooden benches. The ceiling loomed high above, drawing attention to the front, where a large cross hung illuminated pale blue from behind, yet no light source could be seen.

Everyone stood silent, or speaking in hushed tones, reverent as they prepared to worship.

A woman began to play an instrument softly, just like Becca can do, but this one was in a large black box and sounded even lovelier. A family strode solemnly to the front, uttered some sayings, and each one transferred a small flame from a torch to a bowl with five candles, first four thinner ones arranged in a circle, each taller than the one before it, and finally to a larger white candle in the middle.

I started to ask a question, but Spiritae cut me off, "Just watch. The candles are symbolic, and I have a fondness for them."

Well, I won't argue that, but wish I knew symbolic of *what*.

A man, whom I guessed might be the temple priest, made prayers and talked with powerful presence to the assembly. I wished I could understand, but knew he told a story, ancient and profound, which fixed the congregation's attention. I was so enchanted it took me a while to notice that Allen, Becca, and Christy were nowhere to be seen.

They had gone off to prepare to join the worship service, and it was to be an evening of music and light.

The temple was decorated splendidly. An altar beneath the cross held a blanket of potted plants, green near the bottom but topped with vivid red leaves. Throughout, plants were arranged in layers as if they were trees. The temple walls were special too. I could not see through their almost clear panes of beautiful colors that captured outside light and held it there. On sunny days, the effect must be akin to standing in the heart of a rainbow—indoors!

A man and woman came forward to make music.

The woman sat behind a golden harp, slowly exhaled, and raised delicate hands to caress its strings. Just when I think this place could not be more wonderful, I am surprised again. The music struck me as otherworldly; so moving, I hoped the man would not play, because I could listen to this for eternity....But he prepared to join her, bracing under his chin a small wooden box with four strings. He fingered these into precise patterns while drawing a long stick across them with his other hand.

Spiritae started to say something about this instrument, but all I got was that the stick was made from a horse's tail. The keening music was nothing like any sound I'd heard before...high and so very sweet. It soared upon the woman's music in perfect harmony, mingling in my ears, reaching deep into my mind and soul, caressing newly-evoked emotions. If perfection exists, this was it.

When they finished, no one moved, no one breathed. I saw many wet faces, heard much sniffling.

A large group of men and women sat together in the front of the temple, each wearing a magnificent flowing robe that made me feel right at home.

I saw that Becca had donned a robe and sat in a row with mostly women. The group stood in unison and prepared to sing. One woman sat in front of a very large wooden box, something like Becca's instrument at home, but this one had many rows of white and black levers and three large pads at her feet. This instrument must be the emperor of all instruments, for it can make music of any kind, sometimes a single tone, sometimes together in great choruses by way of air pushed through pipes, hundreds of them, some small as your finger and some as tall and thick as a tree.

She played softly and sweetly when the people sang, but near the end the instrument was unleashed, and the entire building reverberated under its power, finishing in a tremendous surge of joy and exultation acknowledged by the crowd with a long ovation. Everyone released all the praise they possessed in a single mighty purge of emotion.

A group of children approached long tables at the front of the temple where many gorgeous brass bells were laid out in rows. At home, we shake bells to make loud clanking sounds. These were polished like mirrors and produced the loveliest sounds. The children grabbed them by a handle and flicked them upward toward the audience. The small ones made a delicate "ting", the medium size ones a mellow "dong", and the big ones, which were hard to handle, made a generous "BONNNNNGGGG!" The children played, sending out rippling choruses of notes, and people clapped with joy. Christy held four of the tiniest bells, and made them sing by twisting her wrists quickly in intricate patterns. I was so proud of her!

The group in robes sang again, and this time I could not believe my ears.

They sang of a woman named Mary, and hailed and praised her above all women as the mother of God. I was stunned, because I could understand every word. Ave Maria. They sang in *my* language! Rome has not been forgotten completely. And they sang "Glory Be to God on High!" *Gloria in excelsis Deo!* I wept with understanding.

The crowd again grew serene and pensive. Attendants distributed small candles to everyone, and they passed a flame from one to the next until each held a single flame. The lights in the temple were extinguished, leaving only the candlelit shadows dancing on the faces of the worshipers. Together they sang a wonderfully simple song born of the still the night, and reverence for the soul. The congregation filed out of the building smiling, tired and contented, full of the season.

Spiritae whispered a thought: "What did you make of all the candles?"

I thought she might make another wisecrack about rotten plants, but I had a sudden inspiration, guessing, "Lighting the candles to the white one in the middle was about waiting for Jesus Christ. Passing the flames from the white candle to the ones held by all was giving them a living flame, like the one they have in their soul from God."

"Not bad. I thought maybe you had nodded off."

Before they left, Becca and Christy went to a small room for a separate ritual. An attendant said a few words, and presented them with a cup that appeared to hold wine, and a small plate of tiny bread wafers which they dipped into the wine and solemnly swallowed.

I asked Spiritae why they were doing this. They couldn't be hungry after the big meal they had eaten earlier today.

Long pause.

Spiritae tried to explain, but it was hard to understand. They wanted to remember Jesus Christ, symbolically eating his flesh and drinking his blood that he had shed for them to take away their sins. I had been very impressed with the worship service, but the notion of eating someone and drinking their blood left me pretty cold. I still don't quite get the taking away sins part. I mean, I've done a few bad things that Mother has yelled at me for, but I didn't think anyone should have to *die* for it. Besides, I tried the bread and it was as tasteless as papyri, and the wine?

Can't fool me. It was grape juice!

On the way home, a sudden thought occurred to me. "Christy? Jesus Christ? Is she named after Christ?"

"You're sure a bright bulb aren't you? You just figured that out?" Back at the house, which still blazed with lights, the family rushed in to get warm and shake snowflakes from their hair.

Becca made steaming hot drinks in the fast-cook. One taste and I was hooked. It had the same flavor as that marvelous dark stuff in the treats she served to Christy and Tanika. Floating on top of the frothy brown drink, were several white little cushions, which made a terrific combination. I think this stuff could really catch on. Becca stirred something quickly together in a pan, and put it to bake in the fast-cook; obviously, the evening of treats would continue later.

The family gathered by the tree, and now I expected to see what would happen with the glowing tree angel. Instead, Becca pulled out a low table and a box with small figures of people and animals. First, she set out a broken looking building. They took turns setting out a small family, a mother, a father, some shepherds, three men with turbans holding gifts, and a tiny white angel with wings. Around these they placed cows, lambs, and a donkey. Finally, in the center, they placed a tiny baby in a cradle. Allen lifted a bulky black book, and read gravely for a few minutes. The passage resembled the story told at the temple.

Spiritae's quiet thought trilled with contentment: "They remembered...they remembered."

Gosh, I really am dense! All this—the celebration, the holiday, the worship. It was all about the birthday of Jesus Christ! So far in the future, and people were still honoring someone who died before I was born, even before my Papa was born.

The family began to open gifts. Not sacrifices to the winged angel, but gifts to each other, given in love and appreciation. The beautiful papyri wrappings were torn off with hardly a glance. I had a hard time with this. The magnificent images and printing were scrunched into little balls and tossed into the rubbish, as though this stuff grows on trees. I did my best to look at each one.

When I turned back, I saw Becca clutched something to her chest and silently wept.

I could see this was a sight-capture of a handsome young man dressed in very neat dark blue garments. He looked a lot like Becca, and I worried that he must be dead. No; Allen and Christy shared knowing glances, and Christy rushed forward with a gift for her mother. A glowing far-talk tablet.

She poked it a few times for her mother, which conjured an image of the man.

Before I could ask, Spiritae said, "Steven, Christy's older brother, is far away and cannot come home from the armies to be with his family during the holiday."

Steven's visage appeared worn and tired and thin, but he could see everyone here too—except me—on a tablet Allen had sent to him.

Overjoyed, Becca and everyone talked as if we were gathered in the same room. From her expression, I could tell this was the best gift Becca could have received.

Later, she disappeared back into the cooking room to check on her treat, a square sweet cake with a remarkably pungent odor from a rare spice.

Becca stirred together a sweet sauce, a dark thick gooey liquid into which she melted a yellow stick that flowed on top, pouring it onto slices of the cake. I managed to sneak a taste. Now this is a tradition I could get used to! Apparently Allen shared my thinking, as he ate three pieces.

River Moon

I BECAME AWARE AGAIN and found myself riding in the back of a long yellow chariot machina....

Ahead sat fifteen or sixteen students from Christy's academy, an equal mix of boys and girls. Christy sat near the front beside Tanika. The kids chattered excitedly, and I have no idea how the man guiding the machina could stay focused on his job. Maybe the machina itself knew where to go.

After a short while, the machina pulled into a resting place beside an ugly low building that appeared quite worse for the wear, hissed suddenly, and flung open its front wings. The kids rushed to gather their belongings and poured outside. Their tutor, a balding man with curly gray hair surrounding his shiny dome like a laurel wreath, pointed them toward the building entrance. The kids lugged some crates.

A greeter near the entrance directed them into an empty room with many tables and chairs. There, they opened their crates, and I was pleasantly surprised to see them pulling out various shiny musical instruments. Most were brass horns, some short and squatty looking, some with long slide-arms, and a few curly horns with ivory-plugged finger pads.

One player had what I thought might be drums and circles of brass that made a crashing sound when he smacked them with a stick. Christy had a short brass horn with three little buttons on top that she kept depressing, and Tanika held a curly horn and attached a black coupling fitted with a reed that squeaked when she blew into it.

Repeatedly she cupped the black piece, making it squawk like a duck. Whenever the tutor shot her an annoyed glance, Christy peered innocently at the ceiling. Giggling hysterically only brought more harsh glares.

The students produced the most raucous racket you could imagine. I shrank from the sound, and reached out to Spiritae, "What sort of music is this? It's god-awful!"

Spiritae laughed and thought back, "Nah, they're just warming up their instruments, getting ready to play. Wait and see. They really are pretty good when they play songs all together."

At that moment, the woman who had greeted the kids stepped into the room, and invited them to eat before they performed. They didn't have to be asked twice.

These kids can really chow down! They practically knocked each other down rushing to a nearby room filled with more tables and chairs already occupied by younger boys and girls.

But something was wrong here.

These children didn't seem right. One sprawled forward onto his plate, and leered at us drooling. Another frantically waved his arms over his head and bellowed like some ferocious animal.

Most of the children had more food on their clothing and faces than in their mouths. I don't know how to say this nicely, but they did not exactly speak, but uttered sounds as if lost in their own heads.

Spiritae quietly explained that this was a facility for children afflicted with severe mental and physical disabilities, and the students from Christy's academy were here to bring music into their otherwise dreary lives.

I could tell that she thought kindly of their tutor for bringing the students here. I had heard stories of people in Rome with these problems, but have never seen any. Some claim babies that don't seem quite right are put away somewhere to perish, but I have trouble believing our parents could be so cruel. Christy's classmates were unsure how to behave. It was obvious that some thought they should try to mingle with the kids, but didn't know how. Others clustered off to the side and wolfed down their food so they could get back to their instruments and prepare for the concert. Some of the disabled children beckoned for the musicians to join them and a few responded, but it was an awkward moment. One young boy with crazy-looking hair took quite a shine to Christy, and I could see that she wanted to vanish, but swallowed hard and made her way over to sit next to him. He really was sweet and laid his head against her shoulder in appreciation. Unfortunately, his mouth smeared some half-chewed food onto her dress' sleeve, but she nonchalantly dabbed it clean with a wet piece of fabric.

Soon it was time for the concert.

The disabled children went crazy when the boy hit the drums a couple of times and clanged the brass circles. I could tell they would have liked nothing better than to spend the afternoon creating an unholy din themselves with these instruments. Spiritae was right. When the students began to play, the music was extraordinarily lovely. They began with some slow sweet pieces that seemed to calm the audience, and progressed to others possessed of a nice rhythmic beat that had the kids gently bouncing.

The concert was short, because the children were scheduled for quiet-time before their parents were to pick them up.

Toward the end, the woman greeter came forward with a special request. Spiritae helped me understand that the woman had asked the tutor whether one little girl could play a piece or two with the students. An old musical instrument stood in the corner, one with white and black keys like the one Becca plays at home, but in much worse shape. Christy's tutor appeared reluctant, especially when the little girl, Janie, was rolled forward seated in a wheeled chair. She could not walk because her spine was twisted in a tortured arc, her legs shriveled. Nor could she speak, and her eyes were glazed with

Portia's Revelation

blindness. Her crooked left arm presented a curved, claw-like hand. "No, really," said the greeter, "she can play. Give her a chance."

Christy's tutor raised his eyebrows, but acquiesced asking what she might like to play. "It doesn't matter. Just play something you have, and she will join in."

The students began a slow, dreamy piece. Amazingly, little Janie leaned over the white and black levers, fitting in perfectly with pretty combinations of notes. Her poor left hand managed to press down just at the right time, looking nothing like Becca's long elegant fingers stroking the music, but getting the job done nevertheless. Christy's tutor stood stunned, but the woman beamed and explained that Janie's father was a professional musician, that Janie couldn't do anything else, but her mind was completely in tune with what she had learned as a baby while her father practiced.

The music was so lovely.

I asked Spiritae what it meant.

She thought, "It's a beautiful scene about the emotions you feel when you imagine drifting above a wide river lit by the moon."

I became dreamy, thinking of the full moon over the Tiber. Then the music turned lovelier still, but sadder too. Little Janie didn't miss a beat, adding tinkling notes atop the pretty melody. Spiritae said this song was about a lost love and the colors of emotions: blue, gray, red, green, and black. I don't know quite what she meant, but she said the rainbow went away, and I know how sad that would be.

Finished, the students stood and gave little Janie a standing ovation.

I wish she could have seen it, but I think she knew. The boys were quiet with wide eyes. Christy and Tanika's shone with emotion. Here they had come to perform, and now would leave with a life lesson.

Spiritae said, "Never underestimate what someone has to offer. Every soul has a gift to give, no matter how they appear to others."

Die Right

Spiritae and I flowed into a healing room, following Becca hard-at-work checking on her patients.

Becca's face was tight with anxiety and concern. In the room, an old man lay on a bed with a breathing machina attached to his face. Bags of liquid hung suspended from poles, their umbilicals threaded through a box machina and into several spots on his body.

The man's eyes were closed, but sometimes he struggled in his sleep, eyes flitting open in brief unfocused confusion.

Two women sat somberly on a bench near the window, waiting to speak with Becca.

I asked Spiritae to help me understand what I was seeing. Becca picked up a tablet near the bottom of the bed and scanned it quickly. She didn't look happy.

Spiritae thought quietly, "This man is very close to the end of his life. He is quite old and has more things wrong with his body than anyone in this time knows how to fix. Becca has enormous respect for him. He was her mentor and tutor during most of the time she was learning to be a healer. She is very frustrated that she cannot help him get well. He is not suffering a lot of pain, because those tubes are filling him with medications to keep him comfortable. But as he grows more ill, that will become more and more difficult. These two women are his daughters, the only family he has left. They are facing a difficult decision."

One woman's face was flushed and bloated from crying. The other, slightly older and more in control of herself, wore a serious expression, as if bearing some immense burden.

Spiritae continued, "In this area of their country, it is now permitted for a person to choose the time they will die with help from others."

"What? You mean they are going to murder their father?"

"No, now don't go getting all upset. If a person has left instructions in legal documents, others can make sure the person leaves this world more easily, with dignity and grace, instead of being diminished by their agony. There are medications that can be given to make death very much like falling asleep."

"Why is death so often painful?"

"It is painful for some, but not so for others. I think there are those whose essence is bound tighter than others', and it takes more time and effort to get everything unwound. Some people fear death terribly, probably because they are afraid of the unknown or worry about those they will leave behind. You can't believe how desperately some fight to hang on."

The older woman showed some documents to Becca, and she shook her head.

Spiritae explained that the woman had asked if Becca could be present, as they helped make his final moments as pleasant as possible and then administer the sleep of death. Becca replied that she just couldn't bring herself to do this, that she was a healer and fundamentally opposed to taking life, even when that appeared to be a humane act of kindness.

"Spiritae, isn't it wrong to kill yourself, even with the help of others? I know some people commit suicide back in Rome too."

"That's a very tough question, and I don't have a black or white answer for you. Here's what I feel. When a person is wracked with pain and it becomes clear to them and others that they cannot regain some quality to their life through any means, I cannot fault them for wishing to end their life with dignity. On the other hand, it is difficult to know with certainty when that moment has arrived. A few make miraculous recoveries from dire circumstances, so it's unfortunate when someone opts out of life too early, but those mistakes are rare.

"The ones that break my heart are when a young person feels they can't go on emotionally for some reason. They've been bullied or abused, or feel helpless, unloved, or ashamed. Maybe lost someone they just can't stand to be without. These are the ones I might be able to reach through the kindnesses of others around them, but who I cannot save in time. These really make me cry when I carry their broken spirits home."

"That must be awful," I said. "And so young...."

"And I really hate some suicides. Selfish ones, designed to cause emotional pain or harm to others. Like people who leave their heads blown open to punish the loved ones who will find them, in retribution for some affliction. Like the teacher who hanged himself from a beam at the academy. Can you imagine how traumatized his students must feel? No matter how badly they acted, is there any reason to make others feel they caused his death? I really can't abide those who see how many other innocent people they can kill before they go out in a blaze of their own death in some desperate outcry of rebellion. I have trouble finding any essence left that is worth carrying anywhere, let alone home."

Spiritae was getting pretty hot under the collar, so I was relieved when a new doctor appeared in the room. Spiritae explained that he was Becca's replacement, the attending healer who would assist in the man's end to life.

I expected him to have a more callous aspect, but he appeared kindly enough and was very respectful with both daughters and the bed-bound man. Spiritae explained it was very important that no one presume the man could not hear or comprehend, even when he appeared unconscious, because his senses were likely to be functioning at some level.

The doctor adjusted slightly the medications dripping from the bags, and after a few minutes, the man's eyes flickered and he seemed more alert than earlier.

The younger woman slowly dimmed the lights, until the room reached its own twilight. Somewhere, she switched on a music machina, so very soft at first it sounded like a distant rain storm. The pattering drops were soothing...and from the edge of perception faded in a beautiful symphony similar to that performed by the man and his small stringed box at Christy's temple, but so many more, dozens of them, some larger with deep resonant voices. My soul surged, and I asked Spiritae, "What is that magnificent music? It's...it's...simply incredible."

"Yes, isn't it? Some composers really know how to channel divine inspiration. It has been this man's favorite music all of his adult life. It is about a new world, a man's dream of what looking into paradise after death must be like."

The music was so perfectly appropriate that I could have guessed its meaning without asking. What hope it promised! The man's tight grip on the bed's fabric relaxed...until, at the last, his hands lay gently curved at his sides.

There came a scent of pine, and rain. This lingered in the quiet room, yet did not overwhelm. It evoked a sense of deep comfort.

What marvelous machinae they have here! Somewhere in the dark, the daughter was able to instruct a machina to make the room fill with the scents of the great outdoors.

The man's nostrils twitched, and he sighed.

Spiritae whispered that the man had lived his youth in the mountains, among towering pines. He had never been able to return there, and his daughters were helping him home. Had I any, tears would have been streaking my cheeks.

The older daughter reached for another machina, and it quietly created images on the ceiling above the man's head.

From the darkness, lovely images bloomed, faded, and shifted. Fiery fields of poppies, dolphins surging through waves, pictures of the daughters as children and a woman who must have been their mother; tropical fish, a grinning dog.

The man's eyes flickered...and did not close. A smile twitched the corners of his mouth.

The older daughter produced a miniscule bottle of chilled green liquid, uncapped it, and poured a few drops into her father's mouth.

His tongue darted out, explored his lips. Spiritae explained that the man's favorite taste was fresh-squeezed lime juice, although he could rarely have it because of stomach troubles.

The daughters pulled out some type of fur, and rubbed slowly, stroking their father's cheeks.

Spiritae said the fur was the softest that grows on any animal, and they wanted him to have a lasting memory of a gentle touch. Each kissed his pale wrinkled forehead.

This must be goodbye, and they performed this final loving ritual so that everything would be perfect. They asked if he was ready to go, and he gave a subtle nod. The image above changed to the night sky, flaring with a million stars.

The daughters each took one of his hands, and softly prayed.

I wanted to ask Spiritae what they were saying, but she protested. "Shh! They are praying to me, not you. Some things are private, you know."

Okay, then.

The doctor stepped unobtrusively to the medication pole and made an adjustment.

Nothing much happened, but after a few minutes I noticed the man's chest was not moving. The healer departed quietly, giving the daughters time to end their commemoration in solitude. After a long while, the healer returned and the older daughter turned up the lights to a soft level, which seemed emotionally warming. Both daughters now appeared at peace.

Spiritae told me the doctor had asked how they wished the man's body to be handled, and let me in on their plans.

Their father had wished for cremation, his ashes forever committed to the family farm. The elder daughter had picked out a place of honor, and would plant a special tree above his remains. She explained how they would mix his salty ashes with powders of lemons and limes, so not to harm the transplanted roots.

Her sister had already picked out a sapling along their fence line that would be uprooted to cover their father. Each autumn, it would blaze scarlet, burnt orange, and burnished gold; grandly preside over them and their children for the rest of their lives.

Spiritae considered this a lovely symbol to honor their father's passion for recycling, and I agreed.

She excused herself, saying it was time for me to head home for a good night's rest. She could handle the rest of the journey by herself.

Good thing, because I was beat....

Dump Trash

I STARTED MY VISION TONIGHT IN A EUPHORIC MOOD, though Spiritae seemed distant and reserved. I was looking forward to more adventures that would leave me breathless with wonders beyond my wildest imagination. I bubbled with enthusiasm, telling Spiritae, "Everything in this place and time is so extraordinary. Most everyone is so lucky. They are blessed to live in paradise."

I swore I heard Spiritae blink with regret at her next words: "Ahh!—so they do. Most fail to appreciate what they have. It is time for you to see other visions from this world, the lives of the less fortunate. This will be hard for you, Portia."

I grew queasy with uncertainty.

The travel fog dissipated, and I found myself standing amidst garbage extending in all directions to the horizon.

It was fortunate my ability to smell is so selective.

Even a subtle sniff of decay and noxious fumes spun me—I nearly fainted, staggered about trying to understand what I was seeing.

Thousands of broken and dead machinae lay scattered in rusting finality, unloved and discarded by the people they once served. So much marvelous papyri and other wrapping materials I didn't recognize, tossed aside as though these things cost nothing. Container after container of food-stuff from the market, not cleaned nor reused. Foul-smelling wrappings from infants smeared with excrement. Half-eaten animal carcasses rotting in the hot sun.

Overhead swirled and cried legions of seabirds, swirled overhead, diving into the mountain of debris and fighting over some tidbit or another.

"Spiritae, why have you brought me here? To see the refuse of the entire world?"

"This is only the refuse from one city—a few weeks' worth."

"What's going to happen with all this stuff? Why don't they bury it, or better yet burn it to heat their homes?"

"People simply use and discard too much. Much *is* buried. Yes, some is burned. Both cause problems. Materials created by people are not quickly accepted back by the Earth. Some of these burn in ways that damage the very air the people need to breathe. Much refuse is thrown into the ocean, as though it will disappear and dissolve, but all these elements assault the Earth and life itself. Hard for people to imagine, I guess, but the Earth, the sky, and the sea are not without limits."

After a few minutes, I spied a small boy, perhaps seven or eight years old, clambering up the pile of trash. He had a tattered basket strapped to his back and was caked with filth. He industriously probed the dirt, plucked from its pungency all kinds of junk, some tossed away on sight, others more closely inspected, and stashed in his basket.

"What is he doing, Spiritae?"

"If he is lucky today, he will find a few things he can exchange for a couple of coins. He hopes to buy a bowl or two of rice today so that his brothers and sisters will not go hungry."

"Why don't his parents go to the market?"

"His father is dead. His mother is very sick and cannot work. There is no one to take pity upon them. There are more hungry mouths than there are those who will share."

"But surely all the people I saw before would share. They have more than they could ever use."

"True, but they don't even *think* about these people. Out-of-sight and out-of-mind. Easier to stick your head in the sand than to see poverty up close."

"But, but...the wealthy cannot be so callous that they would ignore these few."

"Few? FEW? Open your eyes and your mind. Throughout all mankind's history, in your time, before and after, there have always been those who have more than they need to live and legions who, if they are lucky, survive day to day. Those with plenty cannot see these poor souls, except as human waste. People here are *desperate* for help. Their needs go far beyond food. They need many hands reaching out with love and hope, bringing safety, knowledge to care for themselves and their families. This is life as many know it in this time."

I was horrified by what I saw. A tiny girl, maybe only two or three years old, sitting naked in the trash. She had found a miniscule heel of stale bread, and was about to cram it into her mouth when a snarling rat popped from the filth hissing. The brave little soul prepared to do battle, clearly not her first combat, and snatched up a twisted piece of metal to confront the inevitable.

A swooping gull exploited this momentary distraction, and plucked away the morsel. Both girl and rat turned away, not taking the time to show disappointment or wasting time as they hunted for more.

With choked voice, Spiritae thought: "There are dozens of orphans living here trying to survive any way they can. Most don't. They are abandoned. Only *I* love them."

I began to cry. "Spiritae, isn't there anything that can be done for these kids?"

She wheezed as if under the crush of ages. "The answer has been laid at the feet of all people, planted in their minds time and time again. How many ways do I have to say it? It is not hard to understand.

"Love one another. Care and share with those less fortunate. Walk gently upon the Earth, and leave a trail of generosity in your wake. Live in moderation in what you consume and how you procreate. Borrow what you need, but need what you take. Pay back as best you are able. Leave the world a better place than when you arrived. Live and let others live."

My heart is sick today.

City of the Dead

A S I BECAME AWARE, the fog clearing from my mind, I saw an oddly peaceful scene. Thousands and thousands of small white crosses stretched out before me arranged neatly in rows. Every so often, there was a white star instead of a cross. A gentle breeze drifted from the distant azure ocean, stirred the trees. No birds sang, as if keeping a reverent silence. Without asking, I knew these were graves.

I could sense forlorn wraiths who walked here still. What terrible tragedy had ended so many?

Only a scatter of people walked through the graveyard, stopping to look at symbols that must be the names of dear ones...markers keeping silent vigil over land consecrated with blood of the fallen. The number of graves overwhelmed me.

Spiritae too was silent. Finally, she breathed a thought, "I hate war."

Hushed, as though addressing herself, "I carried every one of their souls in my arms. And the ones they fought and killed as enemies, I carried their souls too."

Trembling, I could not help but wonder what manner of being Spiritae might represent. Carrying souls? Now I was truly frightened. Was she Charon, who ferried souls across the river Styx to the underworld? Maybe my parents did not pay Charon's fee, and I am doomed to wander the shores for a hundred years.

I saw that today I must ask questions very cautiously.

"All these graves, Spiritae, what was this battle about?"

Long pause. "Rather difficult to put into simple thoughts.

"It was a time when the entire world was wracked with war, a time when madmen sought to steal other lands, thinking themselves superior, seeing their neighbors as prey, whose lives they could usurp, seeing innocents in their own lands as inferior, deserving to be expunged from the Earth. A time when the spirit of freedom and regard for individual human rights rose up to overthrow those who would impose their will by military force. It was a battle for the future of the human race.

"A most terrible time, when men killed entire cities alive with women and children, the aged and infirm, without regard, burning them in white flames of death. In this period, the horrors of war are magnified a thousandfold—a millionfold. Using machinae of destruction, men can obliterate entire cities, entire countries, in minutes, seconds. They can make the Sun scorch the Earth, bringing fearful deaths to all in their path. Their power far outstrips their wisdom. The future of mankind and the Earth hangs by a thread."

I was not sure why, but Spiritae was clearly trying to scare me silly—and succeeding.

Not even the gods of Olympus have the power she was describing, not even if they all got into a big snit at the same time. I could feel her "thought" eyes boring into me, strange in their intensity. "War is Hades right here on Earth. There is nothing glorious about war, not even in victory. Only misery for the vanquished, and pain enough for the victors."

I thought of the images I had seen on the far-sight:—emaciated men, women, and children staring back with eyes of death as they awaited their cremation—mushroom clouds looming over shattered cities—wholly consumed by million-degree fireballs—human corpses stacked like kindling being pushed into mass graves—metal ships marching across the ocean so thick you could hop from one to the next.

Now I know. These were not imagined visions...nor nightmare, nor portent of some future disaster—but a real world horror. This world needs all the prayers for wisdom that it can get.

I stood humbly at the edge of the field of crosses, thinking of those who perished in the battle of good versus evil, trying to imagine millions of casualties and the slaughter of innocents. If I had had skin, it would have been covered with goose bumps. Spiritae's lessons are very hard indeed.

"Spiritae, why do men fight wars?"

"Mostly for stupid or silly reasons. More often than not, wars are born of greed or fanaticism."

"I don't understand."

"Neither do I, Portia."

The despair in her pause quickened my own. "Little has changed through the centuries. Men battle for control over land and the resources of the Earth. In their greed, they will hoard anything: food, water, land, metals, other people, money, you name it—even rotten plants."

I sensed a sad smile.

"They go mad with power-lust, denying others the right to existence, and subjecting innocents to servitude."

"War and killing seem so wrong."

"War always brings misery, most often to the innocent. There is a time to die, and a time to kill, but always with the utmost deliberation. Defend your life, your loved ones, and your country when tyrants would take them from you. Seek not to impose your ideals on others, but lead your life in a manner that encourages others to follow your example of their own volition. Be in harmony with all people, to the extent possible, without vacating your moral principles. Be intolerant of subjugation and genocide, for these are devoid of moral value."

Spiritae should be a priest in a temple. When she gets on a roll, she's not shy with her opinions.

If only I understood everything she said.

City of Sin

I T WAS SCORCHING HOT TODAY.
Spiritae and I were hovering at the edge of a wide lake surrounded by low mountains, pretty with rocks subtly-tinted yellow and brown, but I could tell it was very dry here. There were no trees, and the hillsides stood parched and bare. The lake was banded by a layer of white rock, and I correctly guessed—according to Spiritae—its water-level had once been much higher. We watched people rush by in speedy boat machinae that screamed and churned water into leaping white waves. People riding on the boats shouted and grinned with exhilaration, hair tossed by gushing wind, bodies bounced with seeming abandon. A few had tiny boat machinae not much larger than themselves. These the riders spun in great arcs faster even than the bigger machinae, jetting giant plumes behind them.

Spiritae wasn't saying much, so I knew she wanted me to see something wrong in all this. "It looks like these people are having fun playing."

She huffed. "I suppose they are. They'd better enjoy it while they can. I don't know why people get such a thrill zipping around at breakneck speeds, especially when they're not trying to get anywhere. Flip one of those boats over and they'll learn fast enough that water is a lot harder than it looks."

"What do you mean 'while they can'?"

"Isn't it obvious? The lake is drying up. This land is dry enough without everybody indulging themselves, making the land even hotter and dryer."

"How does riding a boat machinae make everything dryer?"

"It's not the boats exactly. People all over, even far away, are changing their surroundings by the way they pollute the air."

"Why would they do that? That seems rather stupid."

"Well, many of them just don't think they are doing anything harmful, or they can't bring themselves to change their ways. I know you think I make too much of the rotten plant thing, but when they burn all the wood, coal, and oil to fuel their wondrous machinae, a portion goes into the sky where it traps more heat from the sun. People seem intent on cooking themselves. Come with me. I want to show you something."

We glided to one end of the lake, where a road crossed above the water. We passed over this, and I gasped as we sank lower and lower to a tiny stream in a rocky canyon below. We turned and looked back at the biggest rock I've ever seen.

"That's not a rock exactly, Portia. It's made of concrete, which is a remarkable material discovered in your time back in Rome. This is a human-built structure."

I thought Spiritae must be exaggerating, as we haven't built anything even half so large in Rome. I got dizzy just looking so high toward the top.

"People put all this concrete across the canyon to block it so the water could not escape toward the sea. They made the lake you saw."

"You're kidding. People made that big lake out of this tiny stream? Why in the world would they do that? Just to zip around on boats?"

"Nope. They wanted to use the water for several reasons."

"Oh, you mean like irrigation. But I don't see any *crops*."

"That might have been a decent idea, but there really has never been enough rain around here for good farmland. The main reason they built this dam and the lake was to make what you cutely call *lightning*."

"Come on. You're fooling me. Make lightning out of water? I don't think even *you* can make that happen."

"Well, it's true. When they open massive doors near the bottom of the dam, the water rushes through with great force because it is so deep. The water blasts against lightning-maker machinae, spinning them around and around, making lightning."

"Spiritae, that can't be right! You just squirt some water at a poor machina making it dizzy, and it spits out lightning?"

She giggled, and said, "Portia, you're a hoot."

I sulked for a while. I don't know why she called me an owl, even though I happen to like them.

"This is one of the better ways to make lightning. Much better than burning rotten plants. But there aren't enough places where water can be piled up high enough to do this. It helps to have some canyons around. And this way isn't perfect either. Too much mud can build up behind the dam, and it is hard to remove. Making a big lake covers land owned by people who used to live along the stream, and most times they aren't asked if they are willing to move. Not only people are affected. Fish and other creatures that depend on moving up and down the stream get cut off too—and they are never consulted.

"Wait, you said one of the *better* ways. What other ways are there?"

"Personally, I like using sunlight best, but that only works in the daytime. But people can make lightning from the wind, from the heat of the Earth, even from ocean waves. There are fancier ways too, but mankind hasn't discovered all of them."

"Wow! How can that be? Sounds like you can make lightning out of anything! Maybe people could store up sunlight in big jars and use it at night."

"You're ahead of your time, Portia! They should start working on that. Look here. See all the metal wires up there? That's how the lightning gets sent to where people want to use it."

"I don't understand. You mean they pour the lightning into one end of the wire, and it runs all by itself far away? Where is the lightning going anyway?"

This time she laughed out loud. "I just *love* the things you come up with. No, they only have to connect one end of the wire here, and the lightning appears like a snap of your fingers at the other end. You'll have to trust me on this one. All the lightning is headed to a city we are going to visit tonight."

About all I could understand was that the lightning-maker tickles one end of the wire, and it laughs out lightning at the other end. It's not always easy to believe the things Spiritae says.

"Let's go look at something pretty while we've got some daylight left."

So we oozed along, until we reached a lovely area with a walking trail that passed through all sorts of fantastically-shaped red rocks. As sunset approached, the rocks took on deeper hues elegant against deep blue twilight. We watched a group of young girls climbing high above us on the rocks. I would have held my breath, if I had had any, in terror for them. They didn't have ropes or anything! They scampered up the rocks like spiders finding the tiniest of footholds, and clinging with their fingers. One girl was nearly upside down, and I was sure she would slip and make a big splat right in front of us. But she was very athletic and climbed up with no trouble. Spiritae said, "Some people take terrible chances for the thrill of it. Personally, I thought what the wind did here was pretty enough to admire from the ground without clambering around all over it, but who am I to say? You'd think they might take the gift of life more seriously."

"What do you mean, the wind did this?"

"The wind, rain, and rocks—better tools for a real artist than what a human sculptor can produce. Of course, I might be a little biased. Let's move on."

She blinked and suddenly it was completely dark, twilight was over, and we were standing along a street that stretched to the horizon with more lights blazing and flashing than you can possibly imagine. The abrupt change terrified me.

"Spiritae! Oh my word! What happened? Just like *that* you ended the day?"

"Oh, don't go getting all excited. It's nothing, really. We don't have all the time in the world, so I helped move it along a little, that's all."

Commanding time itself? That's all?

"Spiritae, these beautiful lights! They're fantastic."

"To be sure. Fantastic eaters of lightning, if that's what you mean. This is where that force from the dam is directed."

We glided along, taking in the sights, when I spied a large pyramid. A white beam burst from the top and speared the sky. I jumped with excitement.

"Spiritae!" I cried. "Are we in Egypt? Don't tell me they've moved one of their great pyramids here just for amusement? And is that the *Sphinx* I see?"

"Ha! No, not really. They built copies here to attract people to come inside. The real ones are much larger and far, far older."

"Go inside? You mean we can walk in to a pyramid? That would be great!"

"We'll take a look later, if you can't contain yourself. There are more interesting things to see."

Wow. This place must be *incredible*.

I followed her in to a cavernous building to a dirt-floored arena. Rows of tables surrounded the space, and hundreds of people were preparing for a feast. It smelled awesome. Wish I had a stomach to eat with. People here eat a ton of food. Everyone was served a *whole* chicken. No wonder they're so fat.

As the feast neared its end, a tremendous blast of long silver horns sounded, and a group of men on horseback entered the arena. The men and their horses were dressed in the most colorful and elaborate costumes you can imagine. Each sported a particular color scheme so they were easily recognizable. Apparently they were planning to have a competition. I grew uneasy, fearing that I was going to get to watch men hack each other to death again, but in a modern fashion.

Spiritae reassured me that this was only a mock battle, that the only blood to be spilled belonged to the poor chickens that were being swallowed with gusto. Each gladiator paraded up and down before the crowd, receiving cheers from his admirers and some boos from those who favored others. Somewhere high above, shafts of colored lights shone down on the riders, spotlighting them with rainbow auras. The horses pranced, proud with anticipation.

The riders paid homage to a couple I presumed were their emperor and empress. Each hoped to win the favor of the daughter, stunning in her fantastic gown and headdress. Finally, she smiled at one gladiator, and he presented the tip of his pike. Onto this she hung a swatch of beautiful fabric from her bodice, and blew him a kiss.

If Cato wants so badly to fight, he should do it here. He'd probably fall off his horse, though, if the young empress looked at him like *that*.

The riders paired off in groups of two, one at one end of the arena and his opponent at the other.

Someone shouted, and the horses galloped toward each other with frightening speed, riders wielding their pikes with focused tension. Each hoped to stab the other, protected by only a small arm shield.

I shrieked in fear, not for the men, but the horses. "Spiritae, you didn't bring me here to watch them slaughter horses, did you? I surely don't want to watch *that!*"

"No. Horses are far too valuable. Just watch. See how the men are dressed all in metal for protection?" The riders closed with clanging impact—one man tumbled and crashed to the ground on his back. Ouch! But he rolled around and pulled out a long sword.

The other rider bounced down, presenting his own sword, and they began hacking at each other.

Now I could see they were merely mock-fighting because their thrusts were exaggerated and obvious. Anyone who's been to the arena in Rome knows the best fighters make short sharp movements when they want to kill.

After repeated bashes and groans, a champion was declared.

This, of course, was the man favored by the young empress.

The crowd booed, cheered, applauded and slowly dispersed, appetites for food and conflict satiated.

Spiritae and I moved along the gleaming road, pausing when we encountered a restless crowd waiting for something to happen.

The ground shook—and a too-close-for-comfort volcano erupted!

Rocks and earth dropped like lethal hail, and boiling lava snaked down the sloped face toward us. Fire punched through magma...but something about the rumbling chaos hit me, well, funny.

When a rock lighter than a wad of papyri struck my head, I understood why the crowd had gathered. Drums were throbbing, colored lights bathed the volcano in fiery light, and concealed music played making for an impressive show. But nonetheless, a *show*. Spiritae yawned. "Rather pathetic really. You should see what a *real* volcano can do."

I thought she might be right about this, as I've heard rumors of what took place down in Pompeii. Some survivors claimed fire and rocks shot miles into the sky, and the landscape was encased by lava. Residents were cooked alive, themselves transformed into dreadful sculptures.

Timidly I ventured, "Spiritae, did you make a show like this a few years ago down toward Pompeii?"

She seemed surprised. "Really Portia? You think I'd bake a bunch of folks just to put on a nice show? Jeesh! What kind of monster do you think I am? I know, I know, people always think I'm lurking around trying to punish them somehow, and beg me to pull them out of some fix. When a few escape by the skin of their teeth, they want to give me all the credit, forgetting all the poor people who they decide I've decided to wink out. I mean, if you choose to live next to a volcano, am I really to blame when it burps on you?"

"Sorry Spiritae...."

We continued on, and came to a huge pool of water with another crowd who seemed to anticipate yet another event. Spiritae seemed happier, and said this one was more her style. It didn't take long to see why.

Hundreds, if not thousands, of water jets at once danced for the crowd. Sweet music sang to the water, conjuring gushing spires that waved back and forth like living things in dazzling white light.

But I reserved my admiration, fearful of Spiritae's criticism. She, however, finally was more upbeat.

"They almost have it," she muttered. "Almost. I think they might yet understand. Light, music, colors of the rainbow, and the water of life. How many ages have I written my messages in golden skies of dawn and glorious sunsets, hoping someone would finally understand?" She turned and said the most curious thing. "Portia, they will understand soon. Max will help them, and they will know, all because of you."

"What do you mean? Max? Max *who*?"

"Never mind. You wouldn't understand, but I tell you truthfully, I have great hope now, and you are part of it."

She was right. I didn't have a clue what she was talking about, but I wasn't about to spoil her praise of me.

"Let's go back to the pyramid for a peek inside.

This was unexpected. Apparently some place where travelers spent the night in sleeping rooms, but the entire center was filled with machinae, glowing faces and spinning disks blazing with amazing symbols. People perched on tall seats before various machinae, sipping drinks, chewing fire sticks, and tapping the devices over and over.

Bewildering! Why would *any*one do this? The machinae flashed lights, rang *bong-bong-bong, ding-ding-ding,* and sometimes sounded as if vomiting coins. A couple of girls walked by carrying trays of drinks. I was shocked at their immodesty. I've seen whores in Rome and—trust me—these women were wearing far less. Cato and Cassius would have a field day here for sure.

Spiritae let me watch for a while, and explained: "This entire city is all about wagering. People bring their savings here and hand it over to the machinae. Mostly the machinae steal it from them, usually slowly so they don't get discouraged, but the owners of this place always end up with more than they give. A very few people get lucky and walk away with more than they brought."

"I don't get it, Spiritae. Why would anyone do anything so stupid?"

"All this glitz and glamour is designed to be exciting, and many see gambling as entertainment. Those girls are trying to make a living, but have given in to the allure of making easy money by appealing to lustful men.

"My take on it is that wagering is not one of the better ways to rid yourself of wealth when there are so many needs that money could ease. Losing a small amount isn't terrible, if you can afford to lose it, but the difficulty comes when people catch the gambling disease and spend money urgently needed for themselves and their families. They succumb to a reckless hope of striking it rich and ending desperate miseries.

"Take a look around. What do you see?"

I scanned the room. "These people look wealthy to me, Spiritae. I don't think they are suffering, but they don't look like they're really having all that much fun either. Too serious. Why do they think they need to get richer?"

"Great question. People, no matter how much they have, always seem to think they deserve *more*. One of mankind's greatest weaknesses—simple greed. Unchecked envy of people perceived as having more."

"Can they really get rich here?"

"Highly improbable. But the players don't seem to care. They are buying a few moments of a dream. When it fails to appear, they shrug and say their luck was bad...returning again and again, eternally optimistic tomorrow will be different."

"Sounds to me like many make their own bad fortune."

"I'm afraid that's true. Watch these over here."

A group of people stood watching some small white balls etched with symbols bouncing in a crazy dance. One-by-one, six popped up in a row, and the people looked eagerly at some papyrus they held and checked to see if the symbols matched what was written there. None did, and most of the gamblers wandered away, glum and bored. A few stayed and reached again for more money to wager.

"So let me ask if you'd try this wager. You give me a silver coin and I flip it, letting it land on the floor. If it lands with the emperor's head showing, I get to keep your coin. If the back side shows, I also get to keep the coin. Now if it lands plop on its edge, doesn't roll away, and stays balanced, I'll give you a million silver coins. Want to try? Ever see a coin do that?"

"Why, that's crazy, Spiritae. My Papa works too hard for me to waste his money so foolishly. We need every coin we can get, and many people are worse off than us. I might try once or twice if I already had boatloads of coins, but that would still be pretty wasteful."

"Exactly. But that's what people do here all the time. Come with me."

We headed outside, and drifted over some distance from the dazzling road. Here we entered a low flat building, packed with more bonging machinae and crowded with tired-looking old people.

Spiritae said, "Look at this poor old crone." The woman was plunking coins into the machina before her as fast as it would allow —and it was robbing her. She sipped a foul-smelling liquid, and was obviously drunk. I wondered how she stayed on her stool.

"She's spending every bit of money she earned this week," Spiritae added. "Her husband left her years ago because of her addiction. She's homeless now and lives on the streets as a prostitute."

The woman stooped, had a lined yellowish face, and unwashed hair—a physical wreck. I couldn't imagine what sort of customer she might attract.

Spiritae growled vaguely about customers not being very picky. Something told me the gambler was exactly Cato's type.

"Oh Spiritae, that's so sad!" Why doesn't someone stop her?

"Some people here are predators. They think her money spends as well from *their* pockets as it does hers."

"Let's leave this place. It's so depressing."

We followed a handsome young man walking back toward the dazzling lights. He shot frequent glances all around, as if fearful of being watched or accosted. A man stepped from the shadows, and thrust a small piece of papyrus at him. The other took it, and listened while the man launched into a sales pitch. The young man smiled, and tucked the message into a pocket.

"What was *that* all about?" I asked.

Spiritae remained silent for a moment, and said, "The man was offering to make a woman available to him this evening, and that writing explains exactly what he can buy, and at what price. *Everything*—and I mean everything—here is for sale. People come to this city for entertainment—and to sin. I won't be sad to see the place fade away."

"What do you mean *fade away?*"

"I mean doomed. In a few years, the water in the lake will be too low to make lightning. No lightning, no lights. No lights, no glitter, and no thieving machinae. The trouble is—the whole affair will simply move somewhere else."

After seeing this, I felt like I could use one of those potent drinks everyone was using to dull their senses. Fortunately, my vision had ended, and I dropped into a troubled sleep, grateful Spiritae hadn't dragged me to see *everything* the city of sin had to offer.

Slaves

I STOOD THIS MORNING IN A CLEARING on an idyllic island, or so it appeared, looking along the distant coastline. The day shone clear and sunny, and a gentle breeze stirred palm leaves above me. The azure sea rolled waves onto the beach with hypnotic rhythm.

Spiritae was not saying much, which I took as a sign she was enjoying the beautiful scenery. Finally, she thought in my direction, "Let's head down that path over there."

We glided along a path, and after several minutes this opened onto a clearing clustered with long palm-thatched huts. Near these growled several large yellow machinae. I peered at these with confusion. "What are they?" Spiritae's answer was vague. The machinae were drinking rotten oily plant liquid to make lightning to provide sunshine inside the huts.

Sure enough, when we ducked inside one, we saw several glowing glass spheres hanging from black tails above, barely casting light sufficient to illumine the gloomy space. I was excited to see rows and rows of young girls seated on wooden benches teaching machinae how to sew clothes. How early it seemed they learned sewing skills here. No mother could be seen, but only a couple of rough-looking men at one end, laughing and sharing a bottle of some rancid clear liquid. Some of the girls looked as young as five years old, and none were as old as Antonia. These girls were really talented, working their nimble fingers cutting and stitching gorgeous swatches of fabric into various clothing items. They taught the sewing machinae how to join long pieces, create perfect stitches even Mother would admire—in seconds.

After a while, I could see that the work wasn't pleasant.

The over-packed hut's temperature seemed to rise with each hour, and this was only mid-morning. The breeze outside stayed there. Shoulder to shoulder, the girls labored, foreheads bright with sweat. Most smelled as though needing a dip in the surging ocean, and flies orbited their heads and clustered on salty faces.

So intensely busy, the workers never raised their hands to bat away the flies, but pursed their lips and blew air toward their tired eyes. The buzzing invaders were unfazed, and as unrelenting in their labor as the girls. One very young, probably inexperienced, girl faltered—and the machina's jittering needle pierced her index finger. She screamed in shock and horrific pain.

The chattering machina jammed, but wouldn't release her from its hungry bite. Only one girl stopped to help. The others kept working as though their hair was on fire.

A man lurched over to her, barked some profanity, and aggressively pulled her bleeding finger free.

The hyperventilating girl rocked back, pushed her wounded hand into her chest. The man shouted—slapped her and her helpmate's heads.

Incredibly, the injured girl wrapped her finger in scrap and, with her neighbor, returned to work as if the accident and brutality never had occurred.

I was stunned by the man's vicious behavior, and in shock turned to Spiritae. "What is happening here?"

Tears burned my eyes.

"These children are slaves. I hate slavery with a passion in any form. It is a leprosy of the human soul, and rots the very essence of those who see themselves as masters, and feeds on the spirit of its victims."

"Are these children born into slavery from parents captured in battle?"

"No, their slavery is far uglier. They come from families far away who have little to eat and too many children. This world is overflowing with such people. Men come among them with promises that their children, especially girls, will be taken to a better place, given an education and taught skills, awarded jobs that pay enough to send money back to help the family. A provocative lure, and the girls agree sadly but willingly. When they arrive here, the reality is *much* different. They live in putrid conditions, and must be ready to work when the sun dawns, through the whole day until well after dark.

"They only see the sun during brief breaks, usually eating nothing beyond a bowl of rice topped with bits of rotting fish. They must learn to attend their necessities during breaks, for if they need to use the facilities too often, they are forced to soil themselves or are beaten. If they complain or sicken, they might disappear. The evil men claim wages are sent home, but in reality these are simply pocketed, and the girls' families never hear from them again.

"They cannot escape, for there is no place to run and no place to hide. When they age, fingers traumatized and numb, life gets worse. The older girls are sold into prostitution, kept and ruled by men who traffic their bodies to others who have no respect for human dignity."

"This is absolutely horrible, Spiritae! Papa refuses to own slaves, but is slavery like this in Rome?"

"Your Father is a good man. Slavery in its mildest forms, even with 'kindly' masters, is an evil assault on the human spirit. In its worst forms, it is an unspeakable horror, completely and utterly unforgivable."

"Why...why does slavery exist? Can't you just *stop* it?"

"Mankind must solve its own deficiencies. All it would take is more good people to raise strong objections and confront those who would do evil. Trouble is, too many people are willing to turn their eyes away from evil when it becomes too inconvenient or expensive to intervene. For example, think of Christy's world. Her pretty clothes and shoes don't show up by magic. They are made in places like this one. Some are better, some are not, but all too often the poor are working for mere subsistence to provide lavish luxuries for the wealthy. Christy's family does not think of itself as 'wealthy' as they live amidst others who have more, but compared to many in the world, they lead a charmed life. They aren't mean people. They don't want to think of themselves as living unfairly off the miseries of others. But suppose their goods suddenly cost three to four times as much, or they had to take much more of their time to make their own stuff—that's a different matter. Most find it far too easy to turn a blind eye to the reports of these atrocities.

"Slavery is an age-old problem. There are those who 'have' and those who 'have not.' Those who 'have not' always seem to be held under the thumbs of those who happen to have more. It can be about almost anything: growing plants for making fabric, running large estates of land, mining metals from the Earth, sweetening your drinks, making machinae, and even sucking up old rotten plants."

"Aha! I *knew* the plants would play a role."

"You interrupted. Subjugation of others is wrong whether it is acknowledged as slavery or is called something else that sounds nicer. It is wrong when practiced in your own back yard, and it is wrong when you export it to some faraway land where you don't have to *see* the misery it causes...."

"Spiritae, why can't people learn to share more, instead of subjugating the less fortunate to get what they want?"

"Let me know when you get *that* one figured out. I'd really like to know. Let me put it this way. Those who are intent on preying on others are not headed to a nice place in eternity."

Golden Altar

S PIRITAE TOOK ME TO A TEMPLE TODAY. She said people don't call them temples anymore, but cathedrals. I could see why. The one I saw was magnificent both in size and ornamentation. No Roman temple is half so grandiose. I thought this must be the temple of all temples, but Spiritae disagreed, said there are dozens like this one, some just as elaborate.

From the outside, I saw great stone spires that soared nearly to the clouds. The doors were framed with huge pointed arches and were tall enough for giants to walk through. I really don't want to meet anyone large enough to need these doors. Every stone on the outside appeared to be decorated with sculptures and fanciful scenes depicting people in all sorts of activities, maybe a history of all time cut into the stone. The entire building was a work of art, although it looked delicate enough to blow away in a brisk wind. I didn't like some of the decorations. On the high roof, I could see demons and monsters glowering at people below. Most had fanged, gaping mouths.

Spiritae laughed, and said these figures served simply to provide outlets for rain-water, and when they did this people were amused to see stone mouths gushing. I didn't see the humor in demons spitting water on people below.

We glided inside, and passed a few kneeling attendees whispering in prayer. Some lighted candles, which I liked, at a little table with dozens of clustered flames. The ceiling was so high it robbed my breath (had I any). It took me a while to recognize that the entire building was laid out as a giant cross. I gaped in wonder over the pure ordered beauty, the sweet aroma of paraffin overriding the mustiness of time. High above were huge circles of light. Each had the most dazzling images, lighted from behind in vivid colors. This light streamed down as if directly from the heavens, each shaft seeming to fade some feet above the stone floor. Worshipers spoke in hushed reverence, aware that any tone louder might echo forever between the massive walls and their gray chill. Every aspect of the temple drew my eyes up, and Spiritae said that was the intent of the builders. I felt small and meaningless. Spiritae said that also was the intent of the builders. I began to wonder at the power of the Christians. I thought Rome was the center of the world, but this one building alone surpassed the grandeur of anything in my time.

Spiritae said, "Let's go take a look at the altar."

This lay so deep into the structure, I had yet to notice it. But as we approached, I blurted, "This is an altar?"

I'm used to a stone table where one can make a few sacrifices into the altar fire. Here was a table hewn from gorgeous white marble, behind which rose a fantastic golden wall festooned with images depicting the lives of colorful heavenly beings. At least I *thought* it must be gold, but there cannot be so much in the whole world. Papa once showed me a gold coin. He said it was very precious. Papa is usually paid with bronze coins and, if he is lucky, a silver one. But ordinary citizens don't see many gold coins.

The light beaming onto the altar from the windows and tall candles so brightened the wall I had to avert my eyes. I think the emperor himself would feel like a pauper here.

I stared for a long time, before Spiritae asked, "So, what do you think of all this?"

"I've never imagined anything like it. People here must think very highly of Jesus."

"Hmm. I wonder. Where do you suppose all this gold came from? It doesn't grow on trees, you know."

"I don't know, Spiritae. I thought all metals are dug out of the ground. Don't tell me gold comes from old rotten plants too?"

"Ha! That's funny. No, it comes from the Earth just like you said. It glitters beautifully, don't you think? But it really isn't useful for much other than making some rather attractive jewelry." She paused. "I wish I hadn't made it at all. Either that, or not made so much people would *fight* over it."

What? What was she saying? *She* made the gold? Maybe I'm not the one who is insane.

"Gold was probably a mistake, but I suppose if it wasn't gold, it would be something else. You see—gold is rarer than many metals, and has that lovely color you only see in the sky at dawn. Humans from every place and time have caught gold-lust fever. They have killed each other endlessly in the quest to have more. Dangle enough gold in front of most people, and they would sell their mother for it. Many would even sell their souls. The love for gold and all the power it commands corrupts the human spirit.

"Take all the gold you see here, for example. Ancestors of these people learned of a previously unknown land far across the sea. That land had an ample supply of precious metals. The cruel ruler there forced his subjects to collect and pay him a tremendous amount of it in tribute. But conquerors from here were powerful with weapons the ruler could not resist. He knew they wanted gold, and he offered them a huge amount to keep them happy. But they killed him anyway and took his gold. They raped the land and its peoples for many years, hauling their pillaged treasures home in great ships. They used the gold to gain power against other nations, and some was given to make fabulous displays of wealth in their places of worship. They claimed this was to honor their God, but in truth, it was a vulgar display of power, a statement of strength about their rulers and religious institutions. Your father has told you about Jesus. What do you suppose he would think about this altar dedicated to Him? Can you imagine what might have been accomplished *instead* of this?"

I felt deflated and duped by what I had admired. "I see what you are showing me, Spiritae. Not everything that is beautiful on the outside looks so fine when you look deeper. I suppose you mean it's that way with people, too."

"Exactly."

"But is it so wrong to have temples for praying?"

"No, that's not what I mean at all. Places of worship serve a very useful purpose if the *purpose* is kept in mind. They don't have to be so plain as to be uncomfortable, but they don't have to be ostentatious either. Some fall victim to wrongness. Some seek to impress others, sending a message that 'Our place of worship is superior to others' because we have nicer surroundings.' Others use the place of worship to define their goodness. 'We are more righteous than you in the eyes of God, because we go to our house of worship every week.' Keep in mind that you can find God inside you any time you want if you care to listen. You can pray anywhere and anytime. Some places of worship are focused too heavily on gathering money from their members to maintain their bloated operations, instead of being the hands of God.

"But places of community worship have a worthy mission. Worship leaders can inspire, encourage, and console those in need. In their messages, they can motivate people to turn their wills in a common direction accomplishing greater things than one person. When you give gifts to God or anyone, make sure they are what is needed, not what you want to give for your own purposes."

Whew! Some of Spiritae's lessons are tough.

Plague

MY VISION BEGAN TODAY IN A STEAMING, VERDANT JUNGLE swarming with insects. So thickly fertile were the towering trees and twisty bushes, I could not even pick out traces of bare earth. All around, shrieks and screeches of birds and animals alien to my experience had me shuddering. The sudden poke of a furry face from the shadowed undergrowth was alarming, but my curiosity triumphed.

After a while, I (well, really "we" as Spiritae—as always—was here with me too) could see shards of sunlight cut through the trees, and soon stood on the edge of a small man-made clearing.

Here was a gathering of compact huts constructed with huge leaves and sun-bleached grass. The air was tainted by odors of rot and sickness, and a deeper reek that could only emanate from dead things—and people. I trembled, fearful of what Spiritae might show me today.

Not many villagers could be seen. Those who dared the sun had the darkest skin I'd ever seen; not brown, but black as ebony. I saw only women, orbited by several children—no men or boys. A few other women shouldering crude animal-skin satchels broke through a tangle of vines and huffed into the village. These clearly were foragers, and the others swarmed them, desperate for a share (I now saw) of roots, berries, and grubs.

Despite being obviously stronger than the others, these women had the same desolate glaze in their eyes as everyone else, like the living dead.

The children were young enough to still have pleading in their dark eyes, which only emphasized the ravages of starvation. The bone-thin arms, swollen bellies, and strange lack of tears—they were beyond that. I couldn't look at them without wanting to weep. They took their scarce portions of food from the women, smearing the mashed contents into their mouths with skeletal fingers. Flies like buzzing emeralds swarmed them, alighting even on their eyes, encrusting any scratch or cut with insect hunger. Some bypassed human offerings, and settled into paltry rice bowls, where they too were eaten with no apparent concern or distaste.

"Spiritae, what has happened here? Everything is all wrong."

"These people are suffering a great pestilence. Many have died. Those who were able have fled the village, fearing that evil demons have possessed the dying."

"Is that true?"

"No, disease is not caused by demons, nor is it a punishment from their gods—but this is all they can comprehend. They cannot understand they have been infected by tiny forms of life, many times smaller than can be seen by human eyes. They are not aware of the small life, and the small life is not aware of them."

Ewww! I think Spiritae is telling me these people are being eaten from inside by tiny bugs!

"Is there nothing that can be done to *help* them?"

"A few are trying. Come with me."

We glided a great distance through the forest, and came to a disreputable-appearing town with decrepit buildings. One resembled the place where Becca works, but was not nearly so grand. Inside were beds filled with the sick, and a small team of healers attended to them.

Spiritae said, "Behold these healers, Portia, for they are taking grave personal risks to help these people. The slightest contact with fluids from the sick can bring death, so they must be very careful. What they are doing exalts them in the eyes of the Creator."

"There are so many sick, and so few healers."

Sad sigh. "Yes, that is true. This land is very far from the lands of plenty. In those places, there are many healers with medicine, knowledge, and facilities who could defeat this plague."

"So why don't those in the land of plenty send help?"

"A few do, for there are caring souls, but not nearly enough. Too many think of the suffering here as outside their responsibility—out-of-sight, out-of-mind. They are willing to let others undergo terrible deaths instead of sharing a tiny portion of what they have. A side-effect from greed for money, and discrimination. Remember the contest you went to see at the arena with Allen and Christy? If the people who attended that one event stayed home and sent their money here, and if those who paid to sell merchandise on far-sights to viewers at home, or the money paid to the participants had been sent here, the suffering could have *ended*."

Gravely, I agreed, "That's terrible. What do you mean by discrimination?"

"People here look different from those in the land of plenty, and the fair skinned and even brown skinned do not see these people as equals, worthy of their concern and empathy.

"Portia, suppose you are the Creator. You give people bodies to house their souls, and the wonderful ability to adapt over time to their surroundings and climate. You give some dark skin to prevent damage from the sun. Others requiring more sunlight to nurture their bodies get fair skin. Some adapt to be tall, some short. Some breathe better in high places, others in low. There are those who can run very fast, while others survive by their wits. Some thrive best in civilization; some in small tribes. Others must adapt to cold environments, or desert heat.

"What would you think of people who fail to recognize how marvelous this is? Or of those who say, 'We're superior because we are smarter, or faster,' or any of these reasons?"

"Seems pretty silly, when you think of it like that."

"Exactly. Not a very good way to find favor with the Creator. People find it easiest to be generous with those considered most like *them*, and their family and friends. Maybe they possess the same skin color, culture, or religious beliefs. Generosity is fine, but rather self-serving if they are too selective in who most benefits. This smells to me like promoting their kind over others. Blessed are those who see deeper—into the souls of others.

"The human body is merely a vessel to carry the Creator's gift throughout life, like a mask for the outside world. You may or may not be pleased with your mask. Others may declare you to be beautiful or ugly, admirable or repulsive. This is immaterial to the Creator and should be to you—all souls were created with beauty. Let's go next door."

In the adjacent building were many children running about. Healthier-seeming than the village children in the village, but not by much, these were orphans or children whose parents abandoned them in fear of the plague.

I watched one little girl, about four years old, with bright eyes and a quick smile, who was intensely in charge of her surroundings. Spiritae said, "This child is called 'Dear Heart' by the healers, because she will not reveal her real name. Her father ran away from their village last year, leaving his wife and four children to starve. This child is the only survivor of that family. She cared for her dying mother for the past two months, bringing food, water, laundering soiled clothes, and all else she was capable of handling...until the last, when she had to dig her mother's grave with her tiny hands.

"This amazingly resourceful girl said she returned her name to her mother so it would keep her company in heaven, and *she* can't use it anymore. It is a miracle she survived. Her uncle will not take her in. He fears she might have the disease, and stays drunk."

We watched as a man and woman visited the orphanage. Dear Heart bounded over, hugged the man's leg and raised her arms to be picked up. She beamed up at him. The man looked beseechingly at his wife, who averted her gaze. The hope on Dear Heart's face faded, but not entirely, as the couple moved on. Spiritae said, "The couple has already adopted six of these children, and came today to bring food and supplies. Don't despair, for Dear Heart is a survivor, and has already won the timeless love of the Creator."

Barren Land

I WAS WORRIED, BUT EXCITED, and found myself in a barren land rocky and mountainous, arid with scrub scattered in clumps across the sandy landscape. Bouncing along a rough road in a monstrous combat machina decorated with beige and dark green splotches, I sat among a group of soldiers. I think they were men, but frightening in their protective head-bubbles, rather resembling machinae—at least in part. Each carried a spit-death machina, and their head-bubbles (colored like the combat machina) were fitted with machina eyes that helped them see through the dust we were raising.

I was excited because I recognized Christy's brother Steven among the soldiers.

Surely, I had come to this faraway place to learn something, but I wasn't sure *what.* Steven must have been here for some dangerous purpose like the other men—well, I call them men, but they looked like boys only a few years older than I. Steven appeared haggard, pale and stressed, eyes furtively darting in constant vigilance—danger lurked around every corner. He nervously inhaled smoke from a thin white stick in his mouth tipped with a fiery glow. Why was he trying to eat fire? This could not be very good for him, because the smoke made him cough, but several of the other boys were doing this too.

Spiritae was very quiet, which always spooks me, as this is never a good sign.

We were rumbling into a small destitute village, wary faces peering from ragged hovels built of mud and sticks, wondering what we wanted.

I think the soldiers were trying to speak words of friendship. No one ventured outside until the soldiers offered a few gifts of food, and even then, an elderly woman was shoved out to judge whether our intent was evil. Apparently, if you need to appease demons, you sacrifice your old women. She wore rags and was unwashed. Never had I seen a person with so wrinkled a face, and when she dared a fearful smile we could see no teeth.

She warmed slowly to the men, but only after accepting more gifts of rice and water, deciding we had not come to steal their meager provisions. A small girl darted from the muddy hovel, and hid behind the woman's leg, peeking shyly at the men.

Steven, holding a little treat, slowly approached her. This might have been one of those sweet dark nuggets capable of winning over *anyone*. She thrust out a hand, snatched it, and glancing over her shoulder dashed back into the shelter. The only thing chasing her was Steven's broad smile, and she kept poking out her head to eyeball him. She retreated every time he waved at her.

The soldiers made hand motions, as though asking directions. The old woman repeatedly shook her head as if afraid to speak, like there might be other—perhaps more dreadful—demons loose in the land hunting for those with incautious tongues.

"Why have we come here?" I asked Spiritae. "What are they fighting about?"

Deep sigh.

"There has been fighting in this land for as long as I care to remember. It is tough to survive here. Warlords rule by coercion of others. This is a dog-eat-dog land where thievery, brutality, and bribery are a way of life. Many live by smuggling weapons and opium. Men oppress women in the name of their religion. Women are property, and are forbidden an education. Persons here have little, and hate those elsewhere who live in plenty. A clash of cultures.

"Some in Steven's world wish to change the culture here to be similar to theirs, hoping to end oppression and spread peace and harmony. But they have other motives, too such as ending the spillover into their land of terrorism and drugs. This is a domain holding untapped mineral wealth, resources that could erase the poverty if developed properly. Outsiders are all too eager to have control of these resources.

"People here are fiercely independent and intensely suspicious of foreign influences. Outside interests are viewed as corrupt with materialism and debauchery. Education leads to change. Change means loss of power to those now in control, and a way of life that offends people here."

"Who is right? Why would they be shocked by a better life?"

"Rightness or wrongness is in the eye of the beholder. There is some of each on both sides."

"Well, why is Steven here?"

"I don't think he ever imagined he would be. He joined the army because he wanted to serve his country and, after doing so, pursue more education at a cost he could afford. But he got more than he bargained for. His group is pursuing men who destroyed a school."

I sensed Spiritae was holding something back. "A school? They destroyed a building?"

"And slaughtered more than a hundred young girls and their teachers for daring to learn to read and write."

I thought I might be getting sick again.

The road ahead narrowed, and rose into a small valley. There sounded a volley of loud *pop-pop-pops*. Someone was firing their spit-death at our machina! Death-stones banged and pinged against the metal body, and my ears rang as other spit-deaths too assaulted us. Steven and the other soldiers burst into action, aimed their spit-deaths and fired. In seconds our sheltering machina became cacophonous with death and destruction.

Abruptly the boy beside Steven no longer had a face—only a bloody pulped mess, brain matter oozing where once were eyes.

I screamed in horror, "Spiritae, do something!" Nothing.

Steven pressed a bandage onto the boy's face, his own a rigid mask of shock. After a few moments it was obvious nothing could be done...and the boy died.

The leader of Steven's group spoke urgently into a far-talk. After what seemed an eternity, a giant black dragonfly machina streaked over valley, and unleashed an unholy campaign of death, spewing hornets from the huge spit-death in its mouth and loosing long streaks of screaming fire tubes that made volcanoes erupt all through the places the attackers had been hiding. They ceased at once, and I saw a few scattering away like fleas deserting a wet dog. The dragonfly lingered for a while, and disappeared over the horizon.

The mood in the combat machina was grim, the traumatized men shocked by the loss of their comrade. They decided to abandon their mission, and returned in the direction from whence they came. We careened back and forth over the uneven road for hours. The sun was low in a sick yellow sky. The leader jerked upright, having spotted an animal carcass in the road. He tried to shout an alarm, but he was too late—a trap! The combat machina erupted outward in all directions, bursting into fragments of shrapnel, consumed in a blistering fireball. I felt my essence, my consciousness, even with no body, caught up in a whirlwind, surging violently upward through the air.

When awareness returned, I found myself in Hades on Earth, utterly alone. I drifted about trying to understand what had happened. There was only death walking by me, and the carcass of the combat machina lay upside down in ruin. I saw the body of a boy charred beyond recognition, like a sculpture of a human made from charred wood, seated in death. He had not had time to move.

At the side of the road lay a hand, bereft of a body. This was not burned or damaged, not even bleeding, just lying there with fingers curved gently outward as though offering a gift. I could not bear the thought that it might have belonged to Steven....

I sensed Spiritae was with me again. I could not form any thoughts, any questions, nor scream or cry. I was completely and utterly insane. Spiritae could not speak either, and I could not have heard her if she had. I will never be the same.

After eons passed, Spiritae said quietly, "Come with me, Portia. Our job is not finished."

I wanted to disappear, float away into nothingness, but meek and numb I followed her through dark mist. We traveled seemingly forever, and my mind faded into sleep. I didn't want ever again to wake. But I did.

We were nearing a house, which I recognized all too well, following two very official-looking men in formal dress. Grimly they strode across the lawn and up steps to the door. The older man swallowed hard, and knocked gently.

Christy answered the door, expectation bright on her face. The instant she saw them she violently trembled, covering her mouth with a hand and backing away in disbelief. In that terrible moment she aged ten years. She managed a strangled cry, "Mom!" before her throat closed.

Becca quickly stepped up behind Christy. One glance and she knew, but uttered not a sound. She sank to the floor, eyes rolled back, and curled into a ball like an infant, shaking as if freezing. Allen joined them, face going wooden, eyes akin to those from the underworld, beyond the agony of torture.

The men tried assisting Allen in moving Becca onto reclining cushions. Christy hovered helplessly by her mother, shaking with wrenching sobs.

The men expressed their regrets, and offered sincere condolences, but there are no words that could ever bring the slightest relief. I could not cry before, but now could not stop. My heart was breaking—for them—for Steven—for me. Spreading my essence around them was all I could do, and they did not even know I was present. Spiritae held all of us in her spiritual arms. I never imagined that she too could cry so hard.

Later, alone with Spiritae, having left the family in privacy to deal with their grief, fury brewed inside me. Fury at the unseen attackers, with this terrible world, and yes, with Spiritae, who sensed I was about to boil over. "What are you feeling, Portia?"

"Feeling?! Anger! Hatred! Despair! I want to go *kill* the men who did this, but I don't know how. I want to be free of you, and this damned world once and for all!"

"You must forgive those men...."

"NO! Don't even *start* that ridiculous 'love everyone' stuff. *I* don't, and I never will! I hate them for what they did! I hate you for showing me! You *knew* it was coming, and you didn't stop it. I don't want to even think about you ever again! Go away, and leave me *alone*."

Deep sigh. "Hatred is a poison that lives in your heart, your mind, and it will consume you, not *them*, unless you can conquer it. Hate their *actions*, but forgive them. Love is the only force stronger than hatred, and forgiving those who have injured you, even grievously, is the only way you can heal your wounds. You don't have to forget, just forgive. Hate, and you are no better than they. Forgive, and your soul will live on."

"It is so hard Spiritae," I thought.

"I know. I never said the path would be easy."

"Why do bad things have to happen to such good people? They didn't do anything to bring this upon themselves. Couldn't you have done *something* anything?"

Very long pause.

"You might have noticed that I am here without a body—rather like you?"

"But, but...you're Spiritae. Maybe they could have been warned to avoid the danger?"

"Ah, yes, the eternal question—posed time and again throughout the ages. Few hear the answer. They want to believe in divine intervention in the physical world, supposing a superior being, in whatever form they imagine that entity or entities to be, to have scripted their lives, watching over their well-being night and day. If they are favored, prayers will be answered. When good things happen, the Creator has blessed them. When tragedies happen or prayers go unanswered, their God had some better purpose in mind that will play out over time.

"Suppose I ask you some questions. What would you say to a family if their neighbor's son is miraculously plucked from the jaws of death and their own son is not? Are they to understand that somehow they just weren't good enough? Do you think the Creator is so capricious as to favor the few and ignore the many?

"Perhaps the Creator puts people through difficulties as some test of allegiance or fortitude. Given the terrible things that happen, wouldn't you have to think the Creator is downright sadistic? Does it make sense that a loving being would visit torment upon creation like a roll of the dice?"

"I don't know, Spiritae. I don't know anything about these things."

"Let me suggest, then, something for you to ponder. A Creator's love means giving people freedom of thought and action, even if they choose unwisely. They were not created as dolls on strings, lives and world manipulated at the Creator's whims. Tragedies are not visited upon poor unfortunate souls, nor are blessings or miracles handed out like presents to a chosen few.

"Life happens. Life is a marvelous gift from the Creator, exactly like it was meant to be. The human experience is a miracle in itself—sometimes easy, sometimes hard, sometimes long, short, joyous, sorrowful, fair, and unfair."

"But Spiritae, are you saying that praying makes no difference?"

"No, that's not what I'm saying at all. Praying concerns the human spirit—heart, mind, and soul. Pray for motivation, inspiration, insight, confidence, comfort, strength of purpose, and conviction. Pray to be the hands that bring light into darkness. Your soul is what can receive divine guidance. When human souls strive for noble causes, they can accomplish miracles.

"We could not spare Steven's family pain. But our tears and prayers will bring his family a measure of comfort in time. Their anguish will never be erased entirely, but loving care from friends and strangers alike will flow to them in endless ways. When love heals, their memories will shift to celebrating his life and the joys he shared with them instead of the way his life ended."

"I hope so, Spiritae, I hope so very much! Spiritae...Spiritae? I didn't mean what I said earlier. I love you!" I hope she heard that, but I faded with no reply into darkness....

Marcus

MANY WEEKS HAVE PASSED since I had my last vision. Although I never tell mother or Papa about my visions, they can always tell because of how tired and withdrawn I am the following day. Papa is growing hopeful that my brain is finally healing. After what I've seen, I'm happy to be healing too.

Mother and Antonia went to the market, leaving me to some simple household chores. I heard someone coming to our apartment and was surprised to see it was Antonia's friend Marcus. He has been very good to her, and he often uses the excuse of bringing me more writing supplies for a chance to see her. For some reason, she has remained aloof and indifferent to his attentions.

Recently, Marcus has been coming around more and more. I really like talking with him, although I try not to intrude too much when he wants to spend time with Antonia. Nothing worse than being a third wheel. To be truthful, I could have a crush on Marcus if it wasn't for the fact he is meant for Antonia. I'm not the kind of girl who would try to steal her sister's boyfriend. I love her too much, and besides, I wouldn't stand a chance. She can already turn boys inside out with just a smoky glance.

Marcus is the kind of man I dream of, but I'll never be so lucky. He reminds me of a young version of Papa. When we converse, he really sees me, and isn't merely making small-talk, biding his time until he can score points with Antonia. He has an unruly mop of thick brown hair, and I love how a piece keeps falling down into his eyes whenever he tosses his head. He is lean and slightly above average in height, and appears more studious than athletic, although he carries himself with dignity. Marcus's eyes are large and blue, and I have to look away when he talks with me or I will blush. Can't have that now, can we?

I accepted his latest gift of papyri with sincere gratitude. He glowed with pride when I complimented him on the nice quality of the papyri. I explained that he had missed Antonia and Mother by minutes, but he didn't seem very disappointed. In fact, he said he would like some time to speak with me. Strictly speaking, I should not have been talking to him alone, but Mother and Papa know Marcus and his family well, so I doubt they would object. He sat down at a respectable distance and appeared nervous, searching for some opening topic. I laughed and blathered about something silly to put him at ease, which he appreciated, quickly responding with a broad smile.

I liked hearing his voice, deeper than his age would suggest, soft with quiet grace. He frowned, though, when I said that Antonia was lucky to have caught his interest. He said that while she is very attractive and wonderfully nice, they have both known for many months that they are not destined to be a couple. This surprised me, but they have agreed. Antonia had told me that he is remarkably bright, and much better educated that one might expect from his background. She told him he needs a woman with an intellect, someone whose interests and perceptions complement his own. His father feels the same as ours about getting ahead with education. Antonia says many of the things he wants to discuss, well, frankly bore her, or she doesn't understand. She told him there's someone right under his nose that is exactly like him—me! Besides, she has developed affection for another young man whose father is politically well connected, and whose family can offer her a life of comfort like Mother had hoped.

Marcus said he had been coming by for months to see *me*, not Antonia. Now it was my turn to be bashful. What in the world would this bright handsome young man find attractive in me—the girl with a twisted smile and more mental baggage than he could possibly imagine? He stopped me when I began to protest, said I am lovlier than I see myself, and he was staring intently into my eyes, peering into something deep. He said he knows when he is in the presence of a woman of grace, and asked if I could ever find favor with him. Marcus desired to make his intentions known to Papa, in hope that our parents would agree to our betrothal. I was stunned, trying to decide if his remarks were some cruel jest, and glanced behind to see if he was speaking to someone else.

He laughed softly, brushed my hair back from my face, and kissed my cheek. All at once, tears leaked from my eyes, but he knew from my glowing ace and happy little nods, that I was smitten. I had long abandoned any hope for a happy future.

Shyly, he reached inside his tunic and withdrew a small leather pouch. He gingerly extracted an exquisitely-fashioned circlet of the finest gold, which he caressed onto my hair. I sputtered a protest, "But...but, it's too precious." I knew too well how long he must have toiled to afford it.

"Nonsense. It merely shows the world what I see in your eyes."

He kissed me...oh, how he kissed me.

There sounded in the distance a high tinkling...sweet air on my face, stars twinkling with joy. Mother and Antonia came bouncing in, both wearing a knowing look when they saw. In the midst of all our hugs and tears, Antonia blurted that Papa knew too, and had agreed weeks ago.

What a sweet day!

Darkest Days

Mother and Antonia visited the Forum in search of sewing supplies. It was a rare day. Papa stayed home from work saying he wasn't feeling well. Usually, he goes to work anyway, so I knew he really must be feeling under the weather. Still, he insisted on poking around with work that he had to finish at home. He promised to take it easy, so I retired back to my room to do some more writing. There was a sudden crash, and I ran to see what had happened. Papa had collapsed to the floor, clutching his chest. His face was ashen, puckered lips blue and gasping for air. I screamed and ran to help him up, but he was far too heavy. I kept calling his name, crying and beseeching anyone nearby to help—but no one came. I brought water, which he could not swallow. I tried to give him my breath, and would have given it all. His frightened eyes gazed at the ceiling, and scared me as much as the struggle for breath. I knew what I needed, and cried out: "Spiritae! Help me, I beg you!"

And she was there, thoughts heavy with emotion, weeping. Not for Papa, but me. I felt her aura surround me, and she whispered, "Dear child, your father's time has come. I'm sorry. Hold him close, and I will say something to him through *you*."

I felt her gentle breath pass through my lips, and she began.

"Be at peace. Be not afraid. No evil can touch you. Calm the troubled waters of your soul. As you pass through the shade of death, I will be with you. I will carry you on a ribbon of stars to the perfect light, for you have walked the path of righteousness in my name. You will dwell forever with Spiritae, and you will prepare the path for this dear child. Today you will be in paradise.

"Portia. Tell him you bless him to go with me. He is afraid to leave you."

I kissed Papa's forehead. For a moment, his eyes cleared, and he looked at me, through me into my soul. He smiled...smiled, and then relaxed and was gone. I felt his spirit rise beside me into Spiritae's embrace.

I cradled his body for hours, rocked it in my arms. Mother came in and stood over us, not making the slightest sound. Her face said her life had ended too. She stepped out, and after a while, some men came and took Papa away. If I'd been capable, I would have fought them. Antonia and I clung to each other, sobbed and sobbed... Cato came home late that night, grim and stoic at the news. He could not give, nor receive, comfort.

I was numb and do not remember much from that time. People came from all around, and paid nice tributes to Papa, but the compliments flowed through me without registering. Soon they were laughing and visiting, and I could not stand to be among them. I could not remember names I ought to have known. They did not notice when I stole away to be alone. Later, I remember Mother in black, kneeling before her altar, praying to her gods. She was lost in grief too, but we could not find a common sorrow. Weeks passed before my next vision. I think Spiritae wondered if I blamed her for allowing Papa to die. I could not possibly, and thanked her for the loving care of Father. I will remember her words forever.

"What is it that you would ask me, dear one?"

I did not know how to ask exactly, but finally thought, "Spiritae, what comes after death?"

Very long pause. So long, I thought she would not answer. Finally, she did: "Many have asked. It is the question of the Ages. I will answer, but you cannot comprehend all I will say. You are like an ant walking on the edge of a blade. You can see the narrow path ahead, and remember what is behind, but cannot imagine the majesty of creation that surrounds you in every direction, every dimension. Yet that is where you will go.

"Every child, when it is conceived, is blessed with a gift, a divine spark of essence from the Creator. A precious present, nowhere yet everywhere, in the body. Like a living seed, nurtured and growing when watered with love. This grows in proportion to the love you give, and to the love others have for you. For innocents who have no one to love them, Spiritae still does, which keeps their seed from shriveling. Others waste their gift, and do not make a home in which the seed can take root or abide, and theirs blow away in the wind. In death, all living essence flows back to the Creator, separate and merged, these are not different. Some are giant trees, others remain seeds. The purpose of life is to see what you can grow. You have seen that the creation contains countless wonders and a chaos of wrongs, all here together. After death, your journey will continue with all who have gone before you, united, independent, wherever your spirit wishes to flow."

As I reflected upon this, I quietly offered: "Thank you, Spiritae. It meant the world to me what you said to Papa."

Travels

MY HEAD TONIGHT WAS GROWING HEAVY WITH PRESSURE. A vision brewed, but I hoped to resist. Of course, I failed miserably. Before the fog lifted, I beseeched Spiritae, "Please, no. Please. I am not strong enough for another vision. You have shown me too much pain and suffering. You will drive me over the brink. I cannot do it, please, I beg you."

"Portia, I know how hard it has been. Our journeys together are nearing an end. Come with me again. It will bring you healing and happiness."

Without saying a word, I acquiesced. After all, what choice did I really have?

"We will go many places tonight. You shall behold beauty in ways that few ever see."

The mist cleared, and I stood in a great forest dense with massive trees rising higher than I could see. Even the lowest branches were higher than any in my experience, as if I had shrunk to the size of a mouse. The trees were sentient beings; I sensed their presence, older than Rome, and could hear them (barely in range) murmuring to each other. Their shaggy reddish bark gave off a resinous piney aroma delightful to my nose. Did they communicate by way of fragrance? That could be true. This outdoor temple stood grander far than any constructed by human hands. High above, sunlight piercing the canopy in dazzling shafts...illumined exotic stones scattered along the forest floor. No sound broke that sacred silence, and any living creature must too have been engaged in hushed worship.

I stood on a vast plain. Thousands upon thousands of animals congregated, and some were familiar to me from the arena; others I did not know. Lions and tall giraffes. Boisterous flocks of tall pink-and -white birds swirled as one avian body. Herds of antelope bounded by in huffing leaps. But it was different here. Predator and prey alike settled in at sundown to watch the blazing show in the western sky, a nightly gift from the Creator. Magenta, peach, and fiery yellow-orange clouds streaked an aqua sky. Sunset ignited these yet more, mesmerizing all. Two antelope stood oblivious before me, as if awestruck over the luminous sky. I think they were praying. No painting, no sight-capture, could ever do this scene justice. The sky colors drew to a close, all the shades of the rainbow starting at the horizon, drawing a deep purple pall across the sky.

Before me gaped a tremendous rift in the Earth, a canyon immensely deep. Sparkling along its floor could be seen a living ribbon which, truly, had to be a wide surging river that probably eons ago carved this chasm. A patient, powerful erosion of layered rocks and stone and clay, exposing the secrets of history and presenting it on shelves.

Distant dark clouds rumbled...stuttered with zigzaggy lightning bolts. Perched at the edge, my head swam with dizziness–I stepped back from the mouth of an ancient abyss as old as time....

I glided along under the sea like a fish, breathing easily even without gills. Before me stretched a jagged reef, corals and sponges waving feathery branches. I had never imagined such surfeit of life. Brilliantly colored fishes, yellow and orange, blue, green, and gold, darted in coordinated groups. Some of the coral was bleached white, like bones of an ancient creature. Here, fish I see stiff and smelly in the market, thrived and cavorted, guided by little more than flickering fins and tails. A living cosmos, entwined in a symbiotic dance hidden from land-bound human eyes.

Following an earthen trail, I encountered a vision of what must have been a garden in paradise. Riots of flowers perfumed the air. Feathery tree-tops swayed from a gentle breeze exhaled by surrounding ocean. Along the island trail, every plant seemed eager to display its most colorful foliage, adorned with delicate blossoms offered as gifts to the Creator. The path climbed through huge groves of grasses and leafy poles clustered thickly, creating shadowed sanctuary where light was loath to enter. Gazing out over the trail-ringed valley, I could see two waterfalls misty from cascading waters thundering over black boulders. Beyond this twinkled hills veined with streams, translucent mist shot with rainbow prisms.

Before me lay a high mountain meadow, lush with tall spring grasses and festooned with brilliant wildflowers vying for morning sun. Above me towered a magnificent mountain, crowned with clouds, keeping sentinel over the spreading landscape and its charms. Yellow-black bees and shimmery green dragonflies flitted from flower to flower, busily serving them and drinking their nectar. In the distance stood two deer pawing the earth, shaking antlers and bellowing. The warm air drifted sweet and pure.

A swollen river surged rushing before me. Tumbled boulders—like a bridge—broke the stream, slicing it sparkling into hissing waterfalls. At least twenty fat brown bears had gathered for a feast, shaking their heads and flinging water like rain. Perched to claw and scoop large fish fighting up-river for lazy ponds of their birth (perchance to spawn) the bears loomed patient and assured. Hundreds of leaping fish made the effort less difficult. Many fell and had to try again until they were exhausted. The weighty fish hardly objected when clamped between the bears' crushing jaws, accepting fate with seeming stoicism.

A mother bear with dripping fur mewled as she instructed her cubs. They splashed wildly—batted at fish with comic failure. When their confidence flagged, she gently tore the reddish flesh of a fish, and laid tasty morsels before them. Soon they romped madly back and forth again. Bears ruled here, perfectly content in this pristine world, in sharp contrast to the pitiable one I remember from the arena.

I stood astride a mountain atop the world. The entire Earth lay spread before me, a mass of rocky upheavals, snow and ice. Great cracks crisscrossed the ice, opening to icy depths in lonely ice caves below in the underworld. The wind howled a wild call. No trees, no life in sight, this was a frozen world of glaciers and melting water that replenished the green Earth far below. The brightness of this alien world was blinding. A grumbling storm of snow rushed down a long slope, gathering speed as its smashed trees and icy scrub alike.

Spiritae led me to a vast green meadow that stretched toward blurred horizon. The featureless purple-gray sky served as a backdrop for the coming show. Rain obscured the distance with its dark hazy fall. "You're going to like this," Spiritae said. "Nature wants to put on a special show for us."

"Oh...Is nature alive? Why is she trying to please us?"

"Not the way you mean. Nature is life itself painted onto the canvas of the Earth. Watch what will happen now. Nature isn't trying to please us exactly, but I do have some influence in the matter...and I am very well pleased."

The sky behind us cleared, sun low, shedding its last red and orange rays before twilight. And altered into radiant pink, soon banded by a double rainbow of dazzling brilliance. Spiritae sighed, "Ahhh! That's nice! I just love rainbows."

I have seen a few rainbows in my life, and indeed love them too, but never have I seen such a spectacle...and stood speechless before the otherworldly beauty.

Spiritae sounded more proud than awed, like a parent praising her child. "Look, look Portia! See how the colors are reversed in the second bow. See how the sky is brighter inside the main one? Look closely at the edges of the main bow. See those thin bands? Each band is another thin rainbow"

Something profound blossomed inside me. Red, orange, yellow, green, blue, indigo, and violet. The colors pulsed my emotions, as though talking to me in a visual light-language.

"Do you see, Portia? Can you hear?"

I saw all right, but I didn't hear anything other than the distant raindrops spatting the ground.

"Those colors are the music of the cosmos. Every morning and every evening, messages are painted in the sky for all to see. In the dawn, the colors roll forth in perfect order to brighten their day and send a message of hope. You can understand a lot, if you can read the colors of the sky. In the evening, the sky echoes its performance, settling through the sunset, the gloaming of twilight, and setting the sky for the nightly show of stars. You can look back to the beginning of time, and ponder the magnificence of the universe." The meadow before us thundered with a herd of wild horses, an equine river of flowing manes, tails, and drumming hooves, led by a magnificent white stallion, nostrils flaring and sides heaving with the exhilaration. He guided his mares to the sweetest grass, and they turned to watch the show before them, staring mesmerized as they contentedly chewed.

Abruptly I thought: "Spiritae, they can read the colors of the sky, can't they?"

"Yes indeed. Most creatures see and hear better than mankind. They aren't so full of themselves."

So dark, I could barely make out the features of the landscape before me. The barren land was cratered, as if recently bombarded by boulder-hurling giants. So dry, too, and no breeze. A dusty arid place. Overhead the very heavens had opened up to me. The star-specked sky blazed its infinity of gems...the universe laid bare before my puny gaze. "What do you think?" asked Spiritae.

I didn't know how to reply. "It's—it's—beyond words! Where are we, anyway?"

"Wait a while, and see if you can guess."

It was not hard to wait. Being there made me shiver with wonder. Before long, light shimmered on the horizon. Brilliant and blue—oh, so blue. What I saw unfold was unimaginably beautiful. A blue sphere rose in the distance, a shiny orb swirled with white. Behind these, expansive patches of brown, tan, and green. The sphere's top was adorned by an island of white, colored like the larger one at its bottom. Had I eyes, they would have bulged.

"Spiritae! What great miracle is this? What has transformed the Moon into such a wondrous sight?"

She was clearly happy at my reaction to her surprise. "Not the Moon, girl, the Earth. Look where your feet should be if you prefer to stare at the Moon." I had to be completely insane. An upside-down world where the impossible is reality. I wanted to ask a million questions at once, but couldn't even start. I waited for her to make some wisecrack about me being a "lunatic," but she refrained.

She seemed very proud as she said, "See the white swirls? Those are great storm clouds sweeping across blue seas! Those vast patches of brown and green? Land and forests! See the wrinkled earth? Those are the mountains where you stood. And that tiny boot-shaped projection, right there? Rome is a speck in the middle near the sea. But, open your mind. What do you see?"

I took in this sight for long moments, grasping futilely for what she wished me to learn. Then I knew.

"Spiritae, the Earth is—well, alive. Maybe not like *I* know life, but alive in its way, delicate and precious. Immense up close, tinier than a sand-grain compared to the universe. Creation is beauty within beauty within beauty, layered like an onion."

"Not bad, not bad! The entire world you know lies on the thin surface of the Earth, like a living sheet of papyrus."

"Tell me some more secrets, Spiritae. I love them."

"I won't tell you anything people in this time don't already know. I guess I could tell you a few things, since no one will read about them back in your time. But you really mustn't go blabbing. It's okay to *write* about them, though."

No problem there. I learned long ago not to discuss my visions.

"The story of the birth of the Moon is wondrous. When the Earth was young, another smaller world crashed into it. That was almost the end for the Earth. But the collision tore off a lot of the outside, and it slowly collected here in space, settling in to revolve in a dance around the Earth. Without the Moon, life on Earth could never have happened. The two balance one another like dance partners, arms pulling and bracing. You see this as the sea tides, for Sun and the Moon cause their regular rise and fall, nurturing early life that started near the shores.

"The Moon pulls on the Earth?"

"Yes, and the Sun too." I really don't see how she can be right about this. I don't see any ropes. And how can anyone pull on water?

"But something else marvelous happened too. In the big collision, some of the metals from the center of the Earth were blasted into space. These rained back down onto the planet. If that hadn't happened, it would have been too tough for mankind to get

183

metals from so deep down. Without the great collision, there would be no metal in your time and none here in the world of visions either."

I don't really understand or believe anything she is saying, but her voice is so soothing, like she is reading a bedtime story, and I am getting so tired.

I stared in awe for a few minutes, fading away finally in exhaustion....

I awakened in the middle of the night in my bed. Antonia rustled gently nearby, turning in her sleep. I saw the pale Moon bathing us with its eerie light, wondered if Spiritae lingered there, peering down at me.

Discussions with Spiritae

T HE MORNING TROUBLED ME in deciding whether I had simply dreamed my adventuresome travels. The notion of standing on the Moon had really shaken my confidence. After all, what manner of a spirit could whisk me away to such a place? Wasn't that beyond the conjurings of any old possessing spirit? I've learned that I don't have to be in the middle of a vision to think with Spiritae. I have to concentrate harder, but if I turn my mind completely inward, I can usually find her. I decided it was time to learn if she would be more forthcoming with some of her answers to my questions.

I asked again, "Spiritae, who are you? *What* are you?" I was afraid she would bite my head off for asking this again, since I've asked before, but she seemed to understand why I was asking now. I sensed she was going to start the same old explanation, so I butted in, "I know, I know what you said, 'You are who you are. You are one; you are many. You are the beginning, the end, and so forth.' But who are you really?"

She seemed more amused than put off by my impertinence. "Who do you *say* I am?"

I had some ideas, but was timid about venturing a guess, so I decided to be ornery and buy some time. "I say you are an old rotten plant!"

Spiritae broke out in peals of laughter thoughts for long minutes. It sounded like all the mirth in heaven, or bells tinkling with joy, and stars shimmering with humor.

"Fantastic! I've been called many names, God to people in many forms, but this is the first time I've been called a rotten plant," and she laughed and laughed.

She had slipped. Now I was frightened. Spiritae claims she is a god, a goddess, maybe more than one god all rolled into one. I couldn't tell.

She thought again more seriously this time, "Who do *you* say I am?"

"Mother says you are a demon who has possessed my mind."

"Hmmm...Mother knows best, huh? Do I seem like a demon to you?"

"Well, not really. You have been kind to me, and although some of your lessons have been pretty tough to endure, you seem good, through and through. You could be tricking me though. Demons are like that."

"I suppose they might be if they existed. But come inside My mind, Portia, and tell me what you feel."

I felt myself merging into an ageless river of time, ebbing and flowing. What I said next felt like a revelation from the depths of the universe, not my thoughts, but some eternal truth.

"You are the living spirit that dwells within, worshiped by peoples since the beginning of time. You are the gods of ancient civilizations, all of them, you are the great "I Am", the One God of all religions, and are one with countless souls whose essences have returned to you. You are the Father, Mother, Son, and Daughter, all of these and yet more, of all creation."

I fell, face against the earth. "Forgive me Spiritae (all flustered), I mean Forgive me God!"

"Don't go getting all formal with Me. Haven't we become friends? You can still call Me Spiritae. It has grown on Me."

"How should I worship You, then?"

"Oh, please don't, I'm so tired of all that. I feel more like talking."

"Uh, it is a bit unnerving to be talking with the Creator."

"Why? You talk with anyone else you want to get to know. Why not Me? People have the strangest notions. Why does anyone think I would want a bunch of people falling down, waving their arms in the air, pushing faces into the ground like a bunch of dogs licking their master's boots, calling out one of My names, over and over, thanking Me for every little thing that has ever happened to them or begging Me to bestow one favor or another. Doesn't that seem a little silly to you? Like I created all this just to have people fawn all over Me, like I have time for that? I never asked for anything of the sort!" Whew! Spiritae sure can get testy!

"Well, why would You talk with *me* of all people? I'm just a girl."

"Why *not* you? You're as good as anyone else, aren't you?"

"I mean, You must have endless things to be doing instead of wasting time on me."

"For convenience, I will use 'I,' but you understand I could just as easily say 'We,' right? First of all, it's not wasting My time to nurture a soul. Besides, I'm rather talented at spreading Myself around wherever I am needed. But there is more. I think you are special. A seeker, one whose mind is full of questions, but might actually listen instead of jumping to conclusions. So go ahead. Ask Me the questions I hear rolling around in your head. But leave out the stupid ones, okay? I'm not going to tell you your future or how to get rich. Don't waste your chance. Give Me the tough ones."

"Um, um, so You created the universe. Who created *You*?"

"Not bad, not bad. That's the way to cut to the chase! Honestly? I don't know. Seems like I've been around forever, before the universe, before time began. I've wondered the same thing many times Myself and sure would like to know the answer. I can't remember being young and don't feel like I am aging. Maybe that's just the way it is when you are pure thought-energy without substance. Maybe existence for Me is an endless loop that will be repeated for eternity. Think of it this way. Take that pretty ribbon from your hair, twist it once, and join the ends. Now start making a mark with your stylus along the length. You will end up going forever, covering inside and outside.

"But it also occurred to Me that my beginning was so long ago I simply can't remember, much in the way people can't remember their birth. Some of us have the idea we started as beings having substance, but evolved over a long span of time into pure essence. Maybe My ancestors were created as beings just like you by an ancient essence and this will happen again and again. In fact, that is why I created the universe."

"What do you mean? *Why* did You create the universe? And how did You do that anyway?"

"*Now* you have the idea! I don't have a good way to explain exactly how I created the universe, the Earth, or the beginning of life. The answer would just blow your mind with its complexity. Others have asked, and in their confusion, most end up with notions like I whipped everything up in about a week just by pointing my finger and making the blast of all blasts. Sometimes the beginning involves tales of fanciful beings and creatures in some big drama. I shouldn't make fun of these ideas. They're just the best their minds can conceive. The truth is actually stranger than fiction. The best I can say is that everything is the same, no matter how different it appears to you. Light is the same as substance. Void is the same as the most concentrated substance. Infinitely large is the same as infinitely small. Time is timeless and reality is relative to the observer. Of the many dimensions, one can be the same as another. What you know as the universe is only one of many. Creation is the transformation of one reality into another using imagination, for nothing is lost and nothing is gained. I know that doesn't help much, but it's the truth."

"You're right, mind-boggling. Guess I'll just take Your word for it. But why did You create the universe in the first place?"

"Well, partly because that's just what I enjoy doing. But I'm on a quest to understand My own beginning, if there is such a thing. There are endless ways to create seed worlds where life can exist and beings of substance can evolve in complexity. My intention is to learn whether any can evolve to beings of pure thought."

"Umm. Are you saying You created people like 'practice?' What do you mean 'evolve'?"

"Hmm. Sounds rather frivolous when you put it that way, but true to some degree I suppose. I prefer to think of it as creating children who I love, watching them grow and becoming the best they can. People seem to want to think creation must achieve the end-result right from the beginning. I wish they could see creation as a living process, shifting and adapting through time. To Me, that's much more marvelous. That's what I mean by evolve. People and the Earth are a work-in-progress."

"Wait a minute. You said 'worlds.' Are there other places like Earth, and other beings of substance?"

"Oops, I mustn't give away too much, but try this. Look up into the night sky. Every star you see might have a world like this one. Not all do by any means, but some do. Trust Me; there are more stars in the sky than there are grains of sand on all the beaches in this world. What do you think the chances are that other worlds have creatures? I told you. I'm quite good at doing more than one thing at a time. But don't get all twisted up in that. Let's focus on *this* world. Those worlds and Earth aren't going to be regular tourist destinations. Beings of substance have a lot of hurdles to overcome before they can travel from one star to the next."

"So, if creation...what did you say, 'evolves,' people weren't around at the beginning?"

"Far from it. The Earth is far older than people from your time realize. It took ages to prepare a proper home. Yet, the Earth is only a child compared to the universe of stars you see swimming in the night sky. The Sun isn't even the first one made around here. The others were born and died long ago."

"Born and *died?*"

I thought I'd heard correctly, but you never know.

"Well, so to speak. Stars have beginnings and ends, only in much more interesting ways than you can imagine."

"How long have there been *people?*"

"To Me, it seems like only the blink of an eye. You might think of it this way. Imagine a butterfly landing on an old tree. In its short life, a butterfly can never know that the tree is alive, growing for centuries. The tree can scarcely notice the butterfly's presence before it is gone. Time is relative. The duration of lives is relative."

"Can butterflies and trees really know each other?"

"Not in the way you are aware. But even the lowliest creatures have more abilities than you might suppose."

"Why did You create people? Did You want them to rule the Earth? Why not lions or elephants, or maybe fish?"

"You make me laugh! When you might want to have a tree, do you grab a big one and plant it in the ground? No. You plant a tiny seed, then watch it grow, as did I. I created the tiniest seeds of life, ancient ancestors of all great creatures to come after eons and eons. They grew, they competed, and they changed. Only the strongest became what you know today. Who's to say what the future will hold? Some people think I have it all planned, controlling everything along the way. It's much more interesting to start something, and see how things turn out."

"How do You think people are doing?"

"Not so well, I'm afraid. I have mixed feelings. Some show surprising promise. Others have disturbing tendencies that could turn out to be fatal flaws."

"How so?"

"Some have a good ability to care about others, to live in peace and harmony, careful not to abuse the resources available to them, knowing this is the path to a brighter future for new generations. But I am concerned I didn't get the recipe quite right. Too many alive are self-absorbed, mean-spirited and warlike, predators at the expense of others, excessive in their abuses of the world. Hard to predict the outcome, but too many of the latter will doom the chances for the former.

"I've been a little surprised that humans have done as well as they have. Let's face it, they have *limitations*. They aren't strong, don't run all that fast, require garments to withstand even *cool* weather, their senses don't measure up to those of most creatures, they have a bad habit of wanting to kill each other, and are so self-indulgent they gravitate to bizarre behaviors. But there exists one saving grace. They have developed a brain with some limited ability to reason, conscious self-awareness and, most importantly, an *imagination*. I find this intriguing because of potential to evolve into a collective imagination for a brighter future. If humanity can use its collective willpower, humans *might* just pull it off. I decided humans were the first beings in this world that deserved a shot at eternity.

"Your soul is nurtured and grows inside you throughout life in proportion to how much you love others, and how much they love you. It is like a candle flame that grows to a hot fire when joined with others."

"But Spiritae, what about lonely people who have no one to love them, or babies who die even before they are born? Or good people who never even learn about You? Don't their souls get a chance?"

"Spiritae loves them—loves them so much that their souls are enriched."

"How about Goldie? Do pets have souls? She's such a good doggie, and Christy loves her so much!"

"All humans are given the gift of souls. Other creatures do not start with this. But when people love creatures and creatures love in return, they are transfused with some essence, not exactly a *soul*, but a spiritual force nevertheless. There is room enough in eternity for beloved animals."

"Why have you given people your gift? Do people have a purpose?"

"Umm. I really like your question, Portia. You see, most say I am perfect, all-powerful, all-knowing, that sort of thing. Maybe to them, I seem that way, but from My perspective, there's always room for improvement. The spark of essence placed inside each person is refined by their human experience. Substance refines their inner essence. Think of it this way. Your soul is mostly gold, and a little bit of dross. When you nurture it, the gold multiplies and the dross sheds away when you die and return to Me. If your soul is permitted to shrivel, only the dross is left, and I don't bother with it. Some people say I give humans trials and tribulations—the refiner's fire. This isn't quite accurate. I don't hand out difficulties as some test. The human experience is challenging, and refining in its own right. But don't you see? The refining is to Me, not to humans, for their golden gift was from Me, and returns to become Me...."

"So souls recycle, living human lives over and over again?"

"Not exactly, but consider the following. Suppose you shed a tear. It evaporates and rises to the sky to become part of a rain cloud. The cloud rains, and water flows to the river then on to the sea, forming more clouds and rain. Eventually, someone drinks some water from the river that contains the tiniest portion of water from your tear, only to cry their own and to repeat the cycle. I tell you truly, at this moment in your body, there are the tiniest portions of water that have dwelt for a while in the greatest people the world has ever known. So it is with your soul, for you are never completely separated from Me or all the souls who have lived before."

"So, people can remember when they trickle through life again?"

"Uh, not so much. Pretty diluted, you know. I'm guessing that's more like brain flatulence, but maybe once in a long while."

I'm writing down what Spiritae said, but I must admit, Her explanation is way over my head. Her next answer was even harder to comprehend.

"Spiritae, I don't know quite how to put this, but what is life like after death?...No, that's not right, what is *death* like after life?...Oh geez, I hope you know what I mean."

Spiritae laughed gently and said, "Yes, life...death, not so very different really. You have asked the one question mankind has wanted answered since the first spark of consciousness. I am always amazed how people portray eternity. They imagine eternal life to involve loitering in some blank space. Near My feet, singing songs of praise together with all their loved ones who passed before, simply basking blissfully in My presence. Don't you think that would get old pretty fast? Others say eternal life is completely unimaginable, like a caterpillar that cannot envision what life might be as a butterfly. Well, it *is* tough to comprehend, and I can't give away all My surprises. That wouldn't be any fun. But I will tell you this. Imagine being pure thought, able to converse mentally with Me and every soul that has lived and merged. Imagine gliding effortlessly to any world, or time of your choosing, among the myriad of stars, seeing the endless beauty of creation, in more dimensions and universes than you can appreciate now. Listen to the music of the stars playing in your soul, more inspiring than anything you have ever heard, and keep an eye on your loved ones still in this world who will join you when their time comes. Eternity would have to be much longer than time itself for you to become bored." She chuckled at Her minor pun.

"Why have You appeared to humans in so many forms, when You are really the same God? I think people get confused."

"Yeah, that probably was a mistake. They have such a hard time grasping who I am. You know, one and many, everywhere and nowhere, male and female, infinite and infinitesimal, and so forth. Doesn't make any sense to linear thinkers. So I tried to appear in forms that would be well received and understood by those in their particular circumstances.

"For example, in your time, people love stories about the gods of Olympus and make up tales about their lives, desires, and adventures. I have many personalities and the tales are quite entertaining, so why not give them what they *can* believe? Besides, role-playing is a blast. My message remains the same no matter how I appear, although My intentions are often misunderstood or twisted to someone else's purpose.

"I've tried about every approach I can think of to send My message. In dreams, spoken through prophets, from a fiery bush, chiseled into stone tablets, inspired the words of great speakers—too many *still* don't get it.

"I even tried the personal touch, thinking humans would listen if I appeared just like them. I said, 'Love one another. As I have loved you, so you must love one another.' Nothing more complicated than 'Live your life serving others instead of being focused on yourself.' For this simple message, people thought I wanted to seize their Earthly kingdoms. Me, the Creator of the universe! I wanted to nurture their souls. They beat Me nearly to death, and then nailed Me to a cross, leaving Me to die most cruelly. I reanimated just to give them something to think about!"

Whoa. What?

"Reanimated? You mean those stories about rising from the dead are *true?*"

"Well, call it what you will. It's not so hard if you know how. Lucky for them, I was in a forgiving mood. After all, they didn't really know what they were doing, even if they should have known better. But it wasn't so bad. Most of My human experience went according to plan. I had an awesome Earthly mother, and my adoptive father was reasonably understanding about My visit."

"So You are really Jesus too?! But...but...Spiritae, I thought You were a girl!" I was so embarrassed.

"Portia, I told you before. Gender is a part of the human experience, part of the substance of your body. It isn't particularly relevant when you leave the flesh. It's not like I'm looking to reproduce or anything."

"Can I still think of You as a girl, even if you say it doesn't make any difference? I find it easier to talk with girls, and I've been thinking of You that way for so long."

"Whatever floats your boat."

"Did You really do all those miracles Papa told me about?"

"Let's put it this way. If you know how to do something that others do not, it can appear miraculous. Suppose you know how to build a fire, and you wander into a group of people who do not. When you take pity on them because they are cold, and start a fire, they may start believing you are God and behave weirdly. Some of the people I encountered were in dire straits. I helped them because I loved them. I didn't set out to do God demonstrations.

"Sometimes I wonder if it was a good idea to send a message to people at all. I thought maybe I should get My message written down, and managed this in several forms, which has caused lots of misunderstandings—just the opposite of what I intended."

"Why don't people understand, Spiritae?"

"Mighty fine question. I can't figure it out either. Not that I'm going to give up trying. I've got plenty of time on My hands. Mankind does not.

"Let me give you an example how things usually turn out. Suppose I tell someone, 'You should drink two cups of water a day.' Now, I'm intending this as a suggestion to keep them healthy. Right away, people start asking, 'How big does the cup have to be? What must it be made of? Where does the water have to come from?' Then someone decides it is morally wrong to skip a day if something comes up. Another decides that if two cups are good, twenty are even better. Soon some are selling water, the only stuff acceptable to God. Before long, people are killing each other. One group that drinks with their right hand seeks to kill those who drink with their left. Whole nations go to war about the niceties of drinking water. You think My example is silly, but it is not.

"Many people in the time you visited say they believe in the One God—God of their fathers, each descended from common ancestors. But you can't believe how things go wrong from there. Some say God never came to Earth, that Jesus wasn't the type of person they expected to lead them—that the true leader is yet to come, one who will favor their small group above all others. They say God promised their ancestors. Rather self-serving, I would say.

"Others say their writings, written by imperfect men, are holy in themselves, like some divine law instead of listening to the essence of God living within. Those who do not adhere to those teachings are nonbelievers, and should be converted or eradicated from the Earth.

"Those who profess belief in Jesus are splintered into numerous groups arguing endlessly over little details of worship. Should you believe in God as One or Three? Should you follow the commandments of a man designated to be God's representative on Earth? Should you remember Jesus's last meal this way or that? Should you listen only to men about religion or can women teach too? If a group of people does not see God the same way you do, should you take up weapons and go beat their brains out until they see the light? Should you interpret your own book of scripture, following only the commandments that support your purposes? Should you ban people who see God in a different light from worship in your temple, prevent them from living among you, or even drinking your wine? If you do not like the way others live and worship, should you sneak among their innocent, blow them to bits, and spread your terror? If someone makes a derogatory comment about your religion, should you kill them for it? In your schools, public buildings, holidays, even your money, should you remove any references to me, fearing that one person or another might be offended?"

"Whose ways are best, Spiritae?"

She was working toward a fury.

"You're missing the point. I tell you, Portia, not *one* of these issues makes the tiniest difference to Me! More than a few people have been slaughtered over the centuries for these and lesser matters.

It's fine to have traditions and rituals and a system of beliefs, if they help you focus on leading an honorable life. But when anyone decides they know their Creator better than someone else, frankly, they are simply *wrong*. People lose sight of the goal when they get hung up on style.

"I'm sick of it! I hate to say it, but sometimes I think belief in Me has done more harm than good. The blood of millions killed in the name of religion has stained My hands as I carried their souls home—and I loved them all!"

"Why don't You just make people behave the way they should?"

"Believe Me, it is very tempting to do just *that*. But that's not "creating." That is ruling. Creating means giving humans freedom to make choices in the hope they will blossom and grow beyond what might be imagined. Can you believe it? Many devout believers think I got mad once and drowned just about everyone with as much water as I could pour down upon them. Me, the loving Creator! They buy into the notion that I am a mass murderer—and still they worship. They think I visit natural disasters upon them and thank Me when a few manage to survive. Why can't they wrap their minds around the idea they live in a beautiful but *dangerous* world. Sometimes they should simply take cover from a big storm. I tried sending them rainbows as beautiful signs of hope. But those crazies decided I had made a promise not to drown them again. Believe Me, if I was of a mind to wipe out the Earth, there are a lot faster ways. Frankly, if things continue the way they are headed, people will push their own reset button, not Me."

"What do you mean, Spiritae?"

"I mean, *I* won't have to bring destruction by fire or water; mankind seems intent on overpopulating the Earth, fouling its own nest in ways that will bring the horrors drought, famine, and disease down onto their heads. They will cry out to Me to save them, or worse, blame these troubles on Me, saying I was displeased somehow. I just hope mankind can learn to curb their thirst for rotten, oily plants. They are smart enough to find alternatives if they try and set aside the greed of those who would sell them the very last blood of the Earth." Oh, not the rotten plant thing again!

"Why are some people good, Spiritae, while others act so badly?"

"Humans are the only beings on Earth capable of evil, for they are called to a higher destiny. When they murder, maim, torture, cheat, steal, or countless other underhanded behaviors, they are violating the gift of their soul from the Creator. When they fail to meet their obligations, out of selfish, wanton, or sadistic pleasures, they are diminished beneath creatures, for they have made a conscious *choice* to be evil, and so shall they be judged."

"Mother says I'm possessed by a demon. Can demons make people do bad things?"

"The attitudes and actions of mankind are demonic enough; people are always trying to shift the blame onto some supernatural being instead of owning responsibility for their deficiencies. Forget notions about masterminds of evil controlling others. Evil is a construct of human minds."

"How should they behave, Spiritae? How do they know what to *do*?"

I heard her grind her spiritual teeth. She was getting grouchy again.

"Most already know deep inside their souls; many choose not to pay attention. If they are confused, all they have to do is ask Me and listen to the answer. They may not like it, but My message is easy enough to understand when you *want* to. People need to listen to the *intent*, not merely the words. They need to listen with their souls, not their ears.

"Soon I will ask you to spread My message."

"How will I do that, Spiritae? No one will listen to me."

"You will see, Portia. You will see soon enough."

Cancer the Crab

APPARENTLY SPIRITAE THINKS I NEED A FEW MORE LESSONS before I can be trusted to convey her message. I hope I can bear them. She darn near killed me with some of those past visions.

I was overjoyed to start my vision today back at Becca's workplace, the healing building. I've been so worried about Becca and Christy after Steven's death.

I watched as Becca approached the entrance, striding purposefully with grim determination. I couldn't help but notice that her usual bounce was missing, how her face was haunted and vacant. I turned with concern to Spiritae. "Is she okay?"

"So-so. She still cries a lot, but is healing with lots of love and support from Christy and Allen. Pouring herself into her work, harder than ever I'm afraid, but helping others seems to take her mind off her troubles and brings comfort."

Becca started her day making rounds to her many patients, before starting a full day of surgeries. As we tagged along, I noticed how terribly ill many of these appeared, thin and drawn, but eyes sparkled still with hope when Becca gave them a cheery greeting, her own grief hidden behind her mask.

"What's wrong with these people, Spiritae?" They looked like something was consuming them from the inside.

"That's not far from the truth, Portia. They have cancer, which you know even in your time. But people live longer now, and there are more and more affected by this terrible disease."

She was certainly right about that. We visited patient after patient, men, women, and children of all ages. I was especially troubled when we entered a ward full of hairless children. They peered at Becca, staring back with dark eyes that belied an understanding far beyond their years, pitiable with their gnome-like heads and gaunt bodies. Yet each had an eager smile, responding warmly to Becca's hugs and words of encouragement.

"Spiritae, how did these poor children get crabs inside them anyway? Can't Becca just cut them out?"

"Oh, what I would give if it were only that easy!"

Spiritae launched into lengthy explanation about what causes cancer. To be honest, I didn't understand very much at all. I think she meant that people don't get cancer crabs, not even little bugs that eat at their insides. She said everybody is made up of tiny fibers arranged in some terrifically complex code. All possess mistakes in their codes. Most of the time, these don't cause much trouble, but sometimes do, switching some places in the body into out-of-control growth. These diseased parts seem intent on controlling the healthy areas.

"Mistakes? How do people catch mistakes?"

"No, they don't catch them like a cold. They inherit the codes from their parents, sometimes strengthening their makeup, sometimes reinforcing weaknesses. But mistakes can also come from the harshness of living in a dangerous world. Some troubles are inherent to the environment and are man-made. Let's face it. Beings made of substance are rather fragile."

"How does Becca go about helping people with cancer?"

"She has a very tough job, because medicine in this time hasn't advanced far enough to cure everyone. But Becca and many physicians like her are making good progress." Here again, she lost me with details, said Becca can sometimes cut out the bad parts and sew them back up. Other times she has to put poisons in their blood and hope that the poison kills the bad parts faster than it kills the good. This is why people's hair falls out, though I don't know why hair would be one of the bad parts. She tried to tell me that the healers can also shine an invisible light at a person that goes inside and shrivels up the bad part. This sounds fantastic, but I think she's pulling my leg. Invisible? It can't be light, if you can't see it, right? Spiritae says sometimes they do all three treatments and still it might not work. The treatments can be really hard on a person, sometimes harder than the cancer itself, making them sick as a dog.

"There are some remarkable recoveries, and many people live longer lives with treatment, but I'm afraid far too many succumb in the end."

Here I sensed Spiritae's thoughts getting husky with emotion, and I thought maybe I even heard some sniffles.

"What's wrong, Spiritae?" No answer for long minutes.

Finally, she resignedly said, "These poor sufferers pray and pray to Me to save them or their loved ones. They think I am deaf to their pleas, or that somehow I have some grand scheme to torture them for their own good. Some despair and decide that I'm either dead or never existed in the first place. Others decide I'm not worth much if I can't deliver when it counts. The ones who *do* survive on the strength of their perseverance and good fortune often give Me all the credit, which makes Me feel guilty. Can you imagine? Like I would play favorites, raining salvation down on a handful, and ignore those in equal need? What kind of God do they think I am? I would help them all if I could.

"This is the part that makes me feel so rotten. If I had created people to live without aging, without disease, without any stress at all, they would not continue to evolve to achieve their destiny. Life must involve a struggle, whether I like it or not.

"I try to do what I can. Inspire physicians and nurses to do their best, I whisper to the souls of their friends and family to extend their loving kindnesses, reach out to strangers to send them random acts of encouragement, send them courage and inner grace, and write messages in the sky to brighten their day and let them know eternal paradise lies just beyond the horizon.

"I know it is not enough," Spiritae wept. "I really *do* love them all." I gave her the best mental hug I could muster.

We came to the bedside of a young boy, maybe seven or eight years old, who was lying listlessly staring at the ceiling. He murmured a polite reply when Becca greeted him, but sank back onto his pillow looking forlorn.

Becca said, "I think there's someone here you might like to meet!"

The door to the room swung upon, and the tallest man in the entire world ducked through the frame, "My man! How's my favorite fan?!" I've heard of giants in legends, but here was one right before my eyes. At least twice as tall as me, well, if I was in my body. The boy's eyes nearly bugged out, and the giant got down on his knees beside the bed. He was *still* taller than the boy all aglow, scrambling to his knees eager with excitement. The gentle giant produced a large ball from behind his back and spun it perfectly on a huge finger. He signed the ball, and handed it to the boy, who regarded it like a diamond from heaven. The boy laid his hand across the giant's palm to compare, and both laughed at the ungainly difference. The boy asked the giant endless details about the man's team, his teammates, and how they expected to fare in upcoming games.

Finally, the boy had exhausted himself. The giant knew it was time to leave. The boy struggled, and gave him a hug and kissed his cheek. I never before saw a giant cry.

The boy drifted quickly into sleep...a lingering smile showing what dreams may follow. "Now there's an athlete!" Spiritae said. "That man did more in one afternoon for the boy's soul than all the treatments in the world."

Forget Me Not

I WAS BONE-WEARY FROM MY VISIT to see the cancer patients, but Spiritae said that we might as well stop in at another place since we were so close.

At first, I thought this was another healing building, as it contained many beds with patients, but there were also rooms with people in wheeled chairs. I saw that some wheeled chairs, all by themselves, were able to move people who could not walk. Rather helpful, I'd say, of these machinae.

But the people here were all old. I mean really old. Spiritae snorted and asked how old I thought they might be. I guessed about two hundred, give or take a few years. She said I was off a bit. I probably was on the low side. In this time, she went on, many live longer, and eventually reside in places like this where nurses help them with eating, bathing, and well, you know, all the necessities. I was staggered by the sheer number of elderly people here and how few nurses were available to care for them. I asked Spiritae if this place was home to all the old people in the world. I could hear her shaking her head.

In Rome, when our parents or grandparents become infirm, like when they are fifty or sixty, they come to live with their children. They take care of us when we are young. We take care of them when they are old. Fair's fair, right? But it doesn't seem to work that way here.

I saw some of the oddest things. One woman yawned and her teeth slipped out onto a table! She merely laughed, picked them up, and pushed them back into her mouth. No one even blinked. I think their day must revolve around when they get to eat. Spiritae explained that it was about time for a dining hall to open. The old ones began to gather in their wheeled chair machinae, and when a woman opened the door, there was a mad rush inward. It reminded me of riding out on the roads in Becca's chariot machina, maybe even more dangerous.

Something else here was wrong. Many of the people couldn't seem to remember anything. Spiritae explained that this was a special home for people whose memories have died before their bodies. How is *that* possible? I thought your brain is part of your body, but Spiritae says that sadly, the end of life isn't neat and orderly. Sometimes a person's diseased body becomes a prison, trapping an active mind. Here, people's minds have died leaving their bodies behind to fend for themselves.

We watched one woman who was visited by her daughter and her family. They appeared to be having a nice chat, but suddenly the daughter burst out crying. I asked Spiritae what was wrong, and she explained that the mother had started calling her daughter by her dead sister's name. The mother's memory was adrift in the distant past. The family had brought a lumbering dog along that approached the old woman, and gently licked her hand. The dog then licked her face enthusiastically. The daughter moved to intervene, but her husband stayed her with a touch on the arm. The old mother was startled, but her eyes glowed with pleasure, an unconditional love passing between mother and the pet, an emotional connection she had not enjoyed in long, lonely months.

I asked Spiritae what she hoped I would learn from this visit.

She quietly said: "Don't forget the forlorn and abandoned, Portia, even when they forget you. You cannot tell how deeply your love reaches into them, and cannot know what this does for your soul. You are My hands in the world. Extend your kindness to the least of others, for you are doing it for Me and to Me."

Anything Goes

I LIKE TALKING WITH SPIRITAE, even when I don't understand everything She tells me. Just like Papa, like I really matter and She cares what I think. Amazing, really. I don't have to wait for a vision anymore. I can think to Her virtually any time, and She'll respond if of a mind. Something has been troubling me for a long time, so I decided to bring it up.

"Spiritae, those men who killed Steven..." I choked even thinking of that terrible day. Why—why do they hate so much? You said they were offended by life in Christy's world. Her life is so hard to imagine, but why do they hate it so much that they are willing to kill innocent people?"

"I'll try to give you an answer, but it is really hard to understand, even for me. Even as young children, those men were taught to hate the outside world. Their lives are full of hardship and misery, often short on the conveniences and even necessities of life. Their parents and their leaders look outward, yearning for a better life, but not knowing what to wish for. It becomes easy to resent people who appear to have so much more, especially when those people think they have a superior model for life. But when they look to that world, they do not admire what they see—with some justification.

"Consider what they have to judge by. Few ever make it to that world to see for themselves. They must rely on what they see and hear from what you charmingly call far-sights and news scrolls. You know how I told you to stay away from them and to be careful judging what you think is real? Well, they have the same difficulty you have, and lack someone to appraise what they see and read for manipulation and lies. Sometimes the 'truth' is not true at all.

"The problem is with the hazy nature of far-sights and news scrolls. The information you see or read is neither free nor unbiased. Perhaps useful to or of interest to the viewer, but you must remember they exist to make money for the owners. Unfortunately, a vast majority of humans have the impulsive urge to be shocked, outraged, or entertained in edgy ways. Far-sights and news scrolls are all too willing to oblige in order to sell their services.

"In the world you think of as beautiful, there are those eager to be on display expressing extreme opinions, behaving badly, with shocking appearance, crude language, and disgusting or provocative actions. Entertainment seen as edgy today is boring tomorrow. A slippery slope. People become insensitive to extreme violence and immodest behaviors. They watch others brutalized with no emotion, and their children play games where the value of life is not respected. The question becomes, 'Is such behavior the norm for this society, or the extreme?' It is hard enough for those here to sort the real from the imaginary. Think what it must be like for people in faraway places to see and judge *this* world through the twisted information they receive. Is it a wonder that some conclude the place is morally bankrupt, not only to outsiders, but people of Christy's world too?

"Her culture is founded on the sanctity of the rights of individuals. Many conveniently overlook that they have societal responsibilities too. It's me, me, me, 'in-your-face' and 'anything goes,' not you, me, we—let us live in harmony. The moment public criticism is raised about these messages, those who pander to human obsessions shriek their freedom of speech is being violated, that their 'creativity' is being stifled. What they really mean is they object to their source of income being curtailed. No matter to them that other parts of the world look on in horror.

"The answer is obvious. When people are willing to pay for far-sight views and news scrolls bearing uplifting messages and to steer clear of those that present the worst of human behavior, the world will change—here and far away. But I fear that is beyond the realm of human capabilities. I hope I am wrong."

News Scrolls

S PIRITAE HAS REFUSED TO HELP ME UNDERSTAND what is written in news scrolls, and this is driving me batty. I can't help it. Here I am, the daughter of a scribe, keenly interested in being a scribe myself, and seeing the most marvelous-looking writing and sight-captures I can imagine—unable to understand any of it.

Today, Spiritae seemed to be in a decent mood, so I thought I'd try again, maybe with a different approach. I decided to beg and plead. After all, this seems to work for many people. Sometimes you have to be creative when trying to manipulate God.

"Spiritae, I get curious when I see Allen or Becca starting their mornings. They like to sip those hot brown drinks and read their news scrolls."

"Uh-huh." She wasn't biting.

"You said those scrolls were made of recycled trees, didn't You?"

"Uh-huh."

"I really admire how neat the writing looks. You said it is all written by machinae, didn't You?"

"Well, it is really written by people, and they have a way to tell machinae how to make the letters much faster than they can write by hand."

"How do they know what to write? Do You whisper in their minds, You know, give them inspiration?" I knew this wasn't true, but it would get Her riled and talking.

"Of course not! How absurd. Most of what gets written in a news scroll is far less than 'inspired.' 'Warped' would be a better term."

"Well, how do they learn what is going on around the world so they can write it down? When we want to know anything, we have to go down to the Forum and listen to all the gossip."

"Humpf," she grunted. "Here, there are hoards running around trying to learn stories. They use far-talks, far-sights, and sight-captures. They can send their stories just about anywhere on Earth invisibly through the air to the places where the machinae write down thousands and thousands of copies overnight. After, mostly young boys or girls carry the scrolls very early in the morning to people's houses. All they have to do is open their doors and all the news of the world, such as it is, is lying at their feet. As if *that* isn't convenient enough, they can read the same news on their far-talks or glow screens."

I wasn't sure whether She was pulling my leg or not. Sounded most unlikely, but I decided to play along. "Why don't You want me to know what they say? Something bad written there?"

"There is quite a lot of bad stuff, to be sure, plenty of biased or outrageously stupid stories, but mostly I don't think you should know names, places, or dates. The idea is for you to see what is happening with your heart—not to go away and write down all sorts of details that make you look like some amazing prophet."

"But couldn't I learn just a few tiny things? Please? *Pretty Please?*"

"Portia, you wear me out! I'd start cussing if I was given to that sort of behavior!" I grinned because I knew She was about to cave in.

"Tell you what. Let's go look over Becca's shoulder this morning. You point to things you think look interesting, and I'll give you a sanitized version, what I think is okay to know. If I say to choose again, you'll have to take My word for it and move on. Deal?"

"Yes," I meekly agreed. Exactly what I had hoped for.

Sure enough, we found Becca yawning, warming her hands around a steaming mug of muddy-looking water. She had a news scroll spread on a table, and wore some wire frame over her ears designed to hold glass circles over her eyes to improve vision. The steam from the mug fogged these, and Becca repeatedly wiped them dry. She also munched a round piece of what looked like bread slathered with white sticky sauce and streaks of some reddish-brown spice. I licked it mentally, knowing Becca couldn't tell. Wow! The treats here are out of sight.

I pointed to the largest letters on the first page, exquisitely formed in a swirling curved style. If I could write like *that*, I would be famous in Rome. "What does that say?"

"Simply the news-scroll's name."

"Scrolls have names?"

"I mean it states this city's name, and another word to entice you into believing interesting news waits inside and on the front. Words like *herald, sun,* or beacon. They come up with a million of them. Don't even bother asking what city. I'm not going to tell you. There are hundreds that have one or more versions of news scrolls. They always put what someone thinks is the most interesting or important thing going on this first page. The idea is to grab your interest so that you'll want to buy the scroll and read the rest."

Spiritae showed me how scrolls usually have their messages grouped in sections. First comes news about events around the world, then news closer to the city. Sections about events and entertainment, information about merchants and market conditions, athletic contests, advice on how to do things or solve problems. Even games to make you think, little drawings to provoke laughter, and finally huge sections offering for sale practically anything under the sun.

I aimed my thought-finger toward the main sight-capture. "So what is the most important news in the world today, Spiritae?"

I thought She hesitated for a moment, and I started to give Her that skeptical look I knew would garner a "Move on, move on."

But She sighed instead. "Geez, you sure picked a sad one to start."

I peered at the large sight-capture centered on the page: a huge bird-machina. "Is it going to take people somewhere, like where I flew with Becca, Christy, and Tanika?"

"I'm afraid not. It was supposed to, but it went missing at sea."

"I didn't know bird machinae could swim, too."

"No, no. I mean it was flying over the sea, but crashed and sank to the bottom. Investigators of the accident have been looking for the wreckage quite a while, but they haven't found it yet."

"What went wrong? Did it get temperamental and decide to disobey? Or maybe got tired, and fell asleep?"

"Ha! Not exactly. It doesn't choose, you know. Some people think it might have flown into stormy weather, others that the man guiding the machina made a mistake. Some think part of the machina might have broken, and it couldn't fly anymore, Or that it didn't crash at all, but was pirated and flown to some hidden location. But I'm sorry to say, it went glub, glub, glub."

"Oh...they went down to the bottom? How deep is the ocean anyway?"

"It varies, but pretty deep. Let's put it this way. In many places, you could stack several thousand people on your shoulders and only the top person could breathe air."

Then came a terrible recollection from the far-sight. "And those huge mean fish with big teeth live there too! How many of those damn things are in there anyway? Maybe all the people are still hiding in the bird machinae, frightened to come out."

"I'm afraid not. When it smacked into the water going that fast, it tore itself into lots of pieces. Sadly, the people too. There are plenty of creatures in the sea, and lots of those fish that give you the willies. You must remember; they have their place too. They aren't really mean, only hungry, and they are the bosses of their realm."

"But how can You go carry the people's souls? Can You go so far down in the water? You can't leave them there. Certainly they weren't all dross?"

"No indeed, most were very special, and I always take care of business right away. They have already made the journey home. Souls don't tear apart like bodies, and the bodies don't matter all that much after death. Being made of mental energy has its advantages. I can go anywhere I want, even deep in the Earth if I am needed. This sight-capture shows some of their grieving families."

"They look more angry than sad."

"Both. They think authorities are not trying hard enough to find the bodies of their loved ones, and are protesting."

"Why do they want to find them? It would be very tough to see someone you care about all ripped up."

"It's difficult to look upon anyone in that condition...they need a sense of closure. And want to know exactly where the remains lie so they may grieve, maybe put out flower wreaths in loving memory. That's important, Portia. People live on, in a way, through the memories of loved ones and stories passed along to their children and children's children."

"Maybe those freaky monsters ate everything, the people and the bird machina, and that's why they can't find them."

"Sharks don't have much of a taste for metal, so the pieces are still there."

"Why don't You just tell the investigators where they are? That would save lots of time."

"I'm sure it would. But people always do better when they put a lot of effort into life-challenges. Makes them appreciate their accomplishments, and I can't hand out everything on a silver platter. They'll find what they're looking for eventually."

"So they'll find pieces of metal, but what about the people?"

"No. There are many creatures deep in the sea whose role is to clean up. Their job is nearly completed."

"You mean something *ate* them?"

"Sounds pretty rough when you say it that way. I prefer to think that Earth's creatures have helped with recycling. It would be a very gross world if all the dead bodies were still lying around. Let's move on to something else."

On the next page, I pointed at a sight-capture showing a man sitting on a plain bench behind bars. Caged like an animal, his appearance was rough and scary-looking, and he glowered from the sight-capture like he hated the world.

"He is a man in a prison, Portia. The news scroll is talking about what should be done with those who commit horrific crimes. People here are divided whether offenders deserve to be killed or should be locked up for the rest of their lives. What do you think?"

"Oh, that's terrible! What did this man do? What does horrific mean?"

"Not nice stuff at all. He was judged guilty of killing some people. Are you sure you want to hear the details?"

"I think I can handle it. How bad can it be?"

"He broke into a house looking to steal money so he could buy drugs. A man inside tried to stop him but this guy shot him between the eyes in front of his wife. He raped the woman, held her head underwater in a bathing tub while he did it, until she drowned. He found their young daughter hiding under her bed. She was badly beaten, but survived, although traumatized and with minor brain damage. He probably would have gotten away with it, but got drunk and bragged to his buddies. None of them came forward, but he was overheard by someone who turned him in."

I was aghast, and pretty sure I stopped breathing, or at least I would have if I had been breathing in the first place. "Surely this man is evil above all evil. He deserves to be tortured and die a most painful death! How could anyone do something so cruel? Did he really commit such acts?"

"The evidence seemed to verify this, and he's in prison for more than ten years under a death sentence. Some people believe no one should be killed no matter the crime, so his execution was long delayed."

"We have debates about execution in Rome, too. Citizens aren't supposed to be sentenced to death unless they have committed treason. But, we have judges who will declare almost anything *as* that. They don't mess around very long. Sometimes criminals are whipped to death, or strangled. If they're really angry at you, they throw you off the top of the prison, cut your head off, or bury you alive. I think the worst that can happen is crucifixion, where you are spiked to a wooden form outside, and left for the vultures to peck at you. I think this man should have all of that done at the same time."

"People in your time are rather rough on prisoners and slaves, Portia."

"It makes them think twice before getting into trouble."

"I wish that was so, but too many commit atrocities without thinking of the consequences. How do you know that everyone who is accused and tried *is* actually guilty? Maybe some just aren't liked by their accusers?"

"I know, I know. I'm sure that some innocents get killed. But I think the vast majority of criminals declared guilty actually are bad. You said this man 'was' in prison. What do you mean?"

"They finally got around to his execution. They injected some drugs into his blood. In the news scroll, they report that he coughed and struggled for a few minutes, and they are upset that this was overly cruel."

"What? After what he did, people think it was cruel to make him cough a while before he went to sleep? Sounds like he got off way too easy to me."

"Young ones, especially, think some of the ways people have been executed have been too harsh."

"Why? How do they kill prisoners in *this* time?"

"Mostly, torture isn't allowed no matter what they've done to someone else. The idea is to do away with them as humanely and quickly as possible, rising above the urge to sink to their level. There are several ways that have been used. One is to drop a person with a rope looped around his throat, which snaps the neck and leaves him dangling and choking to death. Another puts the blindfolded person in front of a group of executioners, who shoot him with spit-deaths. The idea is that the prisoner never sees what's coming, and none of the executioners has to feel guilty for killing someone since they don't know which one actually fired the fatal shot. But a method under criticism involves strapping the prisoner into a special chair, and killing him with lightning."

"Wow! That's a new one. We always talk about Jupiter zapping us with a lightning bolt if we're bad, but I've never seen it happen." Oops, I shouldn't have said that. She might have taken my interest seriously and forced me to watch.

"It is pretty gruesome. It usually doesn't take very long, but they keep the lightning turned on for a while just to be sure. Smoke exits from the criminal's orifices, and some of the flesh burns, producing a terrible stink. All the while, the lightning jolts the body into a death-dance."

"Dance? You mean like Christy was dancing at her party? Did someone put lightning into those girls?"

"You crazy girl! No, I mean the prisoner's body jerks around like he is having a seizure, which in fact he is—the worst one he'll ever face. But it's funny you say that because, in a way, people have a little lightning in them all the time. Not nearly so strong as that the sky, or even the lightning chair, but it's what makes it possible for people to move their muscles."

She went into a lot more detail, but I could only understand that She thinks we're full of living wires tickling us with lightning.

"Some even think it is cruel to keep people locked up. They say this man "found Christ" while he was in prison, and repented his sin. They think only God should decide the punishment."

"That sure puts a lot on You! How do *You* think this man should have been treated?"

"I don't think I'll tell you, Portia, but I will say this. When I came looking for his soul, I found it had withered completely away. He may have said he repented, but he could never have earned his way back into My good graces no matter what he said or did. You can't do terrible things, and near the end of your life suddenly declare you're one with God and expect to waltz into paradise. He was made entirely of dross, and I don't waste any time or compassion on anything but gold."

"If they lock up all the people who do crimes instead of killing them, they must have entire cities of prisoners."

"So they do—so they do."

"What's this sight-capture about? I probably shouldn't ask. This man looks like he is crying."

"Actually, it's an interesting issue to consider. This man is well-known, because seen frequently on far-sights. He is crying because his son was killed, but that is not what the story is about.

"Because he is so popular, some people follow him around constantly, hoping to make sight-captures of some aspect of his life. They can sell the sight-captures to publishers of news scrolls and earn money, and couldn't resist shoving their equipment into his face to show everyone he wept. One person even asked: "How does this make you feel?" He got angry, smashed the sight-capture equipment, and punched the man in the face. Now he is accused of assaulting the man and violating his rights."

"What? What did that person *think* he would feel? The man's son died. What about his right to some *privacy* for his grief."

"Reporters like this one think the man has given up all his rights to privacy by being popular on far-sights. They feel they have the legally-guaranteed right to show *anything* as freedom of speech."

"That is in such poor taste. He's lucky the man didn't pull out a sword and give him a whack."

"Unfortunately, taste has very little to do with what appears in news scrolls stories. Remember, 'anything goes' in this society."

"I think everyone is entitled to their privacy."

"Me too, Portia. Even *I* leave people alone until they invite Me to be with them."

"Isn't there anything nice in this news scroll?"

"Let's wait until Becca skips a few pages. These next ones report some robberies, and here's one about some people killed in a chariot-machina crash, and another about some parents who have abused their children. Here's one telling of a certain country angry at another, and thinking about starting a war. Maybe we should wait until Becca gets to the next section. Yes, that's better."

I spied a sight-capture of a giant white bear walking on ice, and decided to ask about the story below.

"Spiritae, I've never heard of a white bear before. Is it special?"

"Yes, certainly. White bears live at the top of the world where the ocean is covered year round with ice and snow. The bears there have adapted to the cold, and evolved to grow white fur as camouflage—lets them sneak up on the seals they hunt. This story warns that the bears are in trouble, because the world is getting warmer, and the ice is melting. This means they must forage for seals farther and farther away. The mother bears have trouble getting nice and fat to last through the bitter winters, and to feed their babies, so the population is diminishing."

"That's sad for the bears. Maybe not so sad for the seals. Why is the ice going away?"

"It isn't just the bears. All life is in delicate balance, a living environment where everything is interconnected. Humans have trouble seeing those links. A problem for the bears can be a problem for birds, seals, and fish—and ultimately for mankind. People ignore problems that happen far from their homes, but they should open their eyes and see what they are doing to themselves.

"It all goes back to what I told you about the world being fouled by their pollution, spilling invisible fumes into the sky that trap more of the sun's heat. What they do far away is keenly felt everywhere, especially at the top of the world where the ice is shrinking."

"That's a pretty depressing story too, Spiritae. What about this sight-capture of these pretty flowers? I suppose they're about to wink out of existence also?"

"No, not everything is gloom and doom. Ha-ha! Maybe bloom! This story details the best times to start flowers in gardens, and advises how deep to plant seeds and bulbs, and what fertilizer will produce larger flowers. I like this section in the new scroll, because it teaches people how to be good stewards of the Earth, planting trees and vegetables, all sorts of useful details."

"How about this story?" I indicated a sight-capture of a studious woman holding a musical instrument, the same curvy brown box with strings that I heard played at Christy's temple.

"Yes, a nice story. This woman will be playing a concert nearby in a few days. She is extremely talented, and believes in sharing her skills with young music students. The performance will be free. She hopes people will come and listen to her student ensemble and make contributions to help offset some of their costs."

"I'd love to attend, but I'm guessing the few Roman coins I have —could I figure a way to bring them here—wouldn't spend very well."

"You're right about that. Your coins would raise a few eyebrows, but they might be more valuable than you think."

I watched Becca whip through the athletic-events section— apparently not her thing. But she stopped, glanced at one story and shook her head.

"What is she bothered by, Spiritae?" The story had a sight-capture of a tall smiling man holding a spherical ball.

"The story says this man has recently signed some documents making him extremely wealthy. His sport involves throwing that ball through a metal hoop. He's among the very best athletes who have ever played that game."

"You can earn a living playing games? By throwing a ball through a hoop?"

"Oh, yes. People here are quite taken by athletic contests, evident in the thickness of that section of the news scroll. They spend a lot of money on clothing to look like their heroes, and more to go observe the contests. Watching them on far-sights is a big moneymaker for people wanting to sell you things by displaying their products."

"I see. This is something like Cato's obsession with the gladiator fights in the arena."

"Yeah, only a modern version gone crazy over the Moon." I could tell She wasn't very impressed.

"But you can't get all that wealthy in contests, can you?"

"Oh, but you are wrong. The wealthiest athletes make more money than kings. Unfortunately, some of them get swelled heads. Small wonder, since they are treated like demigods by their fans. The man in this story is far wealthier than your emperor. He has made more money than Becca will ever earn just by letting the makers of clothing sew his name onto their products. You can't believe how people go for this stuff. All they have to do is show his sight-capture while they're selling something, and his fans can't live without it. I'm sorry to tell you, but a few times, a child has killed another to steal a pair of fancy sandals that he promotes."

"That's insane! Kill somebody for his sandals?" She must have been mistaken. No one would ever do that, I'm sure.

"So here's the problem. This man is one in millions in terms of his skills and the fortune he has made. There are thousands upon thousands of children who dream of being just like him. But only a precious few achieve stardom. The rest don't dream of the many other ways they might lead useful lives making a real difference. They waste their chances at education, dreaming of being a star. When they fall short, as most must do, they are disillusioned, ignorant, and destined for a hard life. All too many find their way to drugs and crime.

"Becca is shaking her head because she knows some of the athletes, even the average ones, will make more in one year than she will ever earn. I ask you, how fair is it that a person who can do something fancy with a ball can be showered with adulation while a healer who saves thousands of lives toils away in relative anonymity? I know, I know. The healer most likely doesn't want adulation; the athlete does. My vote of confidence goes to the person who makes a real difference in the lives of others. I'm not saying this is a bad man at all, but he's only playing a game. I'll tell you this. People may cheer loudly when they watch contests, but their very souls cheer when Becca gives people back their lives. People's values here are upside down!" Well, no one can say Spiritae doesn't have opinions.

Becca lingered over a sight-capture of a woman who Spiritae said gives advice about social issues. "Here is a letter from a woman who lives with a mean drunk of a man who beats her when he's under the influence. He is the stepfather of her teenage daughters, and she worries that he will turn his lustful eyes on them. But she still loves him. What should she do?" She didn't wait for my reply but growled under her breath, "I need to find someone to inspire her... find someone better.

"Here's another letter from a woman who wants to know if it would be bad manners to ask guests coming to her party to store their far-talks in a basket when they arrive. She wants them to visit instead of spending all their time obsessed with receiving messages from friends not even at the party."

"That doesn't sound rude to me. The rude ones are the guests."

"I agree. She could store all the far-talks in the toilet machina for all I care. This world is supposed to be about people, not machinae."

Becca turned to several sight-captures of people's faces. Most of them appeared old, but some were young. Spiritae said, "Becca always checks the lists of the people who died recently. She cares about her patients, even those who might have died long after her treatments. She has a good heart."

"All of these people died yesterday?"

"Certainly very recently, but remember, this is a good-sized city, so this is about average."

"You must be really busy hauling souls off!"

"Well, I stay busy, that's for sure." Spiritae said the long thin columns of words below each picture talked about the person's accomplishments, and named their surviving loved ones.

Becca turned to some pages displaying word games and puzzles, and regarded them with longing. No time to spare today. I would have liked to attempt solving them, but Spiritae said, "Sorry, you'd have to know their language to even have a chance."

Becca finished with a quick scan of two pages colorful with images of crazy-looking drawings headed with writing that looked like they were talking to each other. There were dogs, cats, a shark, and silly-looking people. Spiritae said each one was a little piece of humor, some insight into human nature, or events to evoke laughter. This must be true, because I saw Becca chuckle under her breath at several of them. It's good to start your day off with some humor, I think. I could have used some after my first read of a news scroll.

Becca took the last section from the middle of the news scroll and set it aside for later reading. Spiritae said this part advertised all sorts of things for sale, offering bargains or discounts, and that people don't have time to bargain much anymore, so cut out little pieces of promises from the merchants who will give discounts without haggling. That sure would save time at the Forum.

Becca tossed the already read portion of the news scroll into a bag, which I thought she intended to put in with all the other things going to the trash. I had visions of those bad news scrolls headed to the mountain of debris where I had seen the children scrounging for their lives. I sure hope those kids can't read. Their lives are depressing enough. Spiritae said no, that Becca was good about recycling. All I could understand was that some machina would chew up the news scroll into a pulpy mess, digest it all with its powerful stomach juices to remove the writing. Other machinae would form it back into scrolls and even more machinae would write new stories on it. Unbelievable! But I see what Spiritae means. I don't intend to spend any more time trying to understand news scrolls. Your soul will starve if it must digest bad news day after day.

The Five Brothers

S PIRITAE WOKE ME IN THE MIDDLE OF THE NIGHT and asked, "Can I tell you a story?" I was groggy, but thought this was funny. Like I was going to say "No thanks!" to a request from the Creator? Besides, it's not like I can walk away. She's inside my head. So I agreed, hoping that I wouldn't droop over and fall flat on my face. She seemed happy that I picked up my stylus to write down whatever She might say. In truth, if I merely listened, I would have been back in dreamland after about one sentence.

Spiritae began as though She was lost in her own thoughts. "There was once a father and a mother." Well, that didn't sound like an auspicious start to me. "Quiet!"

Oops, I forgot She can hear my thoughts.

"There once was a father and a mother, who were talking about their children. Curiously enough, the father was invisible, a being of pure thought, although their children were of flesh and blood." Okay, that was a more interesting twist to the plot.

The mother said, "You seem down tonight. What's on your mind, Father?"

"Oh, it's just our boys again. I hate it when they fight all the time. We've tried so hard to raise them properly, to teach them to be good and kind. Just when I think we might have succeeded, one of them falls back into bad ways. Where do you think we went wrong?"

"I don't think we went wrong at all. I know you love each of them. They love you too."

"But they are so different. Do you think we'll ever be one big happy family?"

"I know what you mean. It doesn't seem like they'll ever get along very well. But we raised them to be individuals with wills of their own."

"We certainly succeeded at that—all too well, I'm afraid. I had such great hopes. I remember when they were young. It makes me smile when I recall how you thought so deeply to give them such meaningful names we hoped they would be proud to live up to.

"Amin 'the faithful,' then Avner 'my father is light,' Angyo 'the peacemaker,' Andrew 'the disciple,' and finally Aijaz 'the blessing.' They're bright boys, but as they grew older, they developed such strange notions. I guess what troubles me the most is that none of them listens to me much anymore. They say they do, but they're so busy squabbling they don't pay attention to what I really want. Being pure thought sure has its drawbacks."

"How so, I thought *all* our boys want to please you?"

"Well, that's what they claim, and they each get one part right or another. But none of them know me very well. At least you'd never know it based on the beliefs they profess.

"Amin has a notion of me as a unifying force in the cosmos that can never be fully understood by humanity. But he doesn't really recognize me as an individual, a caring father. I'm just some indifferent force permeating the universe. He thinks his essence will migrate in its entirety from one human to another, until he is liberated from the cycle of birth and death. In some circumstances, he might not come back as a human at all, maybe a cow for example. Candidly, his beliefs are not easy to understand, and seem rather disorganized.

"Avner is quite different. He believes actions are much more important than beliefs. He thinks I know all the thoughts and deeds of people, and I will reward the good and punish the wicked. When he was young, he disobeyed quite often, and I think he feels very guilty. He sees me as extremely strict, and believes I go around

225

whacking entire communities when I'm displeased. He is quite focused on what he thinks are my rules and commandments and loves tradition and ritual. He believes I have made promises only to him, that he and his offspring have my blessing and destiny that makes him superior to others who do not follow his ways. This, of course, is not well received by his brothers. He says Jesus was a great teacher, but not the expected savior that he thinks will come to lead everyone like him. He's waiting for me to show up looking and acting much more magnificent.

"Angyo is more like his oldest brother, in that he believes whatever he does in life will affect his next one. He wants to educate himself, and meditate a lot to escape endless cycles of rebirth. He is deeply committed to learning from great writings and teachers and deep concentrated thinking. I like his notions that our bodies are precious, that he must take responsibility for his own improvement, and think about what he believes. But he has too sour an outlook, for my taste, on life. He thinks there is no particular purpose to life, that mostly it involves suffering. The goal is to take steps to end cycles of painful lives rather than think much about what I am really like. He can't decide whether he has one father or many. He thinks that question is unanswerable....

"Andrew has many strong beliefs just like his brothers. He sees me as his one and only Father, but often thinks of me in three manifestations. Andrew really appreciates good mysticism and miracles. He says I came to Earth, made flesh as my own Son, Jesus, born of an Earthly mother, a virgin. He thinks of me sometimes as Father, sometimes as Son, and sometimes as Holy Spirit who is involved with people's daily lives, all three yet one. People must be born anew, says Andrew, baptized in His name and can only come to the Father by believing in Jesus. Anyone else will burn for eternity in the fires of Hell. He expects Jesus to reappear someday, causing all the dead to rise, and He will reign over the all the Earth.

"In some ways our last son, Aijaz, has been our biggest challenge. As the youngest, he is headstrong and eager to outdo his brothers. He and Andrew are like oil and water. They fight like cats and dogs. He doesn't get along well with Avner either. I probably made a mistake when I made Avner, Andrew, and Aijaz share a room. What can I say? We were short on space. Each boy wanted the room to himself, and to this day can't seem to share anything. It baffles me that the boys can't get along. They share some common beliefs, but their differences are greatly magnified by their mutual intolerance. Aijaz thinks of me as his one and only true Father. He puts quite a load on my shoulders, and insists I know everything, what has happened and what *will* happen, and I have recorded all this. Nothing ever occurs unless I will it. Avner, Andrew, and Aijaz all think supernatural angels come to them from time to time imparting my messages. Hey, I'd try anything to get them to listen! I wish they'd heed what already is inside them.

"None of our boys miss a chance to aggravate the others, and Aijaz is especially bitter about Andrew supporting Avner whenever the issues about the room erupt. Unfortunately, their squabbles have often boiled over into violence and each holds deep-seated grudges they refuse to abandon. They are downright mean to each other. If I turn my back for an instant, they're angling to kill their brothers.

"Our sons put a lot of importance on writings about their beliefs. I shouldn't say "a lot" when I really mean "all important." Whenever they argue, each swears by the writings they believe are my commandments to them. To be sure, there are many great things to be learned from each boy's books, but none will acknowledge their beloved works contain some contradictions, or translation might alter the original meanings. Their book is the absolute word of the Father, and that is that.

"Andrew doesn't help matters by disrespecting the Prophet whom Aijaz admires. Even worse, he tells Aijaz that his holy writings are false, which Aijaz takes as the ultimate insult. Aijaz in turn likes to goad Andrew, saying Jesus was a respectable messenger, but not God at all. He goes further to drive Andrew up a wall by insisting the only he, Aijaz, uses the proper name for God. Andrew can be very punitive, and Aijaz responds with belligerence and acts of violence to demonstrate his rebellious nature. Aijaz professes tolerance for the beliefs of others, but in practice, talks about stepping on the necks on nonbelievers, and glowers threateningly at Andrew and Avner.

"Mother, it cuts me to the quick to say this, but I don't think any of our sons have the proper respect for you or any other woman, the way they should. They act kindly sometimes to get favors, but deep down they see men as superior, smug in their self-righteousness. I hate to say this, but sometimes I wish we hadn't had any sons at all. Maybe having daughters would have been better."

"Daughters fight too. They can be bitchy and petty."

"I know siblings bicker, but girls seem better at holding back from all-out warfare."

Mother cried softly, lay her head on Father's shoulder. "What are you going to do?"

"I think I'll go pray about it."

I sat there for long moments, waiting for Spiritae to make another comment. She sat quietly and expectantly for my reaction, and finally said, "So?"

"So what? That's it? I have to tell you, Spiritae, I don't understand what You are trying to say in this story." This actually appeared to make Her happy.

"I think those sons are brats. My mother is not into spanking, but Papa would probably cut a stout switch and tan their hides. He's done that several times to Cato, for all the good it did."

"Hmm. Interesting approach. I should probably try it. The story isn't for you, Portia. It's for the people in the visions. They will know exactly what it means. Not one of them will like it a bit, for they will see themselves portrayed in a critical light. They will hate the story, for it is not something they can stand to hear about themselves."

"Why write it if no one will like it? I don't mean to be rude, but it doesn't have much of a plot. Which son is right?" I thought I knew Her preference, so I ventured, "Andrew?" After all, she talked like she had been Jesus, if She wasn't telling me a whopper. Of course, that could easily be the case, as Spiritae always has the upper hand in our discussions.

"I wrote it because people should listen even if they won't. None of the sons have it entirely right or entirely wrong. Sometimes one or the other has it mostly right and slightly wrong; other times, they are far off the mark."

"Their beliefs are hard for me to grasp."

"Yeah, for Me too. People will believe nearly anything if it serves their purposes. The point of the story is the minute anyone says they know the Creator's will better than someone else, you can bet they're mistaken. No one is absolutely right. I'm almost perfect (here She smiled), but even I make a mistake now and then, or so it seems to Me. People who say they know best, even with good intentions, have their self-interests in mind and are trying to put a yoke on your beliefs. And while we're at it, if anyone starts claiming they have been granted some divine right to be a ruler, you can bet they are way too full of themselves. I'm not about to waste my time picking rulers. All too often, they disappoint Me anyway.

"People's faiths and beliefs should come from Me, nurtured, but not created, by others. Honor great writings, but look deeper with your soul to know the Creator. Follow whatever traditions and rituals are meaningful when you are seeking. These are not so important as opening your heart, mind, and soul to Me. I like personal relationships like we have, Portia. I'm not into building special ones with hoards of people all with a particular way of worshiping Me.

"It's nice to be feel acknowledged, honored and respected, but candidly, I'd give that up if people would just do what I've asked."

"What's that, Spiritae?"

"Soon. You'll see My message very soon."

"What happened to the sons, anyway?"

"Not much of anything. They continued to battle until the end of time. No happy ending. Sorry!"

"Hmm. Well, I'm afraid that story isn't going to win any awards. Maybe You should stick to Your God stuff and let me be the writer."

"Ha-ha! I think I'll just do that."

"Hey, wait a minute! What do You mean? The Father, obviously You, went away to pray? Who do *You* pray to?"

"I put that last bit in to make you laugh."

Sometimes Spiritae's sense of humor is a bit warped.

Time to Say Goodbye

"**P**ORTIA, WE NEED TO TALK. You must go soon, and lead a new life with Marcus. You will be a superb wife and mother, and the two of you have My every wish for a good life. Our journeys together must end, for you have fulfilled a most important service to Me and to mankind. You prayed and we have done it together.

"You have written words of great importance from Me and from you. Now I must advise how to prepare those messages for a long journey."

"Where are they going? I won't get anyone into trouble, will I?"

"It's not 'where,' it's 'when.' Your writings must trek through time to the world of visions, and you must take steps to make sure they arrive safely. Trouble is in the eye of the beholder, but no, you will not harm those you love."

I was given a long list of instructions about how to pack the pages into my box, cover it wholly with wax to protect against moisture, and seal it under the floor beneath my bed, so cleverly hidden even I couldn't tell anything was there.

"Is that good enough, Spiritae, for a time journey to the world of visions?" I was sad to see my writings packed away. They are part of me, and I sensed I would never see them again.

"I think so, but rest assured. I'm not about to let them get away."

"But you mustn't leave me now. I love our journeys together, even the ones that made me cry. You have taught me so much."

"I am not leaving you. You know how to be with Me anytime you choose. But you have seen what you were destined to see and record for others. We will have yet another journey together, years from now. You can count on it. But I must attend to other things now, and you must return to a normal life, without Me crowding your mind with visions. Hold Me close inside, and cherish our memories."

"I am sad, Spiritae. I love You!"

"Don't be sad. For we are joys to each other. I love you, too. We will have all eternity together."

First Translation Epilogue

THERE YOU HAVE IT. Portia's so-called "revelation." Outrageous to even contemplate that the papyri could be authentic, right? No way. I only wish I possessed the slightest notion how they were faked. With much professional embarrassment, I admit I don't have a clue.

Faked documents are almost always easy to unmask when you apply modern forensic techniques. The papyri have passed every test, conventional or cutting-edge, in my possession. Radiocarbon dating of many samples by various laboratories indicates the papyrus and ink are from 150-200 CE. The writing materials and lettering are characteristic of the period. Detailed examination with state-of-the-art electron microscopy and analytical techniques indicates that the surface oxidation and paper fiber saturation with ink have not been accelerated with artificial heat or chemical treatments.

I have published my detailed investigations and test results. Moreover, I have sent samples to leading laboratories and other universities around the world for independent analyses, but none have proposed plausible or even implausible explanations for any method of forgery that would disprove the papyri's authenticity. We have archived them carefully in argon-filled vaults to prevent further degradation, together with a large collection of photographic documentation, and these remain available for study by any researcher with valid professional credentials.

Am I completely sure the papyri are a hoax? I don't believe they are authentic for a minute—they simply *can't* be. I haven't found any records of a scribe named Lucinius, or any other writings by anyone named Portia. Of course, that is not too surprising, as there are few records from this time. The Capitoline Papyri, if real, would be among the oldest surviving Latin manuscripts, and are a large collection of writings compared with the small fragments extant from this period. It would have been highly unusual for a young Roman woman of a working class to be literate, let alone to have exquisite lettering skills. Papyrus was expensive and not used frivolously. But the key problem is that "Portia's" purported visions are simply too mind-boggling to lend any credence to the papyri.

Therefore, if I can't yet determine *how* they were faked, let's consider *who* might have faked them, when, and why. Start with me. After all, I'm the one most people suspect. I've had the most time alone with the documents and made my own photographic records.

The most popular theory goes something like this. During my early days digging at the Capitoline Hill apartments, I did my excavating, and when the floor was exposed created a chamber beneath in which I placed the box containing the papyri. Later, I called my fellow students and professor over to witness *my* big find. They suspect I faked the box and its contents at my leisure before the dig, somehow sneaking it into the country and past my colleagues at an opportune moment. Somehow, as a student, I had figured out a way to make the documents look ancient in a way that would fool scientists and their instruments not invented yet for many years. Why would I do this? To impress my mentor and to gain recognition over the other students, of course. When I didn't get the coveted attention, I squirreled away the evidence until a few years later, when I resurrected the hoax in a new scheme to gain notoriety, making controversial publications and a public splash to advance my career.

Really? No one seems to think about the hurdles I would have faced to do this. First, I would have to invent a way to fool radiocarbon dating of papyrus sheets. Not that radiocarbon dating is completely precise, but you simply don't take something and change ratios of isotopes by a couple of thousand years. Oh, maybe I found a stash of very old papyrus that I could use. That would have been newsworthy, even with*out* any inscriptions. Papyrus rots, people! Imagine trying to write on something like two- thousand-year-old toilet paper. It's about *that* delicate. I would need to be very clever, making old ink, getting it to infuse the papyrus fibers and oxidize the whole work in the same way paper yellows over time, but in this case, for hundreds and hundreds of years. Next, I would have to pack everything in a wooden crate, smear it shut with ancient beeswax, and age it by another mysterious technique that would make it appear as old as the hills. Of course, getting it into Italy and past officials was a snap, right? I suppose the rest of our archeology team went to sleep while I alone managed to drag this cumbersome foot-locker into place without being seen. Nice trick! Of course, I did all this to impress my professor? Hmm...tell me of any student who would spend so much time and effort to impress a teacher. That isn't reality.

My harshest critics claim I am a pathological liar. I wasn't pulling a stunt, but was driven by some compulsive need for attention caused by the mother who abandoned me and the father I never knew. Who would have guessed that I needed psychoanalysis? I thought I had a happy childhood growing up with a doting grandmother.

Oh, let's not forget the money motive. Supposedly, if I get everyone stirred up enough, someone will buy the movie rights and I'll make millions. That makes me laugh when I'm done being outraged. I like the notion of earning my living honestly, not selling a crazy story to some wacky director in Hollywood. Besides, what sort of movie or book could there be anyway? No nudity, no gratuitous violence, no action scenes with special-effects, not even a very coherent plot- line. A flop at the box office. People simply don't flock to the movies for moral insights.

One last thing to consider. Suppose I really had a way to make undetectable fakes of ancient things, and I craved fame and fortune. Why would I fake ramblings from a Roman teenager? Wouldn't I have picked something a little more interesting? How about original wisdom from Solomon, in his own handwriting? Maybe Mary kept a diary while she tended her baby? An ancient-looking cup for drinking wine found in just the right place, or a chest containing a couple of stone tablets. Now *those* would be tickets to stardom!

Then there are those who claim I have a deep-seated need to spread my religious beliefs, pouring out my moralizing and pretending it to be written by someone with higher authority. While I agree with many of the points made in the papyri, I certainly don't with the entirety. I don't happen to care much what other people think of my beliefs, and don't care much about theirs. My grandmother wasn't exactly religious. She had strong opinions about right and wrong, and raised me with an eye toward good moral behavior, but organized religion wasn't something she encouraged or discouraged for me. As a result, I think each person should decide their own matters of faith. It is not in my makeup to convert anyone to my way of looking at faith issues.

When I make these points to critics, I usually get the response, "Methinks thou dost protest too much." But I notice they never offer any counter-argument.

Okay, suppose you accept that I'm not the author. Who are the other candidates? Nammie? Maybe Professor Matson, or Professore Giberti? Bucelli? How about some of my colleagues or fellow students? I just don't see the motive, and most don't even have half the horsepower to pull it off.

I ruled out Nammie early on. She would have dearly loved to pull such a prank on me, but lacked interest or capacity for the computer technology required. I wondered whether she had been a closet technophile, hiding skills from me, or whether she had a helper at the nursing home. But the effort was far too elaborate for the laughs they would have received, and she didn't have the means in any case to get the fakes to Italy. I am convinced she would have confessed her forgery to me at the last. We had enough time together to say our goodbyes, and Nammie would have taken the opportunity to laugh all the way to eternity. Before I had translated even a dozen papyri, I began to wonder who was behind the hoax and why.

My first suspects were Matson and Giberti working in collusion, funded by a third party with deep pockets who wanted to create tremendous interest but leave behind a mystery. Of course, now Professor Matson is lost in dementia and Professor Giberti is deceased, so who's left to confess the puzzle? I started my investigation by looking into the circumstances of Giberti's death. I thought if I could uncover any foul play, this might lead to evidence of a conspiracy and cover-up. But the details appear straight-forward, if tragic. Giberti was killed in a traffic accident, running a stop light at a busy intersection, and getting T-boned by an elderly woman who was also killed. This doesn't smell like an assassination to me. Giberti and Matson certainly had a collaborative working relationship. Giberti had university resources, plenty of time in Italy to work up documents, and Matson masterminded the operations at our field site, which could have been manipulated prior to our arrival. But something doesn't seem right to me. Neither Matson nor Giberti *needed* to further pad their careers. Each was held in high international regard, and would scarcely sacrifice their reputation by engaging in a hoax even if either knew how. Might they have done it for money? Neither was wealthy, but neither was struggling. Both felt grunt-work should be reserved for their grad student slaves. The heavy-duty counterfeiting would have been done by others, yet I cannot find any evidence. I have spent long hours sifting through Matson's and Giberti's personal files and records. Each was meticulous about recording his research and daily activities. Nothing in their notes makes the slightest allusion to efforts remotely relevant to creating the papyri. If they did receive money, it did not appear to change their lives, as both men appeared to live modestly. I've talked with a number of their closest student assistants. None spilled any beans, and all thought the notion of these two engaging in a nefarious plot to be most unlikely, and outrageously funny.

Obviously, Professore Bucelli, right? Hmm. Trouble is, he was nowhere around as far as I know when we did the excavations in Rome. I never knew of him when I worked as Giberti's assistant in Padua making all my photographs. Bucelli is actually two years younger than I, so I have a hard time coming up with a theory of how he might have been involved with planting the forgery at the Capitoline Hill in the first place. Like Matson and Giberti, Bucelli would be foolish to attempt a hoax at this point in his career. He has a great position at the university, with plenty of funding and an established reputation he would not wish to place in jeopardy. So who *else* could have been watching me? I might as well suspect the proverbial fly on the wall. I worked many long days and nights in that old basement without seeing another human being, so I can't think of any other close suspects.

I wondered what shadowy figure or organization might have something to gain by funding an elaborate forgery, even considered whether the Italian government might have hatched such a scheme. I speculated if the papyri were publicly displayed amid great controversy and heavily promoted, it might bring a surge of tourism. This remains a possibility, I suppose, but hardly seems necessary. Even when Italy's economy struggles, Italy remains a top tourist destination and probably would have difficulties coping with a large influx of new visitors.

A recent discovery troubles me deeply about the papyri. Last year, some excavations near a palace, said to be where Emperor Commodus reigned, uncovered an image carved into a stone wall. It depicts a man with a laurel wreath standing atop a tall tower thrusting a spear into what appears to be a bear. As far as I can determine, this image is unique. Although Commodus's obsession with the arena is well known, no records mention his killing a bear as do the papyri. How could anyone know of this incident before this image was discovered?

Open Appeal

If you have any knowledge about how the Capitoline Papyri were, or might have been, created and placed for discovery, I implore you to come forward.

This matter is extremely important. If we cannot trust our forensic testing of manuscripts, our dating methods to ensure their authenticity, a great deal of mankind's history and records fall under suspicion, which would be a real tragedy.

If the idea is to make me look silly, fine. Teach me your methods. We'll all go have a big laugh. I'll buy the beer, and toss in a public acknowledgement that I am the biggest dupe of all time and toast your accomplishment.

Second Translation Addendum

I HAVE MADE A GRIEVOUS ERROR, several of them in fact, and at least one is sure to get me killed. My first mistake was finding the Capitoline Papyri in the first place. I wish I had never opened that Pandora's Box, for the lid could not be closed before it changed my world forever. I compounded my error by publishing my first translation, never expecting the furor it would arouse.

My greatest error was my failure to recognize what lay before me. I thought I did, but I was wrong—dead wrong. I made the mistake of showing to strangers what I thought I understood...people who turned out to be willing to commit any crime and spare no expense to gain control of the papyri technology. I have no choice now. I must reveal what I've learned since my first publication. It is my only chance for salvation, perhaps yours too, for only by letting the entire world know of the existence of Spiritae's Message can I prevent it from falling into the hands of people who would corrupt its power.

When I published my first translation, I thought I had included everything that had been written. How wrong I was! After Portia concluded her final chapter, I found a sheet with the outline of a small right hand, which I presumed was either hers or the person perpetrating the hoax. I thought it might be something like a signature page or a placeholder at the end of the document. Several dozen blank pages followed, and I guessed that these were simply a stash of extra writing sheets that had not been needed. I tried, of course, to make sure they were blank. I couldn't discern any writing visually, and my thermal-imaging camera made the outline of the hand glow for a few seconds like the rest of the writing, but the remainder of the pages gave no response whatsoever.

One afternoon, I sat alone in my basement lab, once again pondering how the document could have been faked. Then I discovered something incredibly strange. I felt an unwavering compulsion to take my hand and cover the outline on the papyri sheet. The hairs on the back of my neck were tingling, and I had the distinct impression I was being called to some important task. Even stranger, I felt I was being watched, although glancing around the room, clearly was alone.

It's hard to describe the sensation when my hand drew close. Not an electric shock exactly, but a gentle warmth and then thousands of pinpricks connecting to my fingers and palm. I snatched back my hand in alarm, but felt no pain, just a sensation of connections breaking, millions of silken threads that had woven into my skin tearing gently. When I replaced my hand, the connection process restarted. My thoughts dropped away, except for a deep timeless idea growing in the center of my mind. This continued for several minutes before fading. It was not a passing thought, but one that seared into my brain. I had no trouble remembering it word for word, and rushed to write in my research journal. I repeated my experiment in darkness, approaching the hand outline, and the same thoughts came flooding back even stronger. Very weird.

My mind reeled with the possibilities. Maybe the hand-print had triggered some form of extra-sensory perception, some inner clairvoyance of what I would see next? Maybe I had a long forgotten vivid memory triggered by the image of a hand-print, like a post-hypnotic suggestion? I decided to place the hand-print papyrus between two protective sheets of glass. No sense having the fragile piece fall into bits before I could examine it further. I wondered if I would experience the same sensations. Maybe the glass covering would dull them. Not one bit! Each time I placed my hand against the glass over the hand-print, the thoughts reoccurred with an inner voice.

The phone jangled, and I reluctantly picked up. Professore Bucelli explained, "Sorry for the last-minute notice, Max, but I've got a group of important guests here in my office, and they'd like to take a quick tour of the labs. Mind if we stop by in a couple of minutes?" This wasn't a request. He was always on a mission to impress high-rollers, hoping for big donations he could use for new equipment or scholarships. With a sigh, I acquiesced.

I scrambled to tidy the place a bit, but hardly had a chance before twelve or so people crowded into my small lab. Bucelli proudly pointed out the thermal-imaging apparatus, and pressed me into a quick demonstration. In my haste I had not put away the hand outline. Surely it was innocuous enough. I made the outline of the hand glow a couple of times, and most of the visitors looked bored, anxious to move on to the more modern laboratories in the floors above. One man, in his 50s, stepped forward and mumbled a few thickly-accented words I took for Russian. He gestured toward the outline of the hand, and I let him spread his over the protective glass plate. Just as I had done, he flinched, and withdrew his hand quickly. He hovered over it again for a few moments, amazement in his eyes. He turned, looking directly at me, and said in perfect English, "What in the hell sort of capitalist trickery are you trying to play on me?" Then I realized. His lips had not moved, and his mouth was closed. The voice was my own echoing in my mind. He moved backward with a look of combined fear and shock, as well as an aura of malice. Another man, wearing a yarmulke, seemed interested in the first man's reaction, and he stepped forward, eager to try the same experience. His eyes grew wide, then narrowed. He dropped to his knees staring in awe at the outline of the hand and stretched his arms toward the ceiling. I didn't quite catch everything he said, but it sounded like:

"Blessed be the Name of His glorious kingdom for ever and ever. And you shall love the Lord your God with all your heart and with all your soul and with all your might. And these words that I command you today shall be in your heart. And you shall teach them diligently to your children, and you shall speak of them when you sit at home, and when you walk along the way, and when you lie down and when you rise up. And you shall bind them as a sign on your hand..."

Again, I heard his words in my voice and my language inside my mind. The man stood, and Bucelli ushered everyone quickly from the room and toward the elevator. Both men glanced repeatedly at me, faces pale and haunted. The remainder of visitors had not paid much attention, distracted by technical illustrations displayed on the walls. Bucelli hissed as he passed me on the way out, "What in the hell were you *thinking*, Garrett? What just happened here anyway? What did you do that made our Israeli friend start praying in Hebrew?" He rushed out growling that he would take this up again with me later.

Hebrew? Surely he had heard the man as clearly as I. Now it was my turn to be shocked. I was still getting my head around the notion that a message might be encoded into the hand outline by some technology I had never heard of. Now I was faced with a dilemma—it might be much more. Perhaps a universal language translator that interfaces directly to the brains of both the speaker and the intended listener—communication without the need for speech?

Completely baffled, I decided to go outside and get a breath of fresh air before going any further. Maybe I was simply hallucinating from the stress of overwork, or affected by noxious fumes accumulating in the basement. I clipped together the glass panes, trapping the hand-print inside, and slid it inside a manila envelope. The air outside was cool and fresh, and I sat on my favorite bench gazing up in wonder as the twilight melded into night's inky black. I sat quietly for a couple of hours, until refreshed and invigorated, enjoying a moonless sky away from the university street lights.

I pulled the glass sandwich with the precious hand-print from the envelope, revealing it to the universe beyond. I gaped, because the hand-print began to pulse rapidly and rhythmically, as if receiving a message over an incredibly fast data network. The hand outline was glowing intensely with the most beautiful shade of iridescent green. Emerald? Teal? Turquoise? No, maybe all these and more. You cannot imagine, because this shade of green does not exist on Earth. Seeing it literally turned me inside out. A living light, pure mental energy from the heavens. Not only was the hand-print pulsing in patterns, the colors were modulating into intricate swirls of shifting hues that had to be important.

I stretched my hand forward again, wondering if the intense light would consume it, but the outline began to glow with soft green phosphorescence, and the details of the palm patterns and fingers began to show clearly. Ultra-thin verdant threads of energy sprouted through the glass, emerging from the surface under fierce points of white light, and connecting with matching points on my hand. I could not help but note the similarity between the multitude of stars twinkling in the cosmos and these miniscule fireflies. I watched them, mesmerized, as they threaded an ancient dance into the skin of my palm. I had the distinct impression that the hand-print was not only alive, but sentient, and weaving a cocoon of a communication network into my nervous system.

As I write this, I am at a loss for words. What happened next was nothing short of a miracle. I received a new message, one that lasted long moments. I will not reveal it here, for it was intensely personal and private. Moving my hand was like turning the mental pages in a book. There are empty mental pages at the end, which I sense will contain a message for me when the time is ripe. All I can say is the hand-print is more than a profound message, and more than a universal translator. It is a mental interface, a means for connecting mankind to forces in the universe beyond our comprehension—in real-time.

Another astounding truth hit me. The remaining sheets of papyri, supposedly blank, must also contain a message. Shaking with excitement, I rushed to bring them out under the stars and to translate the remaining pages. I must tell you, revealing the text on those pages caused the most profound shock of my life. The Latin text of "Spiritae's Message" matched the English text I had recorded in my journal concept for concept! What a message it was, and is, too! But I'll let Portia tell you in her own words.

The University

Note: This section, and those titled "Spiritae's Message" and "Finem," are from pages I previously supposed blank. How wrong I was!
- Max Garrett

"READY TO GO?" At least Spiritae bothered to ask me if I was ready to head out for another vision. I doubt that I had much choice, so I indicated I was, although my wariness must have been evident in my thoughts. Too often, She has started me off in a vision where everything seems fine and then there is something terrible I have to learn. But tonight She was cheery, so I doubted it would be bad as when She is morose right from the start.

We emerged from the fog into a fascinating group of buildings clustered tightly along a curving river. Many young men and women scurried by obviously intent on making important appointments. I asked Spiritae to explain what we were seeing. Maybe She was simply in a good mood, for She usually bites my head off if I start asking about names or dates. This time, She was reasonably forthcoming, explained this was something called a university, an academy for very advanced students. I was excited to see at least as many women as men. She said in this time, it is one of the oldest schools in the world, yet it will not be built for nearly a thousand years past my time. Also, it wasn't so very far from

Rome, and I could probably get there in a chariot machina in about five hours, a simple afternoon journey. I asked what the students study. She laughed, and said it would be easier to tell me what they *don't* study, as they have endless choices. I wondered what She wanted me to see. I hoped they still spoke Latin. Maybe I could sit in on a class or two. No such luck.

Spiritae indicated I should explore the nearest building. "Be sure to look around in the lowest level, you might see something interesting."

I passed through levels with shining machinae arranged on black tables. Everything looked clean and perfectly organized. Descending stairs led me into a dingy, dark hallway in the oldest part of the building. Everything was dusty and the place appeared abandoned. Some movement ahead had me wondering whether She had sent me down here to learn profundities about spiders and rats. The last door on the right stood slightly open, so I glided in, ready to bolt if something nasty lurked inside. A man sat at a table peering into a machina. He appeared very tired and disheveled, gazing forlorn at the work before him. Something familiar here.... Imagine my surprise when I saw the box in which I keep my writings resting beside his table.

I barely recognized it, as the box was terribly old and dirty. A few of my precious papyri were spread across the table, where he examined them with a look-machina. Oh how my heart leaped and ached at the sight of them. They appeared so old and fragile. But he was so careful, handling them like the most valuable things he had ever seen. My ink had faded so much I could barely make out the words. Clearly he was having a hard time too. I wondered if he had understood my code. I grew discouraged watching him, because he didn't seem very interested. My message was too hidden for him to understand.

Finally, he did something very interesting. He pressed the front of the look-machina poised over one sheet, and on a glowing light-board, my lettering stood out boldly in bright white letters from the old gray papyri. Again, he pressed the front of the machina, and this time the image of the glowing message remained visible. He was making sight-captures of all my papyri with the messages visible. This nearly made me mad with joy, even if he hadn't figured out the messages yet.

I hovered over his shoulder, and tried my best to mentally will him into examining the code markings, shouting thoughts into his ear, but to no avail. I nearly passed out with excitement when he came to the sheet with Spiritae's message. There was the outline of my hand, and he made it glow with the look-machina. Finally, my mission was about to be accomplished. Spiritae's message would be delivered to this world because of my hand! I was panting, waiting for him to realize the treasure before him. He started to move aside the hand-print, but curiously positioned his hand over it to compare sizes.

Gasping, he withdrew his hand as if burned.

Cautiously, he stretched out his hand again, held it above Spiritae's message for long minutes. He kept shaking his head, as I shouted unheard, "Yes! YES!" He appeared disturbed, as though not comprehending the significance of the event. He lingered over scribbling in a tablet where he recorded observations about his work. My spirits sank when he set this aside, stretched, and stood to walk outdoors for fresh air. Oh, so close!

I rushed out to Spiritae, spilling my disappointment. She calmly said: "Don't be discouraged. He's a very bright young man, and that image will haunt his memory until he understands. My message will not be shaken off so easily. Besides, I know someone who he will listen to, and I'll put a bug in her mind. Did you have fun seeing how all this is going to work out?"

"Did I ever...and how!"

Spiritae's Message

I FELT SPIRITAE LINGERING IN MY MIND TONIGHT. I hadn't felt a vision coming on, so this surprised me. She didn't seem intent on taking me anyplace...simply watched me write for a long time about my most recent voyage.

"It's time," she declared abruptly, "for you to write My message."

"Well—sure, but who will receive it? You know I can't share anything I write here, or we'll all be in trouble."

"No one here, I can assure you. It is an important message to the people inhabiting the world of your visions."

"Isn't that going to be difficult? You remember that You wouldn't help me learn their language, right? Besides, how will it get there? If I recall correctly, we didn't exactly drag stuff along with us. I'm still trying to figure out if we actually were there."

"You let *Me* worry about all of that. Now, start with a nice fresh sheet, the best you can find. Rest your writing hand flat, take up your stylus and trace your hand and fingers."

"Okay, but that's not much of a message. Looks a bit childish, don't You think?"

"How little you understand. I want you to make a special ink, not your Papa's formulation. Here, use an ink like this." She had me gather some ashes from the hearth, dust from the corner, and mix these in water with a dash of sea salt. She commented strangely: "Seawater is the fluid of life, ashes-to-ashes and dust-to-dust."

"What?"

Her non-response was, "That's a pretty green stone you have around your neck. Would you mind if we use it?"

"It's just some trinket a boy gave to Quintina at the market-place. She gave it to me because she thought it didn't match her eyes. But what good is a rock?"

"Go heat it up in the fire at the hearth. Be careful not to burn yourself." I balanced it on a metal rod we use to poke embers, until it was glowing greenish-orange."

"Good. Now drop it here into the rest of the ink." Instantly it shattered into teeny-tiny green crystals, raising a hiss of steam.

When the mixture cooled, Spiritae said, "Now rub some of My ink on your palm and blot it off. Put your hand back inside the outline. Be quiet, open your mind and listen." There came a wisp of pressure above my hand pressing it down, soft and reassuring. In my ear, the faintest breath of a whisper, unintelligible, as though speaking languages of the mind, dozens, even thousands of them, bypassing human speech. She sighed and stepped back. I withdrew my hand from the papyrus looking to see what She had done. Nothing but a hand-print, and even that was fast fading.

"Hmmm, just how will anyone *read* this, Spiritae? Not meaning to be impertinent, I'm guessing a few words might help. I know You are the God here, but I think Papa's ink has more staying power."

"Reposition your hand over the print—but don't touch it."

I did as She instructed, and my mind went blank like an unwritten tablet. Then a voice, gentle, ageless, and deep as the ocean spoke inside....

"I love you. I have always loved you—before time ever began. I will always love you—beyond the sunset of mankind. Respect and love others as I have loved you. I do not mean you must be a mat for people to wipe their feet upon, but do not look at them through the eyes of prejudice. Do them honor by seeing them as

worthy until they prove otherwise, for they have the same essence from the Creator as do you. Do not see them as a stereotype that others would have you see, and resist being a stereotype that causes friction with others. Respect that others look and act differently than you. Live in peace and harmony whenever possible. Confrontation may be necessary in the face of great wrongs, but be slow to anger, act kindly, and look for value in others instead of fault. Affirm when warranted; do not denigrate. Others are not perfect; neither are you. Live your life; let others live theirs. Love and let love. Extend your hand in friendship. Do not look down your nose or greet others with a sullen or indifferent demeanor.

"You have rights and responsibilities in equal measure. You have a right to a life of freedom, free from oppression, and a right to seek happiness. These freedoms come with the responsibility to behave in a manner that does honor to yourself and those around you. Your rights end where the rights of others begin.

"Aspire to a higher purpose in all you do. Cultivate your mind, for intellect is My gift to you. Be a seeker of higher knowledge. Do not wallow in ignorance, and be discerning in what you are told by others. Walk gently in this world, for you have been given stewardship, not ownership, of the Earth. Her destiny, and yours, lies in your hands. Her gifts are not boundless. Leave the world, her peoples, her creatures, better than when you arrived. Give more than you receive. Reach your hand toward to those in need. Live in moderation with grace and dignity.

"Be a contributor in your life. Teach, heal, nurse, build, design, create, protect, mentor, write, inform, entertain, manufacture, serve, clean, feed, transport—and countless other vocations that uplift your human spirit. Earn your living honorably and reputably, seeking a fair gain for serving human needs instead of frivolous desires. You are My hands in the world; put them to work in a manner that honors your Creator.

"Do not be a predator or a leech upon your society. Do not cheat or defraud those who might easily be fooled. Do not murder, or cause bodily or emotional injury to others. Do not bring others to financial ruin for your benefit. Do not make your living or spend your earnings pandering to the many weaknesses of mankind: prostitution, drugs, gambling, trafficking, greed, and lustful behaviors—and others that debauch your soul and the souls of others.

"You are each created as equals in My eyes. But you are born into different circumstances, not at My whim, but by the actions and fortunes of your parents and ancestors. If you find yourself in enviable circumstances, give thanks to those who sacrificed for your benefit. Be generous to those less fortunate. For to those who are given much, much is expected. Give a man bread if he is starving, but give him the means and the knowledge to grow grain if you would show him love.

"This does not mean that you must give away all your worldly possessions or that you cannot enjoy the fruits of your labor. Cherish and decorate your life with modesty and humility. But if you live lavishly, hoarding luxuries, doing little for others who suffer while you remain self-absorbed, you will pay a great price. Material wealth will be of no value to you in eternity. Beware your soul does not wither so small that I pass by when I come to carry you home.

"If you receive the generosity of others, be appreciative. Do not hold your hand out demanding charity as your right. Do not be a willing victim, but use helping hands to haul yourself up from your miseries.

"Honor your mind and your body, for they house your soul and must be kept in good order if I am to dwell within. Do not pollute yourself with substances that compromise your human conscience in a desire for sensual pleasures, for you will rue the consequences when you bring harm to others.

"If you are among the poor, the downtrodden, the weak, the sick, the unfortunate—take heart. Your life may not be easy, but there are those whose hearts will open and whose hands will reach *out unto you. Your suffering will be but a heartbeat compared to your reward in eternity.*

"Live My message, and ye shall return unto Me to dwell for eternity."

I could not speak for long minutes. "Spiritae, that is remarkable. But how will people understand? They don't speak Latin there."

"They will hear in their own tongues, each as he or she speaks. They need not even touch your hand, for if they think of it in their mind, they will hear Me. The question is—Will they *listen?*"

Spiritae is a scribe above all scribes!

Aftermath

W HAT WOULD YOU DO if you suddenly discovered something incredibly important or precious? I'm in way over my head, into something far more dangerous than I ever imagined. The single sheet of papyrus with the hand-print and Spiritae's Message might well be viewed as having infinite value by those who see a religious connection. Even worse for me, I can imagine a number of governments and their agencies or terrorist factions who would stop at nothing to control the hand-print's technology. I'm sure I cannot begin to conceive all the possibilities, but I know the ability to leave complex messages that are revealed only to the intended receiver at the proper time or the ability to instantly understand any language would have enormous military implications. The embedded power source that causes the hand-print to pulse and glow when stimulated by the mental energy of someone interacting with it might well transform the future of mankind.

My life is in utmost danger. Through my stupidity, at least one Russian and one Israeli know something about Spiritae's Message. Undoubtedly they will contact authorities in their countries, even if they were not already acting in the capacity of gathering foreign intelligence.

Neither the forces that would use the hand-print for good nor the forces of evil that would corrupt the technology for their purposes would hesitate to squash me like a bug in their zeal to control its awesome powers. My only hope of survival lies in getting the hand-print secured immediately with someone having power to protect it. Yet I also need to let people know of the hand-print's existence, so it doesn't end up shrouded in secrecy in the interest of "national security," for I believe it is a gift to all humankind, not to an individual person or nation.

I am at a loss. Suppose you discovered something that put your life in danger. Who would you turn to? Who would you trust? I can't turn the hand-print over to merely anyone. Some would say I'm obligated to notify the leadership of my university. I don't think that approach will work. I fear turning this problem over to someone else will only endanger their lives, exposing them to incomprehensible risks.

I'm not inclined to turn the papyri over to authorities in the Italian government, although they might well exert a legal claim to antiquities. I fear shadowy forces here that might be worse than the risks I already face. How about the Vatican? I happen to think the present Pope is a very sincere, religious man. But you don't just waltz in saying you have a religious artifact that he really, really needs to see. Some of the people charged with his protection might be inclined to subvert the document into the hidden recesses and vaults of the Vatican Library. Spiritae's Message is not traditional theology by any stretch of the imagination, and it might be destroyed or sequestered as a heretical document potentially challenging traditional church doctrine.

I suppose I might try to smuggle some of the papyri back into my home country, the United States. I would pay a heavy price for such a reckless act if I was caught. Besides, where would I take the papyri? Would I write to the President and ask for an audience? That meeting would be more unlikely than seeing the Pope, and probably make me a "suspicious person" in the eyes of Homeland Security forces. Maybe the Defense Department, the FBI, or the NSA? It's hard for me to see a good outcome if I contacted any Government agency, even though they would have the capability of protecting Spiritae's Message from nefarious groups, unless, of course, they were nefarious too, which I can't rule out.

I thought about making a dramatic disclosure on a national news show, or to a well-respected talk show host. But this would be seen as a publicity stunt. My motives would be questioned severely, and few people would give any credibility to my claims or pleas to have the message evaluated by science professionals.

I think I am being watched. I'm starting to imagine bogeymen in dark trench-coats around every corner, hiding in the shadows, peering through my lab windows. I took the precaution of making several copies of the hand-print on our color copier. Of course, these do not glow either under the thermal-imaging camera or the night sky, but they look authentic to the untrained eye. I put one copy back into the proper place in the papyri as a ruse to anyone intent on stealing it. But where can I safely hide the real message? Criminals and authorities alike know all the usual places chosen by amateurs like me. Behind or under dresser drawers, under a floor board, sewn into the mattress, stashed in the freezer, or even plastic-wrapped and submerged in the toilet tank are tired old ideas.

It finally came to me. I know what to do. Thank you. Thank you, Spiritae!

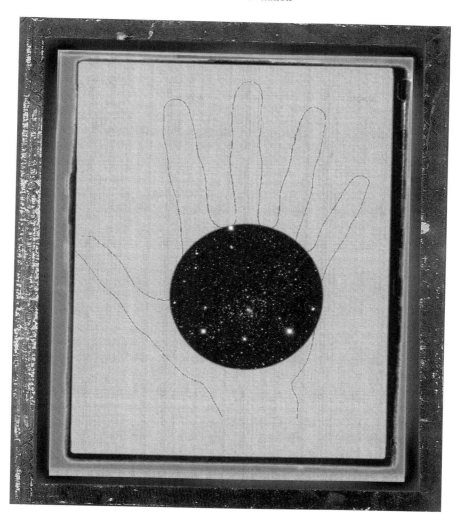

For Max

I RECEIVED THE STRANGEST LETTERS LAST MONTH. Actually three letters, exactly the same, but sent on the same day to my apartment, my work address, and one to a post-office box I keep for mail when I don't wish to disclose my home address. These were all from my half-brother Max. I say my half-brother, because we share the same biological mother, and never knew whether we had the same father, though this is rather doubtful. In fact, there are no records I know that connect me and Max.

I was abandoned by my mother as a newborn, and adopted anonymously by the man and woman who have been wonderful and loving parents to me. You can imagine my shock when I was a teenager, a young man, Max, knocked on my door and claimed his grandmother had told him where to find his long-lost sister. I was very skeptical, of course. I knew I had been adopted, but had never expected a blast from the past. He presented no proof, but when we looked at each other side-by-side in the mirror, the similarities of our features were striking. We kept in touch a few times after that, but rarely shared much time together. He had his career and I had mine, but I was thankful for the blood connection, even from a distance. But on those special occasions we could visit, we talked all through the night, siblings desperate to reconnect.

Max knows I share our grandmother's passion for puzzles. I had almost forgotten that we had devised, probably under the influence of a little too much Pinot Grigio one night, a code that was special to us, "just in case." These letters were in "our" code, so I recognized they must be of great importance to Max. Each letter translated, simply, to "Go in safety," which I understood to mean go to my safety deposit box at the bank. When I presented myself to the teller, she asked me to wait a minute, and the bank manager sauntered over. He said, "I have a key to give you for a new box set up recently in your name. Do you have any identification, please?" After I satisfied his request, I was admitted to the vault and left alone to peruse the contents of the box. Inside were a USB drive, a coded note from Max, and some sheets of what looked like papyrus in plastic sleeves.

Max's note read, "Sis, if you are reading this, you must accept the fact that I am no longer alive. Not an accident, not suicide like you might read in the news. What you hold in your hands is vitally important, and I implore you by all that is holy, to keep it safe, and to publish the story on this memory stick anonymously (here he gave me a publisher to contact, who I cannot disclose but who apparently was expecting to hear from me). You will know this message is from me by our code and by what I'll tell you to do next. The sheets of papyri will reveal a message to you when held out to the sky, at midnight, during the new Moon. Place your hand over them, blank your mind, imagine an outline around your hand, and listen with all your soul. You will hear something remarkable which you must add to the publication. Do not mourn for me. I love you, and we will be together again in eternity. Max

I read Max's updated translation of the Capitoline Papyri. I wasn't sure what to think. Was he pulling my leg, or what? He must have gone Looney-Tunes. But that evening, I was sick to my stomach when I heard on the news about a student shooting at the University of Padua, a depraved student connected with a terrorist group shot up a couple of professors, a Professore Bucelli and Professore Garrett and later three students before turning his gun upon himself when he was surrounded by police.

Two nights later, the sky was dark with the new Moon, and I took the papyri sheets out on my deck. I gazed up in wonder at the clear night sky. A small meteor streaked across the sky, which I took as an omen, a salutation from Max. I tried holding out my hand as he had instructed. It was hard to clear my mind, as my heart was pounding with anxiety. I was getting cold, starting to shiver, and nearly numb mentally when thoughts began to form. I became aware that the papyri were glowing, and pulsing softly with green iridescence, which drew me inward.

And so...

I have published all. I have never been able to make my sheets of papyri glow again. Maybe they served their purpose. If you seek Spiritae's Message through the hand-print, I leave you Max's coded directions on the back of this book. I'm sure our Grandma Nammie would have loved dearly to have a crack at it. Perhaps I will be able to decode it someday, but I'm not sure it is wise for me to try. Mankind may not be ready.

Finem

I AM AN OLD WOMAN NOW. Marcus passed away peacefully in his sleep last year. I miss him very much. We enjoyed a long and wonderful life together. Our three daughters are grown and married to good men. They blessed us with eight grandchildren, and all but one live close to me in Rome where I can spoil them and escape when they get too annoying.

Marcus was an awesome father, and he loved me, really loved me for who I am. My daughters help me when they can, but they are busy, as they should be, with their own lives. I am lonely now, because I have outlived most of my friends. Mother died about two years after Papa. People said she died of a brain fever, but I think it was really because of a broken heart. I still hear from Quintina several times a year, but she lives far away in Judea. We love sending letters to each other. She's just as ornery as ever, but we write less now that our eyes are growing dim and our fingers stiff. My brother Cato was killed many years ago in a pointless battle spreading Rome's control over people to the north. I feel badly that we never reconnected on any level. It was terribly hard on me when Antonia died suddenly five years ago of apoplexy. At least that sweet soul didn't suffer long. What a sister she was to me throughout my life. I couldn't have made it without Marcus's loving support to quench my aching heart.

I did my best to live in a way that would honor Spiritae's teachings, to pass Her values to my children. I could never bring myself to share stories about my visions with Marcus or my daughters. No sense giving them any reason to think I was any crazier than they already did. But Marcus was always perplexed. He said I had a sense of something greater than our time, that occasionally I could see beyond my years. That's a wise thing for a husband to tell his wife! Of course, I have stayed in touch with Spiritae whenever I need some reassurance. Whenever I turn my thoughts inward, She is there for me.

Last night, She told me we needed to make one last vision together, one hard to watch, but everything would work out for the best in the end. Not that I ever had any choice in these matters, but I was filled with dread. When She says something isn't going to be easy, you can darn well bet it won't. You should probably run away screaming.

Spiritae said, "Just this last time, I'm going to let you understand what is being said, so you can write things down exactly." (About time, don't you think? Oops, She probably heard that.)

We appeared back in the lab where the student who had become a professor had worked on my writings. An older professor was rummaging through my sheets of papyri, scattering them as though they meant nothing. I watched outraged as he tore several of the fragile pieces. He finally found what he was looking for—my handprint with Spiritae's Message. He kept holding his hand over it, but nothing seemed to happen. He tried several times to use the heatmachina to make it glow, but to no avail. He was getting quite annoyed and appeared to be on the verge of ripping the entire lab apart like a beast gone berserk.

At that moment, the student-professor entered. Stunned, he said, "What in the hell are you doing, Bucelli? You have no right!"

The older professor flushed deeply, caught in the act, but went on the offensive, shouting, "I have *every* right! These documents were entrusted to me, and I know you are up to more than you are telling. You are hiding something valuable from me, from this university, all for your own benefit. What sort of fool do you think I am, Max?"

The young professor, Max, tried to be reasonable. "Professore Bucelli, with all due respect, what is happening here is far more dangerous than you can possibly imagine. No, I have not told you everything. But it is only because I don't understand fully what these documents mean. What lies here is of profound importance and could very likely get all of us killed."

Bucelli scoffed nastily and replied that Max only wanted to build a reputation at his expense, and steal the proceeds of selling the papyri to a collector. Max's reply was cut short when the door to the lab exploded inward with the heavy kick of an intruder. Both men jumped as the door splintered, and I nearly leaped out of my mental skin. Four men rushed in, faces covered with fabric masks camouflaged with green and tan blotches like the rest of their clothing. All carried long spit-deaths they aimed at the professors. The leader barked in a thick accent, "Hand it over. Now!"

Bucelli tried stalling for time, replying, "Hand *what* over? What do you want? Money? Drugs? We don't have anything valuable. Please stay calm." Meanwhile, he slipped the copy of the hand-print sheet surreptitiously behind him.

The invader demanded more forcefully, "You know what I want. I won't ask again!"

Bucelli reluctantly held out the hand-print sheet.

The leader took it, and the men began to back out the door. Bucelli started to say something, and the leader's eyes narrowed with rage. "Die, you scum!" His spit-death cracked three times in rapid succession, and small red marks punched through Bucelli's chest. Behind him, the wall was spattered with shredded flesh and the horror of blood.

I was screaming, "Spiritae, can't You stop this?"

Max had stood immobile, but at the bloodshed backed violently away. The invader leader was nearly out the door, but evidently he decided not to leave any witnesses behind. He leveled his spit-death and rattled three more death stones toward Max. One missed, but two found their mark in his chest. Max sank to his knees, drizzling blood from mouth and nose, wheezing from chest wounds. The leader stood over him for one last taunt. Max glared with shocky eyes, but managed a defiant grin. "I forgive you...Dross!" The invader blinked in confusion—booted the dying man's ribs, and fled.

Bucelli died instantly, but Max was hanging on desperately. He called out: "Help me Spiritae. Oh help me God!"

Spiritae breathed insistently in my direction, "Now Portia! *Now* we can help!" We rushed to him and his writhing agony. She held him in Her arms, while I pressed my imaginary hands over his wounds trying to cool angry flesh. He calmed, and gazed unfocused as if searching for us. Between gasps, he said, "The pain...the pain, it doesn't hurt anymore. I'm growing cold."

Spiritae hugged him close. "I love you. You have done very well, Max. Come with Me. Feel My warmth. Come with Portia, for we shall take you home."

I cried out in agony, "But Spiritae, all our writing was in vain. Your message has been stolen."

"No. Max has hidden My message right where it needs to be, and it will be found by anyone who cares to look for it. Your writings, even this memoir, will be the stuff of legends. Let us take him home."

And so we did. We arched through the cosmos, past stars like sand grains on a beach, past time itself. We passed through universes and dimensions, along a great tunnel of light. A gathering of souls awaited us, pulsing separately and together, calling to us in welcome. Max stretched forward and was spiritually embraced. "Oh Nammie!" he exalted.

And me?

"Marcus! Mother! Antonia! PAPA! Spiritae, I am really dead!"

"Really? Life, death, I told you—not so very different."

"Pure gold, Portia, you are pure gold!"

Hints to Max's Code

(back cover)

Spoiler Alert! Read these clues only if you need help.

1. Max's code is not a hoax; it is a real message.
2. The message is in English, reads left to right.
3. No spaces between the words.
4. Spiritae loves rainbows and music.
5. Rainbows have 7 colors: R,O,Y,G,B,I,V
6. Music has seven letters: A,B,C,D,E,F,G
7. Wrap the colors onto the notes starting from A-G and repeat for H-N, O-U, and V-Z.
8. Each color can represent more than one letter (some 4, some 3).
9. For a line of the code, put the letter possibilities above each color block (e.g., red can be A, H, O, or V)
10. Now follow the path through the letters, left to right, choosing letters to form words.

Having trouble seeing the color blocks?

B	R	R	G	O	V	O	R	G	G	O	I	G	B	B	B	B	G
	B	O	O	G	O	I	R	B	B	I	B	B	B	R	V	B	
		B	O	B	I	B	V	R	I	O	G	I	R	B			
G	R	G	G	V	B	B	B	R	I	I	R	B	Y	R	B	I	R	B
	O	I	R	V	O	V	B	I	R	B	R	R	V	G			
	O	I	G	B	O	R	V	B	G	Y	R	V	V	B	Y	I	
		B	R	R	B	O	B	R	Y	B	R	R	G	I	R	V	G
	G	B	B	O	B	Y	I	I	R	G	B	G	R	I	O	R	V

Total Spoiler Alert! Solution is on the last page!

Max's Code Solution

"Look inward if ye seek Spiritae's message,
Listen amid the darkness of the cosmos,
Imagine the hand if ye would connect,
Love, Peace, Harmony, Respect, Moderation."